TRIAL

BY

MURDER

ISBN-13: 978-1-63696-413-3

ISBN-10: 1-63-696413-3

Cover design by: Damonza

Printed in the United States of America

www.righthouse.com

www.instagram.com/righthousebooks

www.facebook.com/righthousebooks

twitter.com/righthousebooks

David Archer   Oliver
ARCHER   BLACK

TRIAL

BY

MURDER

A **Ben Carter** LEGAL THRILLER

R

RIGHTHOUSE

1

SOMETHING ABOUT THE INNOCENCE IN THE GIRL'S EYES WAS what first drew my attention to Katherine Wright, a girl who would end up changing the course of countless lives. She had already lived a hard life herself, the stone-faced expression conveying experiences far beyond her years. This was a girl who had cut her teeth for life on the streets, finding safety within the shadows others cowered away from.

At just eighteen years old, this was a girl whose life could have taken many alternative routes, all of them better than the one she'd ended up on. Reading through the file, I couldn't help but wonder what tragedies her childhood must have consisted of for her to believe that she'd be safer alone out on the streets. From what I had read, her childhood home didn't appear to be anything out of the ordinary. Her parents were still together, and looking at the photos of them, they were still very much in love.

A murder charge was what brought the Wright girl's file

onto my desk. Actually, it was *two* murder charges that she faced, one for Amadore Costa and one for his wife, Ersilia. The Italian immigrants came to the US in the early '80s as newlyweds with hopes of starting a new life and raising a family. The couple ended up doing both, only to end up brutally gunned down in their own home some forty years later.

While some random couple's names contained in a case file shouldn't have stirred up further emotions, seeing the Costas did, and not in a good way. It wasn't so much the names Amadore or Ersilia that triggered me but their connection to another Costa, their son Riccardo. Pick up any recent newspaper containing crime-related incidents within the greater Pittsburgh area, and chances are you'd read some sort of reference to Riccardo Costa.

The city of Pittsburgh and the local Italian Mafia shared a history stretching all the way back to the late nineteenth century, and Riccardo Costa served as just the latest in a long line of wannabe gangsters. He began young, growing his own empire over the course of a decade to rise up as one of the city's heavy hitters, and if there was one thing I knew from the beginning, it was that the killing of his parents wouldn't go unanswered. Was this a case I *really* wanted to get involved in?

After spending time going through the file, I'd made up my mind, dropped it into my briefcase, grabbed the keys to my Mustang, and headed out of the office. Challenges were what I thrived on, and aside from the whole Harold and Max Dunning thing from the previous year, I hadn't had a meaty case in quite some time.

"I'm off to the jail," I told Grace Tanner, my associate, on the way past her desk.

She looked up at me from her computer screen with a smile. "Want me to come along?"

"Not for the first meeting," I said and checked my watch. "I should make it back afterward, though, if you want to help me go through the case in more detail."

"Of course," Grace said and returned her attention to the file she'd been working on.

The one thing I'd learned about meeting new clients was that without a certain sense of trust between them and myself, defending them in court became far more difficult. It only took me about a year's worth of cases to figure out that the serious ones, like murders, required a certain approach in order for a connection to grow. In short, I needed them to open up to me, and if they didn't, then the chances of me helping them beat their charges vastly diminished.

Twenty minutes later, I pulled into the Allegheny County Jail parking lot, found a space some four rows back, and grabbed my briefcase. When I climbed out, I took a moment to look at the buildings before me, the tall red brick façade with its recessed windows a foreboding sight. I'd walked into the place to meet with clients plenty of times before, but never for any as young as Katherine Wright facing murder charges. The closest in age to her I'd defended was a twenty-year-old named Emelia Hendrickson, a woman who fought back against an abusive boyfriend and accidentally killed him during a fight. It was a case I lost after she broke down on the stand and confessed.

The thought of a girl as young as Katherine being held in

such a place didn't sit well with me, not knowing the kinds of things that went on in a jail like the one before me. I'd also heard plenty of stories from clients about the horrors beyond the walls and was thinking about one in particular when a voice pulled me from my thoughts.

"Ben Carter, right?"

I looked around to see two men approaching me, one walking slightly behind the other and looking every bit as threatening as a bodyguard should. I'd known when I saw the names of his parents in the file that Riccardo Costa would eventually make himself known to me, but I had no idea it would happen so fast, especially since I'd only taken on the case within the past hour.

"Yes, it is," I said as I tried to picture who in the office would have made the call to the underworld boss. I had my suspicions.

Costa stopped a few feet in front of me, and instead of holding a hand out to shake with me, he instead clasped his hands together in front of his groin as if guarding his manhood. For a second, he just stood there staring at me, his eyes hidden behind the dark sunglasses he wore. The two men looked almost identical, both in appearance and stature, but it was obvious who the man in charge was. Costa carried himself with a lot more confidence, and there was just an extra shine to the suit he wore, a shine that conveyed value.

The man took a deep breath and sighed loudly for what I could only assume was dramatic effect. From what I knew of him, he loved to employ intimidation tactics on his adversaries, and since I was the one defending his parents' killer, that made me enemy number one.

"I hear you're representing the killer of my parents" was what he finally said to me.

"Now why would you think that?" I asked, trying hard to sound jovial.

He tilted his head just enough to indicate hearing me but didn't immediately answer. It was another one of his tactics to try and intimidate me, something I was more than used to. Sometimes, defending people drew the attention of those who might suffer because of an unwanted outcome. Costa wasn't the first big-name opponent to a client of mine.

"Don't play games with me, Mr. Carter," he finally said.

"Yes, I am, if you must know," I said, refusing to let his intimidation work on me. "Everyone deserves a good lawyer."

"Is that what you are, Mr. Carter? A good lawyer?"

"I can hold my own, I guess."

Not happy with my response, Costa took a step forward while his hands remained in the same position. The bodyguard stood his ground, but I could see the muscles underneath the material tense just a little, preparing to unleash at the first hint of retaliation. A bullet to the head wasn't something I particularly wanted that day, and I made a mental note not to make any sudden moves. Costa lowered his voice to try and intimidate me even more.

"I want you to deliver a message for me. I want you to tell your client that she doesn't stand a chance of seeing another sunrise, Mr. Carter. I want you to tell her that." As if needing to amplify his words, he took another step forward, slowly peeled his sunglasses off, and stared me directly in the eyes. "You tell her that for me, Ben Carter."

There's something about a man grieving the death of his parents. It's not anything specific that can be pointed out, and yet I could tell the man was hurting, all of his mannerisms tensed up into a tight ball held deep within him. His eyes didn't show the kind of bloodshot trauma indicating endless crying, and I doubted he would have shed a tear anyway, especially within view of anybody else. No, this was the kind of man who swallowed his pain deep down and held it within the confines of his soul. It would simmer there until ready to unleash on whoever was unfortunate enough to be in the firing line.

I could have responded in another way, of course, but with the tension between us balanced on a knife's edge, I didn't want to push my luck. I didn't think Costa would have reacted rationally, given what I already knew of the man. Throw in his recent loss, and you had the makings of someone prepared to kill at the drop of a hat...or a wayward comment.

"Innocent until proven guilty, Mr. Costa," I said, refusing to back down completely as he leaned even closer toward me to listen. He turned his ear slightly toward me to highlight his listening—yet another attempt to intimidate.

"We know she did it, and that's good enough for me," he hissed through clenched teeth. "You tell her for me. You make sure she gets my message."

He didn't bother waiting for me to respond and turned his back after sliding the sunglasses back onto his face. The bodyguard held his position until his boss had walked past him by a good number of yards before he, too, backed up. I watched until they climbed back into their black BMW parked a few dozen yards away, where the driver sat waiting for them. Just as I knew they would, the car slowly rolled past me, and the window was already down so Costa could eyeball me.

I waited until it left the parking lot and disappeared from view before I turned back to the jail, considering my next move. If I knew one thing for certain, it was that his threat was real. If he intended to have Katherine Wright killed for the murder of his parents, then it would definitely happen and sooner rather than later. This wasn't a man who held back revenge, not when the fragility of his family had been exposed.

Weakness wasn't something a mobster displayed. It opened up all manner of issues, and the death of his parents showed others that their family was vulnerable. I'd read about gangs descending into years of conflict for such incidents, turning city streets into war zones while fighting for both honor and turf. If Costa felt the slightest hint of someone seeing the death of his parents as a sign of weakness, then he would waste little time to hit back, and that spelled certain doom for my client, a client I still hadn't met.

Bail was my only option to save her. I couldn't leave the girl in a place where she would be a sitting duck, not after such a direct threat. Men like Riccardo Costa paid big money to be able to extend their reach into inaccessible places like county jails. With corrupt city officials and cops on their books, I had no doubt that a few lowly-paid prison officers would also be on the gang's payroll, not to mention those among their own ranks already serving time inside.

Speaking of time, I knew I'd be pushing it, given the hour of the day, but after hearing the threat firsthand, it was a chance I had to risk. I took out my cell phone and sent Grace a message asking her to get me an urgent bail hearing down at the courthouse for that afternoon. I made sure to capitalize URGENT so she understood...well, the urgency of the matter. If I was going to have a chance at saving a young girl from the wrath of a Mafia mobster, then I would first need to get her out of a place bursting at the seams with potential hitmen.

2

I'D WALKED INTO PLENTY OF PRISONS IN MY TIME, BUT I CAN swear hand on heart that I had never felt as cautious as I did that day. Maybe cautious isn't the right word; perhaps intimidated is a better one. What it came down to, and it's a fact I hate admitting to, was that Riccardo Costa had managed to get under my skin. After one single meeting that lasted less than five minutes, he'd filled my head with enough insecurity about my client that I began to suspiciously eye every person I came into contact with. A man like that knew people, *lots* of people, and usually people holding positions in places like the one I was in.

It wasn't until I was safely sitting in the interview room that I finally relaxed enough to breathe, although I did check under the table and chairs to make sure there weren't any rogue listening devices planted. As I said, the mobster had managed to get into my head within a matter of minutes of our very first meeting, and I wasn't about to ignore the warning signs.

Planted bugs weren't exactly impossible in a prison, especially in a place where snitches were known to spill their secrets.

When the guard escorted Katherine Wright into the room a few moments later, the first thing I noticed was just how young she really looked. The innocence I'd seen earlier in her eyes in the photograph paled in comparison to the real thing and yet failed to hide the harsh exterior of someone who'd lived through hell. I think it was that very conflict that left me wondering how to best handle a person like her.

I waited until the guard left us alone, the lock of the door closing with a metallic echo that hung in the air for a few seconds. Katherine sat with her arms folded defiantly across her chest while staring at the top of the table. Given the kinds of people she'd been in contact with since being imprisoned, I wasn't at all surprised by her demeanor.

This was one of those moments where I had to tread carefully, knowing that first impressions mattered, and I needed her to eventually open up to me. Trust is something I cannot even begin to explain the importance of. Without it, a case would never get off the ground.

This was a girl who I imagined would have had plenty of adults talk down to her. Perhaps that was one of the reasons she had such a resistant exterior, one capable of easily deflecting yet another grown-up wanting to direct her. The last thing that was going to work was for me to start talking, speaking words she wouldn't listen to anyway. If I was going to help her, I needed the girl to first accept me, and the way I would do that was to wait for her to make the first move.

Instead of asking questions the way most lawyers would have opened the meeting, I instead sat in silence. A *long* silence. Seconds turned to minutes as I watched the girl slowly begin to grow curious about the person sitting quietly before her. My intention was to wait for her to make the first move. This part of the game I sometimes compared to a poker match, where we each held our hand, and the first to reveal theirs would lose. I had no intention of showing mine, and it became clear that neither did she.

The first indication of the uncomfortable silence affecting her was when she shifted her weight from one side to the other. I saw her fingers twitch just a little before she took a quick look over at me. I barely had time to respond before she dropped her eyes again, but the resistance didn't last long. A few seconds later, she finally broke when she asked the first question.

"Aren't you like supposed to tell me stuff about court?" She tried to add as much attitude as possible, but I could see through the façade. This wasn't anything new to me. I came with experience, and attitude wasn't something I took offense to.

"Maybe," I began, "but then again, I'm curious as to whether it's going to make any difference to you."

"What's it matter? They're going to lock me up whatever happens anyway," she said, her tone matter-of-fact.

"Well, not necessarily," I said, doing my best to keep my own tone neutral. "I'm not your average court-appointed attorney, Katherine, and I have an excellent track record when it comes to murder trials."

"I didn't murder anybody," she mumbled under her breath as if using the reply as a comeback.

"Then that's perfect," I said, tricking her into thinking she'd given me valuable information. "It makes my job so much easier when a client is innocent."

My response seemed to surprise her as she took another look across the table, this time holding my gaze long enough for me to offer a smile.

"I *am* innocent."

"So let me help you," I said, and then, not wanting to upset the flow, I continued to roll with the conversation. "My name is Ben, Katherine. I'm here because somebody thinks you might be worth offering a second chance."

"It's Kat."

"Excuse me?"

"Kat," she repeated. "I don't like being called Katherine," and then more to herself, she added, "It's what my *mother* calls me."

"OK, Kat it is." I paused and waited for her defenses to lower a little further before continuing. "You say you're innocent. Does that mean you have an alibi? Maybe something or someone proving your whereabouts on the night of the murders to be somewhere else?"

"I already told you," she snapped. "I didn't *kill* anybody."

"Yes, you already said so, but unfortunately, the judge and jury will need something a little more than hearsay. They're going to require concrete proof of your innocence, and the only way we're going to get that is by you telling me what you know."

"What's this *we*?"

That was when I knew I had her...or at least to a certain extent. Questions were good, especially ones involving me. All I had to do then was get her on my side.

"I don't know whether you've noticed this yet, but there aren't exactly too many people rushing in here to help you." I remembered her history and tried a different approach. "I know you may not have had many people on your side before, Kat. Or even anybody you might have trusted, but I can assure you—"

"Is this the part where you tell all about how wonderful you are and how you know how to talk to kids and stuff?" I wanted to grin but resisted the urge. She had spirit, that was for sure.

"Actually, at eighteen, you no longer qualify for that title, and to tell you the truth, I don't have a lot of experience with kids. But if you ever want to see the outside world again, I'm about the best chance you have."

I expected her to bite back, but to my surprise, the only reaction I noticed was her lips pursing ever so slightly while considering my words. When she didn't respond after a few moments, I continued trying to reel her in.

"Kat, have you ever heard the expression *innocent until proven guilty*?" She didn't answer but also didn't turn away, so I continued. "That's only partially true. The prosecution believes they have enough evidence against you, which means you will need to face their accusations. Only by proving your innocence will we be able to disprove their charges."

"But if I didn't do it, then why do I need to prove it? I didn't kill anyone."

"I know it's not exactly black and white, but unfortunately, the law rarely is."

"So what do I have to do?"

"Tell me what happened." I was beginning to feel the last of the walls crumbling as Kat sat up a little higher in the chair. It was a sign that she felt a glimmer of hope in my offer. "Can anybody vouch for you not being at the home?" Surprisingly, she shook her head. "You were there?" A head nod.

"I was hungry," she said. "It had been a tough couple of days. Raining, cold, I just...I saw their front door open and went in."

"When you say their front door was open, open how? Somebody walking in and out carting groceries or what?"

"I'm not sure. All I know is that it was late and I needed food. I'd begun shaking and feeling sick."

"That's low blood sugar," I said, having experienced the same sensation during a particularly long court session.

"Anyway, I went in, and I couldn't hear anything and so figured if I was quick I could find something to eat. I found some plates of leftover food on the kitchen table, so I ate some."

"And?" I could tell by her shoulders slumping that she knew what I meant.

"And that was when I saw the purse."

"And that was when you took Mrs. Costa's credit card," I corrected her.

"I wouldn't have if there had been more cash," she cried out defensively. "But twenty bucks was all there was. I figured I'd just tap a few quick transactions and get myself some extra food and drinks, and I'd be OK."

"And that was how the police caught you, wasn't it? One of the storekeepers spotted Mrs. Costa's card and called the cops." She nodded, her eyes downcast as she shook her head almost apologetically.

"But I didn't kill anybody; I swear to you I didn't."

"I believe you, Kat, I do, but we need more than that if we are going to have a chance at proving your innocence."

That was when I knew I had to tell her the accurate scale of the matter, a matter she would need to fully understand if she was going to comprehend the danger she now found herself in.

"I know you didn't kill anybody, but just so we're on the same page, do you have any idea who the murdered couple are?"

She shook her head. "Just their names."

"Amadore and Ersilia Costa were the parents of *Riccardo* Costa, and he just happens to run a local crime syndicate." She appeared not to understand what I meant. "Kat, he's a very bad guy who does bad things. He ran into me outside just before I came to see you."

"What did he say?"

"That he wants to avenge his parents," I told Kat, knowing the days of people sugar-coating things for her benefit to be over.

"But I didn't kill them," she snapped, more out of fear than frustration, and I waited a second before answering with a lowered tone.

"Which is why I'm going to be attending a bail hearing just as soon as I can get one arranged. In the meantime, I'm going to request the jail to keep you isolated until I have a chance to figure out our next move." She didn't appear to have heard me.

"He needs to believe me," she said, more to herself than me. "Someone else hurt his parents; it wasn't me."

That was when I saw the panic take over, Kat's face contorting into a mass of fear and confusion as her lack of years betrayed her. The tough outer façade she'd hidden behind on the street melted away as a scared child looked back at me, the gravity of her position finally hitting home.

"We're going to get through this together," I said, lowering my voice to a much more empathetic level. "I'm going to do all I can to make sure that he can't hurt you, OK?"

She nodded as tears slowly rolled down her cheeks, each glistening line highlighting the youth within her. Realizing them for the first time, Kat rubbed a finger across her face, flicking each tear away like traitorous soldiers. I didn't think she was going to respond, but eventually, she gave me a nod, albeit a slight one.

I stayed with Kat for perhaps another ten minutes, more so to help calm her down enough for me to feel comfortable enough to walk away. When I first saw the case notes, I knew from the date of birth in the file that I would be representing the youngest defendant of my career. The last thing I expected was to find myself immediately drawn into her world like an overprotective brother.

3

When I first walked out of the jail a good hour after going into the place, I did so with the feeling that my life had taken a significant turn. In fact, I could feel a new kind of heaviness weighing down on me, an uncomfortable urgency in my middle that just didn't sit right. Half a dozen steps toward the parking lot, I had to stop and take a look behind me to make sure the memory of the previous hour had been real and not some out-of-body experience.

The jail loomed large, just as it had when I'd first arrived; its foreboding presence, secondary to the secrets I knew, remained hidden from public view. Inside, in the brightly lit pods dotted across every floor, hardened criminals spent their days in a place where the laws of the jungle applied. This was where only the strong thrived, feeding off the fear they generated among the weaker inmates.

This was also the place now holding a young girl barely old enough to do the things most adults took for granted, thrown among some of the worst society had to offer. I knew Kat wasn't the only eighteen-year-old inside, but she was the only one I now represented, and I had a genuine opportunity to save her from such a place.

My phone began to vibrate, pulling me out of the dream-like state, and I grabbed it out to find Grace's number staring back at me. Thumbing the Answer button, I turned and began walking back to where my car sat waiting for me.

"Hey, how are you?" I said, at the same time pushing the unlock button on the key fob.

"Ben, sorry to push you. I've got you the bail hearing, but you'll have to get your skates on."

"You did?" I grinned, not surprised by my assistant's efficiency. "You know they're not paying you enough."

"Downside of owning the place, I guess," she mused. "Now hurry. We only managed to snag the slot because of another hearing getting postponed. Judge Becker is expecting you at eleven sharp." I checked my watch and saw I had less than twenty minutes.

"Eleven? Talk about cutting it close."

"You'll manage," she said with a definitive grin in her tone, and before I could answer, Grace ended the call.

She was right, of course. Not only did I know my way around town quite well, but I also had the right kind of car to get me through it. I'd found myself caught short of time plenty during my years working the courts, learning which shortcuts worked best at particular times of the day. It paid to know the flow of traffic when entire verdicts depended on it, and this was no different.

Most people look at cars and see nothing more than

shaped materials, maybe fine lines blending in with particular colors and patterns. Not me...and not thousands of other car enthusiasts who drive their particular vehicles for more than just looks. When I jumped into the Mustang, it wasn't until I pressed the Start button that the real connection came to life, the sound of all eight cylinders immediately waking the neighborhood.

It was the sound of that engine that sent goosebumps breaking out along my arms, that unhinged trickle of electricity running down the length of my spine hard enough to push my foot down harder on the gas pedal. Weaving in and out of traffic felt more like an obsession than a need, a thrill ride without limits. Yes, I loved driving my car, even more so when time felt against me.

I barely slowed when I eventually reached the courthouse parking lot, finding a spot as close to the front as possible. I spotted Grace already waiting for me on the steps and barely looked behind me when I climbed out and half-ran toward her, locking the car over my shoulder with a quick press of the fob.

"Judge Becker? Really?"

Her grin matched the one I had when she told me she'd managed to get me a hearing. "It was either him or Judge Blamey next Friday," Grace said as she turned to follow me up the stairs and inside the courthouse. Inside, I shuddered at the thought of Kat remaining inside the jail for another week.

"Becker is fine," I said.

"I thought you might feel that way."

We pushed through the doors into the foyer, where the

smell of lemon-scented floor cleaner hung in the air. The janitor handling the mop to clean up a spill had set up a warning sign almost directly in front of the door, and I had to sidestep around it. The lemon smelled pleasant but not as pleasant as the underlying tones of what I always felt was the building's true essence, its soul. To a lawyer, that scent smells sweeter than anything else.

"Carter, I hear you're representing the Wright girl," a voice called to me, and when I looked to my left, I saw Xavier Bartell walking toward me.

"Ah, Bartell," I said, not bothering with pleasantries. He didn't slow when he reached me, and together, we headed for the courtroom.

"I hope you don't think that we're just going to let this girl go," he said as we walked side by side. "She killed two people."

"*You* might think she killed two people, but I sure as hell don't."

"The evidence is clear, Carter. You'll never—"

"Watch me," I said as we reached the door and continued on. Bartell slowed to let me in first, and I obliged, not bothering to look back. As far as I was concerned, the conversation had ended.

Bartell knew how to work the system to his advantage, and I expected him to put up a worthy fight, which was why I didn't hold back when the time came. From the look of Becker, the judge appeared to have already had his last remaining nerves squashed by previous matters, that one single eyebrow of his already raised before I'd even stood up.

Shit, I thought to myself as I listened to Bartell lay out the state's case to the court. If Becker was already as pissed as it appeared, it meant my job had just grown in difficulty.

"Your Honor, we strongly object to bail in this matter given the accused's history and the brutality of these murders. An elderly couple gunned down in their own home, the wife left to die as she lay next to her deceased husband of forty-plus years."

"Your Honor, the evidence against my client is circumstantial at best, and none of it has to do with the actual murders."

"She was in possession of the deceased woman's credit card, Your Honor, proving she was in the house at the time of the murders. The first transaction occurred just ten minutes after the determined time of death, meaning—"

"A transaction to buy food, Your Honor," I said, cutting in. "Food to feed herself. Katherine Wright was looking for something to eat, and when she saw Mrs. Costa's purse sitting open on the kitchen counter, she seized the opportunity."

"Two innocent victims murdered," Bartell repeated.

"Not by my client. The murder weapon still hasn't been found, and no traces of my client being in the house have been found other than the open purse. It's only because of Katherine Wright's police interview that her admission to being in the house is known at all."

"An admission to being in the building places her inside at the time of the shooting. Add in the credit card in her possession—"

"All of which is still circumstantial when it comes to the murders, Your Honor, and while the prosecution forgets about the basic laws of investigating, my eighteen-year-old client is sitting in a prison cell with a direct threat from the victims' son. I don't think I need to remind anyone here about the links between Riccardo Costa and the criminal underworld of this city."

"Your Honor, as a—" was as far as the prosecutor got before the judge held a hand up to silence him. I could see the look of victory on the man's face, and a quick glance in my direction confirmed his win.

"All right, all right, Mr. Bartell," Becker said as he shut the arguing down. "I hear you loud and clear…"

Shit, my brain repeated for the second time as I pictured Kat sitting inside a prison cell surrounded by those waiting to take every advantage of her.

"However," Becker continued. "I also know that Allegheny County Jail is no place for a young girl, and after reviewing the accused's record, I see no reason for her to be held in custody while awaiting trial."

"But Your Honor, if I could just—"

"Thank you, Mr. Bartell, but my decision is made," Becker continued before turning to me with the biggest surprise of all. "I'm going to grant your client bail, Mr. Carter, which I'll set at $100,000 but with the strictest of conditions. I order the accused to be monitored via a tracking device fitted to her by the state of Pennsylvania, as well as order her to remain confined to a suitable residence until her trial date, which I set as…" He paused as he looked at the screen of his computer. "July 11. That's seven weeks from today."

I think I felt a physical weight lift off my shoulders as Becker slammed the gavel down a single time, the echo bouncing around the room several times. Either that or my breakfast shifted in a way I didn't care for. I was buzzing. The idea that I would now become a direct target for Riccardo Costa far outweighed the jubilation of being able to take Kat out of that hellhole, but I didn't care. My first duty was to the client, and it was that first duty I intended to hold close for the next few months.

With the bail hearing effectively over, I turned to leave the courtroom but not before meeting the gaze of the prosecutor. He didn't look pissed, instead grinning at me, the message behind it pretty obvious.

You and me in the ring, Carter, that grin said, Bartell throwing down the challenge to me. He would no doubt be looking forward to the eventual fight, the one that would see us once again go head to head and decide the fate of an accused. The question I needed to answer was whether this client really was as innocent as I believed.

4

WHILE I PRACTICALLY RAN FROM THE COURTHOUSE TO GET back to the jail, Grace remained behind to take care of the formalities and to make sure the paperwork for Kat's bail went through immediately. She and Dwight had set up a special trust fund several years earlier for just this type of situation, so the funds were already available. Back in the Mustang, I felt the thrust of all eight cylinders pushing me back into the seat. Minutes mattered, especially when it involved someone held inside a prison cell, one I still wasn't sure was as isolated as I had hoped.

Thanks to the time of day and a lack of incidents, the traffic along the route wasn't too bad, the other cars stretched out enough for me to slot in and out like a regular speed freak. I hate to imagine what the other drivers must have been thinking, the 'stang sounding every bit as thuggish as a regular rabble-rouser.

The only call I made along the way was to Linda, who answered on the very first ring.

"Howdy" was how she greeted me. I hadn't spoken to my investigator in more than a week. She'd been in LA for a few days to catch up with an old college friend and only arrived back in Pittsburgh late the previous evening.

"Howdy, yourself," I replied. "How was the break?" She hesitated to answer for a few seconds.

"Hmm, I'd have to say eye-opening."

"Yeah, that doesn't sound all that positive."

"Well, let's just say twenty years is a long time between drinks, and the girl I knew back in college is definitely not the one who came to greet me at the airport." I could hear the television in the background.

"That definitely doesn't sound positive," I repeated. "Listen, if you think you could drag yourself away from *Days of Our Lives*, I could use your help down at the county jail."

"For your information, it's *Young and the Restless*."

"Whatever," I said with a grin. "We have a new case."

"Tell me more."

"When I see you. In a bit of a rush. How quick can you get down there?"

"Be there in twenty?"

"Perfect," I said and ended the call.

Despite us getting caught with our pants down with the whole Max Dunning thing a year earlier, it was a lesson Linda and I took seriously. Serious enough to make sure that we would never find ourselves caught short again. Katherine Wright, to me, felt like another Max, someone needing to stay out of the public eye and stay alive long enough to get through her trial.

That was why we ended up renting a cabin on the outskirts of Pittsburgh owned by a very close friend of Linda's. The old guy owned a bit of farmland about thirty miles out of the city, and while his house sat near the front of the property, a self-contained bungalow sat near the back, far enough away to ensure privacy. It was there that I planned to take Kat and hide her until such time as she needed to come out of hiding and head to the courthouse.

Ten minutes was how long it took me to work my way through the traffic. This time, when I climbed out of the car in the prison parking lot, I managed to reach the front entrance without getting stopped by a Tier-1 gangster first, although, in all honesty, I did take a look around just to be sure I wasn't walking into an ambush. Let's just say I know what it feels like to have a brightly illuminated target on one's back, and the uneasiness felt uncomfortably familiar.

Given the sheer number of cars parked in the lot, it made spotting a gangster-style European luxury vehicle a bit more difficult, but I didn't see anything untoward while running my eyes across the multiple rooftops. No shiny black duco stood out to me, and figuring I'd take it as a sign to get things done, I continued on to the entrance. I hoped Linda would be ready and waiting by the time I came out again.

As it turned out, I shouldn't have bothered, as the on-duty officers running the show had other ideas about the meaning of efficiency. Not only did they shelve the paper-work regarding the release of Katherine Wright for at least an hour, but when they finally did pick it up, I had a second hour to wait while they transferred my client from the unit to a holding cell.

"They're bringing Wright down shortly," the officer dealing with my request called out as I sat in the reception area next to Linda. One look at her and I could tell she felt exactly the same as I did. Frustration.

"Let me bring the car closer," she said when we finally saw some movement farther down the hallway—a good move, all things considered.

I don't think I breathed easy again until we had Kat safely seated in the backseat of Linda's car, and even then, it was short-lived. The hardest part was still to come. Trying to move her discreetly out of the jail proved an impossible task, given the openness of the exit door. If any of Costa's goons had been assigned stakeout duties, I had no doubt they would have picked us out from a mile away, a situation I couldn't get around. In any case, I waited until Linda was already moving off before calmly walking back to the Mustang.

For the next twenty minutes, we made our way through Pittsburgh traffic as a split-up convoy, with me constantly keeping at least three or four cars between us. For one, it gave me a chance to monitor the cars following Linda while also keeping an eye on those following me. There was every chance that Costa's men might already be monitoring us, especially if he heard that the accused killer of his parents had been granted bail.

The problem I faced, or should I say *problems*, was that Kat was already being tracked thanks to her newly adorned ankle jewelry. There was no getting around that, and the only hope I had was that people charged with doing the monitoring weren't prone to cash handouts in large yellow envelopes from filthy-rich mobsters. If they were, we'd be in some serious shit and a lot earlier than expected.

The other issue I had was that I couldn't call through the news of Kat's bail to the office. I already knew we had a spy in our midst on account of how fast Costa knew of my appointment to the Wright case in the first place. That wasn't a small inconvenience, and I intended to bring the matter to my boss's attention. Unfortunately, that was something else I needed to time. I'd also asked Grace to keep the update to herself until my return, which meant the only way Costa would know about her release was through a paid contact either at the courthouse or at the jail. It was the jail I had my money on.

That overwhelming sense of urgency finally began to abate once we reached the city's outskirts, and I watched the cityscape make way for greenery. A few more miles down the road, my pulse rate dropped to normal levels again, and by the time we pulled in to Marlon Shaw's property, I felt a lot better about our decision to hold Kat there. With nobody following us, as far as I could tell, it appeared we had achieved victory after the first round.

Linda drove straight past Marlon Shaw's residence and followed the narrow track through several thick tree clusters before reaching somewhat of a clearing. The small cabin standing at the outer edge appeared isolated enough from the main road, hidden behind a wall of thick vegetation that Linda parked in front of. I pulled the Mustang up immediately behind and climbed out.

Being a city boy from way back, the lack of noise immediately stood out to me, with nothing but silence hanging in the air. An occasional piece of birdsong rolled through the trees, just enough to let a person know that time hadn't frozen in place.

"Welcome home," I said as Kat and Linda climbed out.

"Why do we have to be all the way out here?" Kat immediately asked, a surprising bit of attitude in her tone. Linda also gave me a bit of a sideways glance, and I could tell there had been words between them during the drive.

"It's not forever," I said. "But the trial is several weeks away, and with Riccardo Costa out there, we can't risk him finding you."

The answer seemed to her satisfaction as Kat's attention turned to the dwelling.

"Can I go inside?"

"Yes, of course," Linda said, stepping forward to lead us to the cabin. "I've stayed here myself when I wanted some peace and quiet."

Kat didn't respond, but she did follow Linda inside. It looked a lot bigger from the outside, but with two separate bedrooms, a bathroom, and its own kitchen, it really did have all the necessities one could ask for.

"Look, it's even got a TV," I said, pointing to the ancient-looking Sony Trinitron.

"I want to go home" was all Kat said in return, and I wasn't sure what she meant, considering she'd spent her recent past on the streets.

"I promise it won't be long," I repeated as I sat on the arm of the small couch. "And Linda will be here to keep you company."

"I don't like company," Kat said, her tone turning more frustrated. "Prefer to spend time alone."

"You won't even know I'm here," Linda said to try and ease the tension. "I spend most of the day on my laptop and live off coffee and pizza."

"What kind of pizza?" I could sense hope.

"Just plain old cheese for me."

Again, Kat didn't answer, but I took the silence to mean a good thing. She checked out the fridge, the small pantry, and the microwave.

"How will we get food?"

"Marlon does the grocery shopping every other day and usually picks up a few supplies if I ask," Linda said, taking the cue to keep the conversation rolling. "If there's anything specific you need, just let me know."

I could have stayed longer, but given the pair seemed to have finally found some common ground, I figured it best to make a snappy withdrawal.

"Listen, I have to get back to the office," I said, hooking a thumb over my shoulder. "Linda, I'll be on my cell if you need me. Kat, I promise you're in good hands."

That was when she offered me a faint grin, just the top edge of her lip curling up enough to make itself known. She didn't speak, but I could see that, for the moment, Kat Wright trusted us enough to play along. The question for me was just how long that was going to be.

"I'll walk you to your car," Linda said and followed me

back outside as Kat took a seat on the couch and picked up the television remote.

"You're going to have to watch her closely," I whispered to my investigator once we were far enough from the cabin. "Even with the ankle bracelet on, my guess is she'll run the first chance she gets."

"You got that vibe too, huh?"

"Got it the second we picked her up," I said as I opened the Mustang's driver's side door. "What did she say in the car?"

"Nothing in particular other than she doesn't care who comes after her. She can hide on the streets. Which I don't doubt for a second," Linda said, taking a quick look over her shoulder. "One sec."

She ran to her car, pulled open the passenger side door, and leaned inside. I heard her open the glove compartment, rummaging through it for a few seconds before she came back, holding a couple of cell phones.

"I've already set these up. My number is on Redial and in the Contacts List as B1. You've got B2." She handed one of them over to me.

"Linda, listen," I said, lowering my voice even further as I leaned in closer. "I'm not sure how secure that tracking bracelet is going to be. If Costa gets his hands on anybody inside the monitoring company, he'll be able to—"

"Find where we are, yes," Linda finished for me. "Already thought about that. I figure I don't have much of an alternative than what we're doing, but if things do go pear-shaped..." She paused and took another look around, this time not just over her shoulder back at the cabin but also toward the outer edge of the clearing. Only when she was sure nobody was eavesdropping did she continue. "There's a tunnel leading from the cabin out to the woods some two hundred yards that way." She nodded her head in the direction just enough for me to see. "This place used to belong to drug dealers back in the '80s. Don't ask me how I know; I just do. If we do get caught unexpectedly, we will have an escape, but I don't know how long we will have before they find us."

"Just make sure you keep in contact. And if you do need urgent help, you know what to do."

"I do," Linda said.

I don't know why I did it, but a part of me needed to feel her, so I leaned in and gave Linda a hug. It was short, quick, and returned just as succinctly. Linda even added an extra backslap to make it feel a little bit more buddy-like.

"Stay safe," I finished and with that, jumped in the car. I saw Linda head back to the cabin as I rolled back down the track and left.

The part that I couldn't bring myself to believe was that, for perhaps the first time in our professional relationship, I feared for my investigator. We'd worked dangerous cases before, of course, but this one felt like it was sitting on an entirely new level. Riccardo Costa represented a level of threat I myself had faced a couple of times in the past but never in the context I was now. This time, it felt like I wasn't just fighting for the life of my client but also everybody else involved with the case.

5

I RETURNED TO THE CITY IN SILENCE. NO RADIO, NO RIDING THE gas pedal for those sweet V8 engine acoustics, just me alone with my thoughts. Within the space of just six hours, I'd managed to gain a new client, win bail for her, come face to face with a significant threat to our lives, organize a hiding place, and realize that spontaneous decisions came with the biggest chance of catastrophe.

Normally, I would have had the window down, my elbow resting on the ledge, and enjoying the breeze ripping past my face. Instead, I drove with one hand resting on the gear shift and the other barely holding the bottom of the steering wheel while rolling endless scenarios around in my head. I knew how dangerous the what-ifs game was, of course, but sometimes the sheer power of them is enough to pull the mind away from everything else that's going on.

The most dominant thought of all playing in my mind was Costa finding where we had hidden Kat. Him sending goons, those goons storming into the cabin and shooting the place up, maybe setting the place on fire after blocking the tunnel. All manner of barbarism filled my head, each thought more intense than the previous. There came a point where I knew I had to stop or else I'd end up driving myself crazy.

"Come on," I said to myself, shifting uncomfortably in my seat.

Whether genuine fear or just nerves about the people involved in the matter, something about the case just felt different to me, different in a *bad* way. Don't get me wrong; I wasn't second-guessing myself for taking on the case, not by a long way. I just had concerns for my friends' safety. I've seen how crazy things get when someone's out for revenge, how far the fallout can reach, and I didn't want that to happen with this case.

I must have driven back to the office on virtual autopilot because I suddenly found myself parked in my usual spot, staring at the wall in front of me and wondering how the hell I'd gotten there. Once back in the moment, I paused enough to remind myself of what I needed to do next, and only when I was sure I didn't look like a guy needing a nap did I climb out of the car.

"That's one hell of a case you got yourself," Dwight called out to me as I passed him in the hallway a minute or two later.

"It certainly is," I called back. "Got time for a catch-up later?"

"Can it wait until five? Just about to head out for my weekly meeting uptown." He lowered his voice and crinkled his face to make it appear like he'd rather not go, but I knew better. With two old college buddies at the meeting and a couple of notable politicians, it was a meeting my boss enthusiastically showed up for.

"Five it is," I said with an accompanying thumbs-up and continued on to my office.

Sitting at her desk, Grace looked up when I approached and picked up a file to hand to me.

"Put this together once I got back," she said and followed me into my office. "Interesting fellow, this Riccardo Costa." Just hearing his name was enough for something inside me to stir. I made a mental note to focus on ignoring the sensation.

"He's even more interesting in person, believe me," I said and accepted the file. "Thanks."

I set my briefcase down on the desk and took off my jacket before loosening the tie. My neck thanked me for the small reprieve, and after considering it, I took it off completely.

"How about Katherine Wright? Any more information on her?"

"I managed to get an updated report on her as well, plus the assistant DA is sending over their files first thing tomorrow morning."

Grace paused for a moment, giving me time to sit down and open the paperwork she'd just handed me. I briefly flicked through the first few pages, spotting familiar names before closing it again. Dropping the file on my desk, I took a deep breath and sighed. Grace recognized the sign immediately.

"That bad, huh?"

I wanted to tell her about the spy at that very moment; the words balanced precariously on the tip of my tongue. Even the muscles powering my lips tensed up, the words a split second from falling out of my mouth.

"I'm not sure" was what I willingly let out as I held the rest of the words back.

"How was Katherine?"

"Trying her best to be brave," I said. "This is one hell of a mess she's found herself in, and something tells me she isn't going to be strong enough to decide her own fate."

That was when a low rumbling rose into the air, my stomach's protest rolling on for almost ten seconds. Grace looked at me with a grin and waited for the sound to stop.

"You skipped lunch again, didn't you?"

She didn't bother waiting for me to answer, perhaps the look of guilt on my face again giving me away the way it normally did when it came to food. Grace had been at me for months to get into a proper eating routine, but with the way my job refused to follow any predictable pattern, it felt like an impossible task.

Grace returned a few moments later carrying a paper plate, and when she set it down before me, I saw several hors d'oeuvres lined up in neat little rows.

"What's this?" I asked, spotting a shrimp skewered to a piece of pepperoni with a toothpick.

"Martin's birthday lunch. Dwight insisted on bringing in some catering."

"Geez," I said, mentally thanking the man for being born as I popped a meatball into my mouth and quickly devoured it. "I hope I get that kind of treatment when *I* turn fifty."

"I guess you will if you're a senior partner," Grace quipped. "I'll give you time to finish that."

She got up and left me alone with what I can only describe as perfection on a plate, each morsel's flavor more intense than the previous. I think I began to groan by the fourth; my eyes closed by the fifth. Fine food, even if in reality it is just an exotic form of leftovers, is another one of the unlisted perks that came with the job and not one often mentioned.

"Would you two like to be left alone?" a voice suddenly interrupted as I continued focusing on the intense flavor. Opening my eyes, I found Beth Sanders leaning against the doorframe of my office, the grin on her face proof she'd been watching me for some time.

"I'm guessing you didn't try these for yourself," I said as I sat up, pointing to the meatballs and shrimp.

"I'm vegan, Ben," Beth said as she walked in and dropped a folder on my desk.

Beth was what you might call the office gossip. She worked as a personal assistant to Miles Hammer. He was another one of the firm's lawyers, albeit one a lot more senior than me, having worked for Dwight going on twenty years. Miles and I didn't always see eye to eye. We'd had our fair share of run-ins, mostly when it came to client allocation. Dwight once told me during a brief moment of weakness that he considered Miles to be an opportunistic snob who craved pats on the back. If it hadn't been for him working his way through a fine bottle of brandy at an office

Christmas party at the time, I doubt those words would have slipped out, but slip out they did, and I was there to hear them.

His assistant, Beth, on the other hand, took whatever information she heard and ran with it, sometimes spreading news like an overzealous teen buzzed up on Slurpees. She thrived on the attention it gave her, and a few in the office suspected her so-called vegan experience was only so she could actually tell people she was one, another form of attention.

"Miles said you might be able to use this," she said as she barely slowed. "He heard you picked up the Costa murders."

"Thanks," I called after her, but she had already taken her leave, not bothering to hang around and watch me finish the last of the shrimp.

Upon opening the file, I found a case pertaining to a business dispute between the recently deceased Amadore and a woman named Sophia Cafaro. Further investigation showed them to be brother and sister. The pair had opened a bar in downtown Pittsburgh during the late nineties, The Trojan Horse. I myself had been in the place a couple of times over the years, so I already knew about it, although not as well as I had hoped. I recalled meeting a client there once, although I couldn't remember if he was Greek or not.

In any case, it looked like the place had gone through difficult times during the onset of the pandemic, and Amadore made a play to try and have his sister removed from the title. From what I could tell, his plan was to close the bar and sell the building, wiping his hands of the business and pocketing a nice chunk of change. Suffering financial woes, Sophia put up one hell of a fight and ended up winning the day when she managed to find a backer at the last possible minute.

The case was eventually dismissed, the judge telling the two siblings to find a good counselor and take their relationship hassles out of his courtroom. Writing the sister's name down on my pad, I made a note to pay the woman a visit at the first opportunity so I could find out more about her relationship with her brother.

While the file from Miles didn't exactly throw the case wide open for me, it did offer a tiny glimpse into a family I knew I would get to know a lot better as the days went on. It also offered me a look at the place where my greatest threat grew up: Riccardo's home, perhaps the best indicator of a man now seen as one of the most ruthless crime lords around.

As I waited for Dwight's return, I began compiling a list of possible scenarios. Not suspects, per se, but instead, a few ideas on what might have happened...how things played out that would ultimately cost two people their lives. At the very top, for obvious reasons, was the scenario laid out by the prosecution, the one law enforcement had pursued since the very beginning. It also served as the foundation for every other scenario, considering Kat had been in the house at some point either before or perhaps even during the murders.

One scenario I did write down and subsequently scratch off the list again was a murder-suicide. It could have been a very remote possibility were it not for the fact that Mrs. Costa would have had to have shot her husband twice in the back and then herself in the stomach and again in the chest before hiding the gun in a place the police were still yet to find.

Another scenario I wrote down involved a third party, and it was one I circled several times while considering the idea. The one idea I couldn't get away from was the one involving the couple's son and how he might have been the reason they'd been murdered. That was when I started another list right underneath the first, this one headed Possible Thirds. I got two names in before I heard a familiar voice out in the hall before Dwight stuck his head in the doorway.

"Still want that chat, sport?"

"Yes, I'll come right over," I called back and dropped the pen onto the desk.

After closing my laptop and securing the rest of my things, I headed out to where my assistant still sat at her desk.

"Grace, would you mind joining us?"

"Yes, of course," she said without hesitation. When she went to grab her writing pad, I waved a hand.

"You won't need that. Just a quick catch-up, that's all."

Dwight was already sitting behind his desk with his feet up by the time his wife and I walked in. I ushered Grace ahead of me so I could close the door, then joined them, sitting in the one remaining chair next to Grace.

"Was talking to Bob Christianson about the Costa murders," Dwight said once I'd sat down. "Tells me the case is drawing attention from across the state. Even the mayor's talking about it."

"No surprise, given who the son is," Grace said, but that was when Dwight's expression changed.

"You haven't come to talk about the case," he said, the wrinkles running above his eyes deepening with curiosity.

"Actually, the case is *precisely* what I need to discuss," I said and cautiously took a quick look over my shoulder toward the door.

"You checking for hired protection? I don't keep any," Dwight said. "What's going on?"

"We have a spy in the office," I said, lowering my voice to ensure the conversation remained in the room.

"A spy? Who?"

"That I don't know...yet."

"What makes you think we have a spy?" Grace asked. "Ninety percent of our staff have been here for years, and you yourself know how rigorous our vetting process is."

"When I took on the case this morning, I'd only made the decision minutes before walking out of this office and heading straight to the jail to speak with Katherine Wright, and yet somehow Riccardo Costa already knew and confronted me in the prison's parking lot."

"What?" Dwight looked genuinely stunned as Grace shifted uncomfortably in her chair.

"He also made a direct threat against my client, and given her young age and vulnerability, you can understand if I've taken extra measures to try and protect her."

"Ben, Jesus Christ, I wish you would have told me earlier," Dwight said, his tone more shocked than annoyed, but I could see he was pissed. "Do we have any ideas about who the mole might be?"

"No clue," I said. "But whoever it is was close enough to my office to find out almost immediately."

"Hun, would you run checks on all outgoing calls from the office?"

"Yes, of course," Grace said, " but they most likely used their cell phone to make the call."

"Or text," I added. "All it takes is a couple of typed words. Could do it in the blink of an eye."

"That son of a bitch," Dwight said as he leaned back in his chair and looked up at the ceiling. He considered the business his pride and joy, his baby, and someone betraying him like that must have felt like a sword through the heart. "If I find out who—"

"*When* we find out," Grace corrected him. They exchanged a look and didn't need to finish the rest of the sentence, Dwight's nod of the head enough to close the point. It was a connection the pair had shared for many years with no words needed to communicate the unspoken ones. Thankfully, I knew enough to guess them myself.

"Whoever it is, we're not going to find them until they make their next move," I said. "Which is why we're going to have to keep all communication about this case strictly between us."

"And strictly out of the office," Dwight added as he began looking around the walls. "Damn son of a bitch probably bugged the place," and then louder, "So help me, I'll find out who you are."

Dwight suddenly pushed himself out of his chair, walked to the wall immediately behind him, and pulled the huge picture of Mickey Mantle away from the wall. The safe kept behind it wasn't exactly a secret, so I wasn't surprised to see it. The real surprise came when Dwight pulled a huge bank-strapped bundle of cash out and held it up.

"Ten thousand be enough to get you started?"

"Ten thousand for what exactly?" I said, too dumbfounded to conjure up anything more sophisticated.

"To ensure you hide the girl," he said. "Going to have to keep completely off-grid, so to speak. No credit cards or random ATM withdrawals. I know how men like Costa tend to operate."

"OK?"

Dwight walked over to me and held the bundle out. When I hesitated to take the cash, he gave it a shake.

"Come on, just grab it. It's not a bribe or a pay raise, for Christ's sake."

I couldn't refuse, nor did I want to. Dwight was right, of course. To keep Kat safe would take a whole lot of money, and if my boss was willing to fund such an operation, who was I to refuse it? The real question was where I'd be able to keep her safe *and* hidden while unable to remove the weakest part of our vulnerability...the ankle bracelet.

6

CALL IT STUPID ON MY BEHALF, BUT I DECIDED NOT TO MOVE Linda and Kat, at least for the time being. While Linda's association with me might have been common knowledge, her friends weren't, which meant that there was every chance we'd get away with them hiding out on Marlon Shaw's property. Plus, it had all the makings of a classic hideout, complete with an underground tunnel that could serve as an emergency exit. I wouldn't find *that* in any hotel room open to the public.

Thanks to the burner phones, Linda and I stayed in regular contact, and with me maintaining open and honest communication with my investigator, I told her about the money Dwight had given me. She texted back almost immediately, telling me to save it for a rainy day. That meant she had faith in their current hideout, and I wasn't about to question her on it. Linda knew her stuff, especially when it came to eluding criminals and staying out of sight. If she trusted Marlon's former drug shack, then so did I.

You might wonder why we opted to text rather than call. The truth is we didn't start off that way. It only changed after I heard Kat in the background a couple of times I did call, and it was hearing those constant complaints that made us switch to a more stealthy form of communication. If she didn't know I was listening, then she might ease up on grumbling about her surroundings.

An hour after reaching home that night, and with my mind unable to switch off, I decided to try and catch up with a friend, an old friend of Linda's and a relatively new friend of mine. After Jack Barnes took off the top of Robert Norris's head during that brief hotel parking lot exchange the previous year, we'd caught up several times not long after, sometimes on official business and sometimes not.

That night, it was Barnes' professional side I wanted to meet down at The Hose and Ladder, Pittsburgh's finest bar for anybody within law enforcement or the services supporting it. That included both lawyers and sheriff's deputies and also a place where we had caught up on several prior occasions.

Jack answered my text not two minutes after I sent it with his usual thumbs-up emoji, a man of few words when it came to the important stuff. Rather than head straight out again, what I needed first was a shower, which was why I asked to meet Jack in an hour and not sooner. It felt like the day's residue clung to my very skin, and only a hot shower and scrub would remove it. Halfway to the bathroom, my plans took another detour as the vibration in my pocket caught my attention.

After pulling the cell phone out, my eyes paused at the name staring back at me from a screen, a name that shouldn't have made me feel the way it did. The thing was, I had felt the text coming long before that evening, the unspoken words already hanging between Gabby and me. I sighed seeing them, something inside me tightening up with dread.

While you might have assumed romance was sparking between Gabby and me, it never seemed to fully play out. Things just always seemed to get in the way. Whenever we went out or sat together on the couch, something would always come up that seemed to pull us in a different direction from where the romance was waiting. A conversation would start up, or something would flash up on the TV that drew our attention away. Sometimes, a phone call or a text cut in, dragging one of us away and diverting our plans down another track.

I liked Gabby—liked her a lot, in fact. She was fun to hang out with, and the conversations we had just seemed to flow. We shared similar interests when it came to just the two of us, and things could have progressed from those basic foundations, and yet...they just didn't. Some might say that the spark we all expected just didn't seem to fire up. The worst part was that the last time I'd seen Gabby, friction I had felt for a while finally surfaced, and we ended up in an argument, one that never actually resolved itself. As I stared down at the name on my cell phone screen, I already knew what the words were going to say, which was why it took me a few seconds before I finally opened the message to read them.

Ben, I'm sorry to say it like this, but I don't think I have the courage to do it face to face. I'm so confused about how things continue to play out between us, and after not seeing you these past ten days, I wonder whether it might not be best if we just go our separate ways. I'd hoped that you might have at least phoned me after the way we left things the other night, but no amount of hope can get a girl through. Please don't respond. I honestly don't think I can keep putting myself out there waiting for you to fall for me the way I have for you. I guess sometimes, things just aren't meant to be.

I don't know how long I stood in the middle of my living room staring at the words before I finally lowered the phone beside me. The three words that hit me the hardest were the ones that effectively wedged us apart once and for all: *please don't respond*, kind of closing the door if I did want to do anything.

Yes, I could have sent a reply. God knows I wanted to. Perhaps the more noble thing to do would have been to jump in my car, drive to her house, and do what I should have done long ago. Maybe push her against the wall and kiss her passionately, let her tear off my clothes and do to me what she'd been insinuating for months. I very nearly did, looking over my shoulder to where the car keys sat on the other end of the dining table.

I can hear you screaming down at the book while looking at my words, calling for me to grow some balls and just do it. It wasn't fair to let her hang like that, but to be honest, and it was the other side I didn't think I could go on with, the part that led her on even longer. Gabby was right. Sometimes, things just aren't meant to be, and after all this time, I simply didn't feel that way about her.

"It's better this way," I whispered to myself as I set the phone down on the table and continued on to the bathroom.

The shower felt like shit. No, that's not true; the shower felt fine, the water washing the rest of the day away. *I*, however, felt like shit, thanks to my ultimate decision to honor her wishes and let things go. I only had myself to blame, of course, but I knew in time I would come to grow used to the feeling and get on with my life just the way she would.

The irony of the whole thing was that I hadn't actually felt like a drink when I'd first made the decision to go down to the bar, but now that I had Gabby's text message weighing down on me, a drink seemed like the perfect solution. A drink or two and Jack Barnes' insights would serve as the perfect distraction.

An hour later, and feeling a lot more casual in my jeans and T-shirt, I walked into The Hose and Ladder. It took me all of a few seconds to find Jack sitting at the bar alone, thanks to the distinct lack of patrons, a half-empty beer in front of him. I gestured to the bartender for one of my own, clapped Jack on the shoulder, and took a seat beside him.

"I see you got a head start on me," I said with a grin.

"What makes you think I just arrived?"

That was when I took a little closer look at my friend and saw the evidence for myself.

"OK, then, it looks like you've gotten a few in ahead of me."

Jack didn't smile, not even the faintest grin. His usual cheery self had been replaced with the sternest of poker faces. When he set the glass down after taking a swallow, he gazed into the bottom of it the way people did when the thoughts in their heads weighed heavy.

"Everything OK?"

"Maddy left me," he grumbled with a tone barely loud enough to travel the short distance between us.

What I wanted to say was, *Oh, you too, huh*, but I didn't, keeping the words held in. Instead, I waited for the bartender to bring me my beer and took a large mouthful, enough to need three swallows to sink it all.

"I knew it was coming, but still kicks like a damn mule, you know?"

"Yeah, I know," I said as I assumed the same posture as him, right down to staring into the bottom of my glass as Gabby returned to mind.

We remained in our assumed positions for the next two beers before I asked Jack whether he was up for some questions about my latest case. He suggested we move our gathering to somewhere a little more private, and I followed him over to one of the booths.

"Tell me about this case of yours," he said as he started on a fresh beer. "Anything to get my damn mind off things."

"It's the Costa murders," I said. "Defending Katherine Wright."

"Holy shit, that's you?" I nodded. "Jesus, man, you really are a glutton for punishment. Maybe you should have called me *before* you decided to take on half of Pittsburgh's criminal underworld."

"I'll remember it for next time," I said.

"*If* there's a next time," Jack said with a suppressed chuckle. "Going to have to survive this one first."

"Well, at least you understand what I'm up against. That's one positive thing."

"I understand, all right. Already heard all about Riccardo putting out feelers for someone to bring him the one who murdered his parents."

"Yes, a little eighteen-year-old girl. That's who he thinks murdered his parents."

"Did she?"

"That's what I need to find out," I said. "And fast."

While I could get all the information I needed from the multitude of files on Riccardo Costa, the best insight would always come from those who worked the cases, the cops personally getting hands-on with the suspects. That's what I hoped for, anyway. As it turned out, that's not what I got from Jack.

"He's the kind of guy who watches his ass carefully" was how he put it. "Costa always pays for someone else to get their hands dirty on his behalf, and he always manages to keep himself separated so as not to get drawn into any investigations. Even our snitches work on nothing more than rumors and assumptions."

"Think he'll stand back and let someone else avenge his parents?"

Jack considered my question by slowly raising his glass, holding it for a brief moment before taking another large swallow and setting it down again.

"Who knows what goes through the minds of these

crazies?" he eventually said. "All I know is that if I were you, I'd start looking over my shoulder a lot more. Maybe check underneath that car of yours as well. I'd definitely be sweating a lot more each time I hit that ignition button."

"Thanks, pal," I said with a shake of the head. "As if I didn't have enough worries already."

"Just telling you how it is, brother," Jack said and finished his beer.

It wasn't exactly the kind of insight I imagined when I'd first messaged him, but I couldn't ignore the fact that he was right. If nothing else, Jack reminded me of just who it was I now found myself the target of. Riccardo Costa was a man with a long history of criminal dealings, living his life above the law that I myself tried my best to uphold. If Costa did, in fact, try to make a move on Kat, it would be me he'd have to come through.

7

AFTER FINISHING THE REST OF HIS BEER, JACK WISHED ME A good night by clapping his hand on my shoulder.

"I don't think I'm the best guy to keep you company tonight, brother," he said, and before I had a chance to respond, Jack headed out into the night. I felt sorry for him. I'd only met his wife a couple of times over the months and always assumed they were happy.

I decided to stick around for one more drink, this time opting for something a little stronger. It would raise my buzz enough to ensure I'd easily pass out once my head hit the pillow. Bourbon just had that kind of effect on me.

"JD, straight up," I called to the bartender once I'd retaken my previous seat, and he slipped the glass in front of me with seasoned efficiency.

"How was Jack when he left?" Simon Winston asked while pouring my drink. The man had worked the bar for as long as I could remember and a great deal before then. He was one of those men who knew faces and remembered most of those he'd served during his tenure.

"OK, I think. Nothing a good night's sleep won't fix."

"She cheated on him, you know?"

"What?" The revelation just about knocked me off the stool. "No way."

"I wish I was wrong, but the guy she was cheating with normally sits at the very spot you're in." I tried to think of who it might have been but couldn't picture the person. Simon wasn't about to let me take guesses. "Joel Peterson. You know, the—"

"Paramedic," I cut in. "Yeah, I know him. He's married too, isn't he?"

"Two families broken by a single betrayal," Simon continued. "Some people don't deserve kids, I swear."

"When was the last time you saw Peterson in here?" I asked, a new realization forming in my head.

"Last night."

I began to wonder whether Jack had not been waiting for the man who effectively broke his marriage. Perhaps I was the distraction he needed in order to save himself from a suspension or worse. Who knew how badly the deception had affected him? Enough to warrant sitting in the very same bar waiting for the betrayer to walk in.

"Well, let's hope they don't cross each other's paths out in the parking lot," I said, raised the glass, and downed the amber liquid in one swallow.

The moment the words left my mouth, an eerie tightening gripped my insides as if I'd spoken some premonition out loud. The bartender had already moved on to another patron, giving me the perfect opportunity to make a quick exit. I don't know why, but I suddenly felt an urgent need to get outside to see for myself, to make sure that Jack had indeed left without first stopping to unalive the man who'd broken his life.

As I pushed through the doors onto the outside decking, I paused long enough to scan the majority of the parking lot. I also listened for any sort of commotion that might indicate a confrontation, although it took just seconds for me to confirm the silence. The only section of the parking lot I couldn't see was the half-dozen or so spaces around the far side of the building, and when I didn't spot Jack's Jeep parked among those cars I could see, I wanted to confirm he hadn't parked around the side either.

The urgency was what propelled me forward, and never in a million years would I have guessed that it would ultimately betray me in the worst way possible. My feet carried me to the corner and should have stopped when I reached a point where I could see the two vehicles hidden beyond, but powerful hands suddenly pushed hard into my back, the momentum immediately working against me. By the time I finally did manage to stop, I'd been pushed almost completely into the shadows and turned to face four men.

"Who the hell are—" was all I managed to get out before two of them lunged forward, the first catching me with a fist to the side of the head. It only skimmed across my cheek, a knuckle flicking the top of my ear, thanks to me flinching to one side, but it distracted me enough for the second guy to land a gut punch.

I stumbled back as the other two rounded their buddies.

One tried to launch a kick, but I easily deflected it, swinging a fist hard at the guy as he tried to regain his balance. I felt my knuckles connect with the middle of his face, and the ensuing grunt confirmed I'd struck gold. He stumbled back, clutching his face, although the lack of lighting kept his injury hidden. A fresh blow landed in my lower back, pain ripping through me like infectious heat. Somewhere in the back of my mind, I could see myself pissing blood for the next few days.

"Take your medicine, Counselor," a voice said from somewhere behind me before more pain exploded in my ear. Stars filled my vision as my knees gave out, and I hit the ground hard enough to feel my knee open up.

Once down on the ground, they knew they well and truly had me, and all I could do was curl up into a fetal position to try and shield myself from the hammering I was about to endure. While one of them continued throwing punches, the other three opted for kicks instead, the boots landing intermittently across my back and head. The one standing in front of me kept trying to kick my face and would have succeeded were it not for me managing to bring my knees up far enough to shield it.

I don't know how long the beating lasted. Perhaps time slowed down, getting in on the action by betraying me the only way it could to ensure the punishment lasted longer than it should. Perhaps the universe hated lawyers as much as everybody else, and all the jokes I'd heard during my years as one only served as a forewarning.

Just when I thought I couldn't take any more and my struggle to remain conscious would be lost, the blows first slowed and then stopped. Heat ripped through the top of my head as someone grabbed a fistful of hair and pulled my head up. Rancid breath filled my nostrils, the stink foul enough for my insides to gag.

"The boss wants to make sure you suffer," the voice croaked bare inches from my face. "If you're dumb enough to defend the little bitch, then you're going to pay the price."

With no strength left to hold my head up, it hit the ground hard when he let go, and I could barely open my eyes enough to watch the four men walk away. I didn't dare move until they rounded the corner, but not before one of them paused to take a final look back at me. He pointed a finger, pretending it to be a gun, and imitated taking a shot. The message he intended to send hit home.

Once I was sure I was alone, I managed to roll onto my back, throbs of pain emanating from every part of my body. I couldn't tell one limb from another and instead focused on the raindrops slowly building in intensity. I tried to remember whether rain had been forecast for the day, a fitting alternative to trying to decide whether I'd ever walk again.

"Ben, Jesus Christ," a familiar voice suddenly called out from somewhere behind me, and a moment later, I felt something brush past my face. "What the hell happened?" Simon said as he looked down at my bruised and bloodied face.

"Think I got jumped," I managed to mumble, the exquisite pain of a busted lip reminding me that speech would take on new meaning for the next couple of days.

While I did try to decline the offer of an ambulance, my

words fell on the deaf ears of a sixty-something-year-old bartender who called for one anyway. Before long, I found myself staring up into the faces of multiple paramedics who eventually helped me sit up and clamber onto a gurney they wheeled to their waiting vehicle. When they asked whether I wanted to spend a night at the local hospital, I politely refused and insisted on getting the rest I needed in my own bed.

What I didn't expect was for Grace to show up while I was still sitting on the back step of the ambulance talking to one of the medics. At first, I thought I was seeing things, but the look of concern on her face quickly proved her to be real.

"It's not as bad as it looks," I tried telling her, but I could see words weren't going to change the evidence staring back at her.

"I think you might need a mirror if that's what you think, Ben Carter," she said with an almost scolding tone as if I'd simply been fooling around.

It's funny how maternal instinct has a way of trumping any other type of emotion when it comes to looking after someone. Regardless of my protests, Grace insisted on driving me home in my car and then ordering herself an Uber to go back to the bar for her own vehicle. I felt guilty, and not just for my predicament bringing her out on such a miserable night. The heavens really opened up during that long drive home, and the silence only further exasperated my already dim mood.

"At least let me stand here while you wait for your ride," I said once we parked the Mustang and headed for the front of the building. When she looked at me with an expression of disappointment, I knew I'd screwed up.

"I'm sorry, Grace, but I'm not sure what I did wrong here."

"You haven't done anything wrong, Ben. I'm just angry that this is the penalty for wanting to help a young girl."

"I'm not sure it's a penalty," I said, leaning against a sign-post for some much-needed support. "I think it's just part of the job."

"To get yourself nearly killed? I mean, look at you."

What I had assumed to be disappointment on Grace's face turned out to be fear, the kind that took a bit to come to the surface. In a way, it scared me to see that fear in her, although I tried my best to keep mine a little more shielded.

"I have to admit, this is probably the worst beating I've received since becoming a lawyer, but if that's what it takes to protect Katherine Wright, then so be it." I felt my fear turn to anger. "And if this is how Riccardo Costa wants to play, then so be it, but I'm not backing down, Grace. Not now, not ever."

At first, I thought Grace might actually try and slap some sense into me, but just as headlights came up over a nearby rise and illuminated the two of us, Grace began to grin.

"You're just as crazy as Dwight said you were," she finally said.

"Dwight called me crazy?"

"Uh-huh, the first week you joined us."

Now it was my turn to grin, and when Grace walked toward the curb, I began to laugh. Multiple parts of my body instantly flinched from the pain, but this was too good to be ignored.

"Well, you tell Dwight he was right," I called after her. "You tell him I'm exactly as crazy as he assumed."

I waited until the Uber took off again before heading inside, Grace giving me a final wave as the car pulled back out onto the road. What I didn't know was that somebody had already taken up a position in the nearby shadows to watch me, their boss paying to know my every step moving forward.

8

WHILE MOST PEOPLE WILL TELL YOU THAT SLEEP IS THE BEST
medicine, I'm here to tell you otherwise. When I woke up
the next morning, I could barely move, each of my joints
feeling frozen in place. Aches and pains came from places I
didn't even know I had, and when I looked in the mirror, I
had to move my head several times to make sure the movements matched. I barely recognized myself.

My left eye lay hidden under dark purple swelling that
extended down the side of my face. Even the ear looked to
have been cut up, with a neat line of dried blood running
across the top of it. The medics had told me that my nose
hadn't been broken, but I seriously questioned that diagno-
sis, given the distinct bend I could see. Both my top and
bottom lips sported cuts, albeit on opposite ends, which
made any sort of movement nearly impossible without the
pain giving me a wake-up call. Even tensing my muscles in

preparation for speech was enough to tap me on the shoulder.

When it came to the rest of my body, that vision sent cold shivers through me once I managed to get my T-shirt off. I hadn't bothered stripping the previous night and simply slipped into bed with the hope of that mythical healing sleep fixing me while I was passed out. No such luck. The bruises from the multitude of kicks dotted my torso from top to bottom, both my front and back resembling a war zone. How I managed to escape without at least a broken rib or two is beyond me.

Grace was right, and I finally acknowledged her words from the previous night about me coming close to death with a simple head nod. She was right. I had come dangerously close to losing my life before the fight had even begun. I needed to be more careful if I was going to be around long enough to see this battle through. How was I going to help Kat survive if I sucked at keeping myself alive?

The real kicker came when I finally relieved myself for the first time since the attack. While the stream looked mostly yellow as it should, a distinct tinge of red began to turn the toilet bowl crimson, confirming that my kidneys had taken a fair beating. I shuddered at the sight, not because I was squeamish about blood but because of what could have happened had they added a bit more oomph into their lesson. Flushing the toilet was more of a relief than the actual urination.

I ran the shower as hot as my skin allowed me to, and a few seconds after climbing in, I added a few extra degrees for good measure. I needed to get some heat into my muscles to get them mobile again. The only thing sleep had given me was cold joints too painful to move, and I had some serious cleaning to do. Five minutes in, I could feel them beginning to let go enough for me to soap up and wash off some of the blood. I figured any that remained after my effort was meant to stay.

Once I climbed out again, I did feel a lot better. I certainly moved a lot more freely, although I couldn't say the same for my face. It was my lips I feared for the most, the pain coming from them the most exquisite of all. Sharp, sweet bursts of torment plagued me whenever I forgot and began to speak, feeling like long needles pushed into the delicate flesh. It's funny how a person forgets just how much they talk to themselves when caught in such a dilemma.

It's also funny how different movements will highlight different injuries. Take my left knee, for example. It wasn't until I climbed into the Mustang and went to push the clutch in that a new uncomfortableness made itself known. As it turned out, the angle at which I needed to raise and lower the foot in order to change gears was precisely the position where the knee sang a chorus of agony like a choir on steroids. Let's just say I made minimal gear changes during my drive to work that morning, most of the time taking off from traffic lights in second gear.

While I'd prepared myself mentally for what I'd ended up seeing in the mirror when I first got home the previous night, nothing could have prepared me for the reactions from my colleagues the moment I walked through the doors. Most tried to hide their shock, either behind hands they used to cover the bottom half of their faces or just looking away. Unfortunately, nothing could hide the shock from their eyes, and it was there that I saw the real reactions.

"I'm all right, Jessica," I told our receptionist when I saw tears begin to well up. "I promise."

"You shouldn't be coming in to work, though," she told me through clasped fingers pressing against her face.

"I'll be fine," I managed before the next person appeared and then the next. I eventually had to address a crowd and reassure them I was fine before escaping to my office.

I'd barely sat down before someone knocked gently on the door, and when I looked up, I saw Grace peering in at me.

"Jessica was right, you know. You could have just stayed home."

"And miss all this?"

"They're a delicate bunch. Maybe I should have forewarned them," Grace said as she walked in carrying a file of some sort.

"What's this?"

"Oh, something I found while tinkering around last night." When I looked at her strangely, she waved it away. "Don't worry, Mr. Carter, I wasn't here on your account. Dwight worked late, and I didn't want to be home alone, so I decided to hang around here and get some work done."

"What did you find?" I asked as I opened the file and scanned the first page.

"A possible answer to who might have had reason to murder Riccardo Costa's parents," Grace said as she sat down in front of me.

"Solomon Malak?" I'd heard the name before but

couldn't quite place where, so I simply shrugged my shoulders.

"He's in the same business as Riccardo," Grace said. "A drug dealer working the city's northern side. I've checked back through the records, and it looks like these two have been going at it for almost a decade."

"OK, but why now if they've been trying to get each other for that long?"

"Six months ago, Riccardo's men took down a meth lab of Malak's, firebombed the place, stole the money and drugs, and left two men dead."

"That's not uncommon in their line of work," I said as I tried leaning back in my chair, felt a bolt of pain deep down in my kidneys, and quickly rethought my decision. "Doesn't explain why someone would go after the parents. Seems like an excessive move to me."

I wasn't trying to be argumentative, although it might come across that way. What I wanted was a clear picture that I understood, especially if I was going to devote precious time to investigating the lead. Call it an unofficial cross-examination, if you will.

"One of the two men killed in that attack was the boyfriend of Malak's daughter. My guess is she took it hard and convinced her father to exact revenge for her."

I didn't answer right away, running the idea through my mind. The thing is, Grace was starting to make sense and painting a very clear picture of the possible explanation, and I wanted to be sure I understood perfectly. As it turned out, Grace wasn't finished.

"There's more," she said as she saw me trying to process all the information.

"Go on."

"A hitman Malak's been known to use landed at PIT two days before the Costa murders." She pointed to the file. "I took the liberty to print out a condensed version of his record as well. If Malak was going to go as far as killing his adversary's parents, that's the man he'd use for the job."

She was right. One look at the file of Mansur Diab was enough to send a cold shudder down the length of my spine. Suspected to be involved in seventeen missing person cases, nine homicides, and two very public assassinations in New York City, this was a man who knew his business.

"This is some serious firepower," I said more to myself than to Grace, but she agreed.

"And he doesn't come cheap, according to the message boards."

"Grace, I need your help with something," I said as I closed the file and gripped it with both hands. It was that very moment when I came to the realization that I needed help, the kind from a person who also understood their business...or should I say *her* business.

"Of course," my assistant said. "It's what I'm here for."

I pursed my lips as I considered the words before speaking. I wasn't entirely sure whether it would matter, but I needed her to understand the seriousness of what I was about to ask.

"How are you with kids?"

For a second, Grace just looked at me before tilting her

head ever so slightly, like a pup trying to work out what a whistle was.

"Kids?"

"I need Linda to help me with this one. I don't think I can do this without her, but she's caught up looking after Katherine Wright."

"You want me to babysit your client?"

"She's eighteen, so not quite babysitting, but yes, would you?"

For the briefest moment, I thought Grace was going to take offense to the request. I should have known better. In all the years we'd worked together, I don't think she had ever turned down a single one of my requests, no matter how crazy they might have been.

"But of course. Just tell me where."

"Before you decide, I need you to understand what you're getting yourself into. This girl...Grace, she's lived on the streets for a long time and knows them like the back of her hand. If she wants to disappear into them, she would, and I highly doubt she'd pass up an opportunity if given half a chance."

"Benjamin Carter, are you suggesting that if this girl decided to run, I wouldn't be able to keep up with her?"

"No, not at all. I'm just saying that she might get a head start...you know...give you the slip or something." Grace chuckled, the look of bemusement growing.

"I'm pretty sure this sprint champion still has some speed left in her."

"Sprint champion?"

"Three years straight back in college, thank you."

I couldn't stop the questions. "Back in college? How long ago was that?" I didn't mean it the way it came out, but of course, it sounded way worse than intended. What I should have done was cut off my foot and jam it into my mouth.

"It may have been some years ago, Benjamin Carter, but I'm not quite over the hill yet," Grace said with a bemused smile. Feeling the heat rising in my cheeks was enough to tell me I'd erred.

"OK, OK, forgive me. I just never pictured you..."

"What? As a runner?" More bemusement. "I assure you that if this girl decides to try and outpace me, she may just get the shock of her life."

"I'm sorry. That came out all wrong," I said, hoping the bruising was enough to cover the flushed embarrassment.

"Hey, kid, go a few rounds with Tyson or what?" a new voice called out, and I looked up to see Dwight standing in the doorway. He walked a few steps farther into the office before stopping. "Shit, kid, Gracey told me you'd been beaten up, but I didn't think you skimmed this side of death. Did you go to the hospital?"

"The paramedics assured me there were no broken bones or a concussion. Just a lot of bruising."

"To the ego, I bet," Dwight said.

"That too."

"Listen, if you want to palm the case off to someone—"

"Not a chance," I said, cutting him off with a hand held up. "I'll see this one through personally, thanks."

"I knew you would but had to ask."

"Of course," I said, and after giving his wife a kiss on top of the head, Dwight left us alone again.

"He wasn't going to ask you, you know," Grace said once we were alone again.

"Ask what?"

"Whether you wanted to keep the case. He had his mind made up to give it to Justin, but I suggested he wait and ask you himself."

"Thank you, I appreciate it," I said. "And you guessed right. I owe it to this girl to go on. I can't imagine how many people she's had give up on her in such a short life."

"Too many, I bet," Grace said. "Still, nobody would have thought less of you."

"I know," I said and pulled out the second phone, the one handed to me by Linda. "Let me send Linda a text to forewarn her, and then we can go."

"OK, let me go grab a few things from home. Pick me up from there?"

"I'll see you in an hour," I said and continued with the text.

I didn't share everything, just enough to let my investigator know that she was about to be relieved by a replacement so I could task her with other things. Linda answered almost immediately, a sign she already had the phone in her hands. After giving Grace enough time to make it home and throw a bag together, I grabbed my things and headed out.

It was when I reached the parking lot that a thought stopped me in my tracks. The notion that they were already watching me wasn't new, but I guess I'd never considered it much of a threat until that moment. Looking around, I couldn't see any suspicious vehicles parked on the side of the road or within view, but that didn't mean I wasn't being tracked. They could use any number of ways to follow me around, and if they found where I had hidden Kat, the game would be over.

I changed my mind in a flash and pulled out the phone again. Instead of taking Grace to the property, I gave her directions on how to get there and asked if she would mind handing her car over to Linda. Of course, Grace agreed, just as I knew she would. The real question was whether Costa had also put a tail on my assistant.

9

AFTER SENDING INSTRUCTIONS TO BOTH MY INVESTIGATOR AND assistant, I turned around and headed back inside, where I began the process of looking into Solomon Malak for myself. I knew going into the case that Costa would have his fair share of enemies and suspected that one of them might have been responsible for the killing of the parents, but I never expected my assistant to be the one to bring me the name.

I was still reading about Malak's history when Linda walked into my office a couple of hours later. She stopped just inside the door, leaned against the frame, and gave me the same look as so many others that day.

"It looks worse than it is," I said, still doing my best to resist annunciating for fear of my cut lips opening up again.

"I'll say," Linda said as she walked the rest of the way and sat down. "Don't tell me. You should see the other guy, right?"

"Well, there were four of them, actually," I said.

"Riccardo Costa's men?"

"Confirmed. Came to deliver a message."

She shook her head in disgust. "I'm guessing you left your piece in the car?"

"Even if I had been carrying it, there was no time to use it. They snuck up behind me and pounced in the blink of an eye."

Another disgusted head shake. "Can't let that happen again. You know that, right?"

"Didn't plan for it to happen the first time," I said and prepared to defend myself again, but Linda didn't push the issue.

"Guess we'd better make sure we give you the chance to put them away then. What do you have for me?"

"Solomon Malak," I said, glad to change the direction of the conversation. "Actually, it was Grace who brought the name to me, him and his usual hitman, Mansur Diab." I held out the file Grace had brought me earlier, and Linda took it as she looked at me curiously.

"Diab?" She sounded familiar with the name.

"You know of him?"

"As a matter of fact, I do. Involved in a case that I worked on quite a few years ago."

"During your time working for your previous boss?"

"No, before then," Linda said, and I felt her close off for just a brief second. If I didn't know her mannerisms, I might have missed them myself, but I knew my investigator and picked up on the pause in an instant. Linda immediately deflected the question and turned in another direction before I had a chance to double down on it. "Diab is one dangerous individual. If this Malak really did bring him in to take care of Costa's parents, then you can rest assured he completed his mission."

"What if he turns his hitman on me next if he suspects us of poking around? Or you?"

"Then we're going to have to move fast. Work the case, get our list of names, and start banging on doors," Linda said as she continued eyeing the file I'd handed her.

I wanted to ask her more about how she knew the name Diab, but I could sense a weird vibe coming from her, the kind of vibe that indicated a lack of willingness to reopen that part of our conversation. I filed the questions into the back of my mind and resumed building our plan.

"OK, why don't you take that file and see what you can come up with? Grace said that Diab arrived two days before the Costa killings, which kind of fits in with the timeline if he was, in fact, the one responsible for the shooting."

"And you?"

"I'm going to look into Solomon Malak and see what I can find about his beef with Riccardo Costa. I also need to meet with Sophia Cafaro, the sister of Riccardo's father. Apparently, Amadore and her went into business together and opened a bar down by the riverfront."

"Definitely not a wise move going into business with family."

"You're telling me," I said. "I already found a lawsuit between the two during the pandemic."

"One of them fell short on money?"

"The sister," I confirmed. "Guessing Amadore figured it

would be a nice little payday for himself if he could sell the building."

"All right, well, it sounds like you've got a bit of work cut out for yourself." She stood and pointed to my face. "And a nice bit of healing."

"Don't remind me," I said. "Just let me know when you find anything we can use."

"I'm on it," Linda confirmed and left just as fast as she had arrived.

I sat quietly, staring at the doorway for a few minutes, the scent of Linda's perfume lingering as much as the conversation. I couldn't get that brief moment of hesitation out of my mind. The thing about Linda was that she was extremely private. Had been for as long as I'd known her. The only reason I hired her in the first place was because of her previous experience working for another lawyer. At that moment, sitting silently in my office staring at that doorway, I realized just how little I knew about a woman I had entrusted with my life on more than a few occasions.

"Earth to Ben," a voice suddenly said, and I looked up to find Jessica staring back at me from the doorway. Just her head was visible, along with some fingers curled around the corner, and from the sound of her tone, I could tell it wasn't the first time she'd called out to me.

"Sorry, away with the fairies," I said with a smile that immediately sent needle pricks through my lips.

"I'll say. Was about to throw something at you."

"What's up?"

"I have a Mr. and Mrs. Wright waiting out in reception for you."

"Who?"

For a second, I had no clue who she was talking about. Not only did I not have any appointments scheduled for that day or any other that week, but the name didn't sound at all familiar to me. Thankfully, Jessica could see my lack of knowledge and added a bit more context.

"They said you were representing their daughter."

"Oh, shit, of course," I said, feeling more than a little stupid.

"Want to meet them out in reception, or do you want me to walk them down?"

"Could you bring them in for me? Thanks."

Jessica didn't respond before disappearing again, and while normally my first move would have been to make my desk look presentable, I quickly headed to my private bathroom and checked the reflection staring back at me in the mirror. Yup, just as I had feared. I looked about as presentable as a half-baked leg of lamb, the color about the same.

Fearing there was nothing I could do to improve my appearance, I ran my fingers through my hair to at least make myself feel like I'd made an effort. When I was sure it had the desired effect, I returned to my desk but remained standing next to it in anticipation of my visitors' arrival.

"There you go, folks, just through here," I heard Jessica say from a distance, and a moment later, she led the two guests into my office. "This here is Mr. and Mrs. Wright," Jessica finished and immediately moved aside as I stepped forward.

"Ben Carter, pleased to meet you," I said and held out a

hand, first shaking with Kat's mother, Lois, and then her father, Brad. Not surprisingly, the two exchanged a look of surprise. "Won't you take a seat?"

I thanked Jessica for her help, and she immediately left the office, closing the door behind her. Taking my own seat, I could see the questions written on the faces of my visitors and knew I had to address them first before anything else.

"Car accident," I said, figuring it a better explanation than the one involving paid men sent to rough me up for defending their daughter.

"Wow, it looks like you hit a brick wall," Brad Wright said, and his wife immediately tapped his leg. He looked at her and shrugged. "What? He does."

"Actually, it was the back of a cab that decided to lock up its brakes without working warning lights."

"Ouch, that'll do it every time," Brad continued. "Smashed my Chrysler up almost the same way."

"No kidding?"

Deciding that there were more important matters to deal with, Lois leaned a little forward and interrupted the conversation.

"Mr. Carter, forgive the intrusion, but when we heard you were defending Katherine, I felt it our Christian duty to come down here and offer our support." She looked uncomfortably at her husband before turning back to me. "It's not exactly common knowledge that our daughter has been living the way she has. As far as our congregation is concerned, Katherine has been staying with her aunt in Upstate New York."

"Please...call me Ben, and I gather you're not close with your daughter."

She looked uncomfortable when the question was asked, a lot more uncomfortable than her husband, who seemed to be paying more attention to the photo of my Mustang on the wall than the topic of conversation.

"Katherine is a...*difficult* child," she began. "She'd never been one to follow the rules, and when we banned a couple of her friends from our house a few years ago, Katherine took it upon herself to run away. We brought her back a few times, but she'd always take off again until we eventually gave up trying. She'd gotten pregnant, you see, and when she opted for an abortion, it crossed every line imaginable for us."

I'm not what you'd call a religious person. It's not that I don't believe in God; it's just that I have my own viewpoint on the subject, and it doesn't involve trying to force others to follow it. Lois Wright, on the other hand, looked to be the type of person who took her faith seriously, right down to the crucifix dangling from a chain around her neck and the husband she used for support. The woman wore her hair tied back and shaped into a neat bun, no makeup, and a plain yellow dress. It wouldn't have surprised me if she had pulled a small Bible out of her purse and begun sharing a verse or two to fill in time.

"Unfortunately, your daughter is facing a double murder charge, Mrs. Wright. The prosecutor has a wealth of evidence against her, and it's going to take a miracle for us to prove them wrong."

I expected her to tell me that she knew just the being to

provide such a miracle, that she would go home that very second, fall to her knees before her living room altar, and begin praying to her Lord and Savior for guidance.

"You see, our family has used the same respected lawyer for years, Mr. Carter, and we would much prefer him to represent Katherine," she said, ignoring my attempt to be less formal. She gave me another up-and-down look as if trying to highlight my appearance, but I ignored it.

"Have you spoken with Katherine about this?"

"We are meeting with her tomorrow morning," Lois said, and I saw her give her husband's hand that she had been holding the entire time a squeeze.

"Yes, tomorrow morning," Brad Wright said, suddenly aware he also had a role to play. "Gordon Woodford represented my father's business for decades, and we feel he might be more suitable for this."

That was when I realized just how much the couple was out of the loop. If they didn't know their daughter had even made bail, how little interest did they really have in her welfare? I could have told them, of course. Perhaps I *should* have told them, but a part of me couldn't bring myself to speak the words. Instead, I decided on a different tactic.

"Is he a criminal lawyer?" I asked the question with a certain attempt to lessen the tone, but I don't think it worked.

"He's a lawyer; that's all that matters," Lois continued. "And besides, we have an arrangement with him when it comes to fees."

"Katherine isn't paying me to represent her," I said, detecting a hint of opportunity. "Our firm likes to offer certain cases free representation that we feel helps the community. Katherine waited two whole days for someone to help her before I showed up."

I didn't want to sound like I was attacking them, but it came out that way, and I saw the woman flinch in her seat.

"Yes, well, Brad and I were out of town this past week. We only arrived back this morning and immediately contacted Gordon." I wanted to ask what had kept them out of the city that they saw as more important than their child's welfare, but I resisted the urge.

"I don't think you understand, Mrs. Wright. Katherine isn't a child anymore, and at eighteen, she's well within her right to choose who she would like to represent her."

That was when the woman didn't bother hiding the offense she took from my words. She immediately let go of her husband's hand and pushed herself out of the chair.

"We'll just see about that," she snapped, and without bothering to wait for her husband, she stormed out of my office. A few uncomfortable seconds passed as the father and I simply stared at each other before his brain finally caught up to the moment.

"Yes, right," he mumbled to himself, and after offering me a weak wave, he followed his wife out through the door.

For a few seconds, I simply sat in my chair staring at the same piece of doorframe I had gazed upon multiple times that day, from Grace, to Linda, to Jessica, and now to a woman intent on pulling the rug out from under me. I wanted to scream, the lower lash of my eye twitching as the anger coursed through me. The arrogance was what got to me...the assumption that she still had control over a child who had so clearly severed herself from such domination.

While I couldn't exactly stop them from seeing their daughter, I decided to make it my priority to visit Katherine myself. First, I would give her parents time to try and meet with their child. To see the look on their faces when they found out she was no longer in prison would have been glorious to see for myself. My only concern was that they would react with extra ambition to meet their needs, a new urge to win the day no matter what. I had a feeling they would try something stupid and take up valuable time, time I needed to conduct my investigation. I had no doubt that Kat would remain with me if given the chance, but I wasn't about to reveal her location for the sake of parental pride. From what I could tell, I had just added another layer to my workload.

10

HAVE YOU EVER MET SOMEONE AND IMMEDIATELY FELT A WEIRD vibe from them, one you couldn't quite put into words? That's how I felt about Brad Wright. The thing is, I totally got his wife, even with the confrontational, over-the-top, narcissistic control she projected. I guess it was one of the things I admired her for, the woman sticking to her true self. Her husband, on the other hand?

Having not had children, it was hard for me to imagine what it must have felt like to be a parent to someone like Kat, but then again, I could imagine how it must have felt to have a child facing such horrific charges. The way Brad Wright had acted during our brief interview wasn't the way I pictured anybody behaving. The man had appeared distracted...uninterested...like someone had dragged him along to a bad musical and forced him to sit through it. I imagined he probably faced a lot of bad musicals, married to Lois, and yet this wasn't some random play. We were talking about the very fate of his child, and he sat in that chair showing more interest in my décor than talking about Kat.

Something felt off. I couldn't quite put it into words, but there was definitely a sense of unease coming off the man as if trying to avoid the topic altogether. While I did have plans to head downtown and meet with Sophia Cafaro, I put that little trip on hold as I turned my attention to the laptop and began searching for anything I could find on the family. Maybe I should have done so earlier, considering I'd taken the case on a whim.

With Linda busy checking into the dealings of Diab and Grace busy looking after Kat, it was time for me to get down into the trenches myself. An hour later, I found myself reading the man's service record from his time in the Army, as well as his current business as a kind of home handyman. Lois, on the other hand, hadn't worked a day in her life, the mother of one, a devout Christian who volunteered her time to the community.

It didn't take me long to find certain discrepancies I wanted to investigate further when I had a little more time. Their lifestyle didn't seem to match the income I assumed someone of Brad Wright's business standing brought in. Their modest house stood in the middle of Squirrel Hill, not quite Fox Chapel territory, one of Pittsburgh's most affluent suburbs, but definitely still up there in terms of wealth. Yes, they might have had a significant inheritance come their way or perhaps won the lottery, but something just didn't gel for me.

I made a few notes in my writing pad to recheck later, mainly the income thing, and to find out how they made their money. I also wanted to delve into Kat's school records to see whether I could get a clearer picture of the person I was representing. Once I finished my notes, I dropped the pad back into my shirt pocket, closed the laptop, and stowed it in my briefcase.

The walk through the office felt uncomfortably similar to when I'd walked into the place. I could feel eyes watching me, and when I glanced in any direction, I found those sitting at their desks quickly looking away for fear of meeting my gaze. What I wouldn't have given for my injuries to heal on the spot.

Stepping back out into the day, I briefly paused as the sunshine hit my face, closing my eyes as I turned my face skyward. The heat felt good, the brightness forming weird patterns in my vision. Opening my eyes, I continued on, and when I reached the Mustang, I gave the roof a bit of a rub before climbing in.

I kept the radio off as I pulled out into traffic, wanting to focus on the woman I was about to meet. From what I had read, Sophia Cafaro sounded like a real fighter, someone who knew how to treat people right and went out of her way to ensure her people were looked after. Reading through the case notes from her brother's attempt to sell the bar out from under her, I couldn't help but note the number of times she brought up the staff who would suffer if she lost the business.

Unlike Amadore, who appeared to want nothing more than a minor addition to his already-inflated bank balance, Sophia showed genuine regard for those she employed and, with the ongoing pandemic, knew that if they lost their jobs, things would ultimately become extremely difficult for them. As it was, she had already put in virtually all the money she had access to, including selling her car and the majority of her jewelry, most of which had been family heirlooms.

Pulling into the parking lot of the bar, I grabbed a spot near the back and sat in my car for a few moments to get a sense of the place. From the outside, it looked like just a regular place, with the usual signage and whatnot spread out along the front façade.

"The Trojan Horse," I read out loud as I gazed upon the name painted under the mural of a black horse.

An enclosed decking sat on one side, complete with stretched sunshades hanging above the area. It was the skewed posts that caught my attention, each leaning in a different direction to create the unique roof covering.

When I walked into the place, I got the feeling I'd walked into a kind of '80s nightclub. Bright purple and teal neon lights decorated the walls, while an unseen jukebox played Rick Astley to the half-dozen patrons seated around the main bar area. The young guy working the bar itself looked barely old enough to be legally in the place, and he, much like everyone else, didn't pay me the slightest attention.

I stood in the doorway for a few seconds while scanning the room. A couple sat in one of the booths, two guys sat on stools at the bar, and a couple of others played pool in a side room. The walls featured various movie and musical posters, all mainly from the '80s. We're talking a number of Arnold Schwarzenegger movies, Madonna, Tom Cruise in *Top Gun*, and several more. What I couldn't see was the woman I'd come to visit.

"What can I getcha?" the guy behind the bar said when I finally made my way up.

"Would Mrs. Cafaro be around by any chance?"

"Sophia? Sure, she's in her office," the kid said. "Want me to get her for you?"

No, I just came all the way down here and wanted to see whether she was in, I felt like saying, but I held my tongue. He looked like a good kid, and I really wasn't the type to call out stupid questions.

"Yes, please" was what I did say, and before I had a chance to tell him who I was, the kid turned around and disappeared through a small doorway halfway along the wall behind the bar. Thirty seconds later, he emerged again.

"She'll be just a minute," he called out to me and resumed his previous activity of wiping the bar down.

The first time I saw Sophia Cafaro, I immediately saw the resemblance to her brother, the chin dimple reminding me of Kirk Douglas. She wore her gray hair tied back into a ponytail, revealing a face still waiting for the wrinkles to catch up with it. She looked incredibly fit for a sixty-three-year-old, the black tights showing the kind of tight buns most women in their twenties would have killed for.

"Hi, there," she said with a welcoming smile. "Alex said you asked for me."

"Mrs. Cafaro, I'm Ben Carter."

She shook with me as her eyes narrowed. "Why do I know that name?"

"I'm the lawyer defending Katherine Wright."

"Oh, yes, of course. I read about you in the paper. How's the girl doing?"

"Fine so far."

"Can't imagine the trauma she'd be going through. Kind of glad the judge granted her bail."

"Her getting bail doesn't annoy you?" The comment surprised me.

"No, why? Should it?"

"Well, it's just that—"

"Mr. Carter—"

"Ben, please."

"OK, then, Ben. My brother was an asshole. The only person I truly feel sorry for is the girl charged with the murders...and perhaps Ersilia, to a certain extent." Another comment that surprised me.

"You don't think Katherine Wright murdered your brother and sister-in-law?"

She smiled, and not in a way that conveyed warmth. "Given the number of enemies Amadore had, I'm surprised he lasted *this* long. It was bound to happen, and from the sounds of it, whoever did it managed to find themselves a scapegoat." That was when she pointed to one of the booths. "Why don't you wait for me over there and I'll bring us a couple of cold drinks. Beer?"

"Water is fine for me, thanks," I said and went to the booth.

I would have been happy with a glass filled with tap water, but what I was served was anything but, the bottle of Pellegrino coming with a frosted glass holding some ice cubes and a wedge of lemon.

"Always preferred water myself," she said, sitting down opposite me. "And please call me Sophia. Everyone else does."

"Thank you." I poured myself some and took a sip. The chill raced through me in a refreshing kind of way, and I ended up swallowing half the glass before I set it down. "Boy, that's good."

"The lemon is the real kicker," she said and grinned. "You're here because of what happened between Amadore and me, aren't you?"

"The case did make it to the front page of several newspapers," I said. "It was hard to miss at the time."

"You'd think with the pandemic and everything else going on, people would find other things more interesting than a couple of siblings bickering over a family business."

"I think it was more about the building itself," I said. "The city's history means a lot to folks."

"Yeah, I guess so. I can't imagine it would have gone down well if he had won. He already had a buyer lined up, did you know?"

"He did?"

"Friend of his who planned to demolish it. Use the land to build a hotel." She took a drink before studying me. "I'm curious as to what your plan is. I can see that my nephew's people have already paid you a visit."

"What, this?" I pointed at my face. "Car accident."

"Those types of injuries don't come from any car accident. Don't bullshit a bullshitter. It was him, wasn't it?"

"OK, you got me," I said. "And my plan is to defend this

girl in court. If I can also find who actually committed the murder, then that would make my case a whole lot easier."

"I bet it would. But you should know that my nephew is a hot head, just like his father. Once he gets an idea in his head, there's little chance of changing it. Been like that since he was a kid."

"Then I'm going to have to do my best to prove him wrong. I think anybody with the slightest bit of common sense knows that Katherine Wright didn't kill those people."

"The prosecutor seems to disagree."

"The prosecutor works for the district attorney, and he is up for re-election later this year," I said. "Votes matter, and this kind of case could attract some negative press if given a chance."

Sophia shook her head in disgust. "You know the world is going to shit when the fate of a little girl is determined by the number of votes a politician needs to secure office."

"Hasn't it always been like that?"

She took a drink and shook her head again. "Perhaps so."

A man suddenly approached us, walking with a slight limp, and after asking where the new invoice books had been put, Sophia introduced her husband, Savio, to me. We shook, and he asked whether I wanted a real drink, which I declined, and he left us alone just as fast.

We chatted for another fifteen minutes or so before Sophia called out to her bartender about an expected delivery, at which point she ended our little meeting. I didn't exactly blow the case wide open by talking to her, but I did manage to gain valuable insight into the victims. The final question I asked her was one

I'd asked plenty of people before and one I regarded as perhaps the most important of all. Her answer would determine whether any of her information would add weight to the case.

"Would you be willing to testify in court if need be?" Her simple nod of the head was enough for me, and as I watched the woman return to her place behind the bar, I wondered how her nephew would feel if he knew she'd just signed up with the enemy.

11

Driving home after my meeting with Sophia Cafaro, I couldn't help but run the final few questions through my mind, the answers more than a little surprising. They also painted a vastly different picture of the man I'd assumed was just a retired grandfather living the final years of his life like most men his age. Boy, was I wrong about the guy.

For one thing, Amadore Costa wasn't the warm and loving father figure to his sons or grandfather to theirs. Instead, Sophia described a man consumed by control, unable to function knowing that his boys might have outshone him in every aspect of life. They were more successful professionally and financially, closer to their children, had loving wives, and all in all, they lived much happier lives than their father. Yes, one of them did run a crime outfit known for breaking kneecaps and destroying families, but that came secondary to the millions of dollars the business brought in.

Amadore Franco Costa was one spiteful individual, unable to see through the jealousy he had for his sons. That was the main reason he wanted to sell the bar so badly, so his friend could build a new thirty-story hotel complex of which he'd be part owner. Unfortunately for him, his sister had other ideas.

Before reaching home, I stopped off at a nearby drugstore to grab some painkillers. While my face might have displayed a visual representation of my injuries, it was in my ribs and lower back that the real party raged. The endless throbbing had been going nonstop since I woke up that morning, and while I did manage to ignore it for most of the time, sitting in the car seemed to amplify the discomfort.

It was when I slid back in behind the steering wheel a few minutes later that I first noticed the Buick LaCrosse. The sun gleamed off the black paintwork at just the right angle to catch my attention in the rearview mirror, and when I absently glanced toward it, I realized that it wasn't the first time I'd seen it.

There was something familiar about the car. It sat two rows back and definitely not close enough for me to identify the person sitting in the driver's seat, but I could still make out the mass behind the steering wheel. Whoever it was was huge, at least six-six, maybe taller. I could also make out a baseball cap but other than that, not much else. An SUV suddenly pulled into the space immediately behind me, cutting off my view of the car, and when I pulled out of my spot a few seconds later, the car had disappeared.

For a moment, I didn't know whether it was just paranoia

or something else. After the direct threat from Costa and then the follow-up beating, the notion didn't surprise me. Anybody carrying the injuries I did would be cautious of anything suspicious, and the idea of a car tracking me wasn't that far-fetched in the context of the situation.

It shouldn't come as a surprise to learn that I drove the rest of the way home with my eyes glued to the rearview mirror, throwing in the occasional over-the-shoulder glance whenever possible. My neck protested each time, but my nervous curiosity far outmatched those brief moments of pain. Who knows what would have happened if I had spotted the car again, but thankfully, I didn't.

The suspicions didn't end when I finally reached my building, and even once inside my apartment, I looked at the rooms in a whole new light. I don't know whether it was my talk with Sophia that raised my suspicion level, but something had definitely changed. Not long after walking through the door, I began running my fingers underneath tables and checking for hidden cameras in several spots. Even the front door wasn't safe, with me down on my knees intricately studying the lock for any signs of tampering.

Only when I was absolutely sure my place wasn't bugged did I sit on the edge of my bed, pull out the burner phone, and call Grace. She answered after three rings with her usual cheer.

"Hello?"

"Grace, it's me. How is everything?"

"We're fine," she said. "Could do with some Netflix, but other than that, I think we're good."

"And Kat? How is she coping?"

"Better than I expected. She's sitting out on the front steps with a cat who just happened to show up this afternoon."

"A cat?" My suspicious mind considered the animal, but I didn't find anything weird. "Probably do her some good."

"I think it has. She's already named her Whispers."

"Whispers?"

"Yes, on account of us only being able to whisper to each other or else getting found out."

"Listen, Grace, I need to talk to her."

"OK, let me get her."

I listened to a muffled shuffle, a few steps first on the linoleum and then on timber boards before a voice spoke some unintelligible words. Next thing I heard was Kat's voice.

"Ben?"

"Hey, kiddo, how are things?"

"Great, I guess. I made a new friend."

"Yes, so I heard. It will be a great distraction for you."

I considered not telling her about the visit I'd had earlier that afternoon, but something inside told me I needed to. If nothing else, I needed to know that regardless of everything else, she would stick with me if given the chance.

"Listen, Kat, I had a visit from your mom and dad earlier." Her tone changed in an instant, any hint of sweetness evaporating under the blazing heat of disdain.

"What did they want?"

"To check on you, make sure you were OK." I wasn't

exactly lying, figuring that even just turning up showed a slight level of interest, even if neither of them actually asked about the state of their child's welfare during the meeting. Kat saw straight through the bullshit.

"You don't have to cover for them, you know," she said with a flat tone. "Now how about telling me what they really wanted?"

"OK, you got me," I said. "But they sounded like they really cared. Anyway, they wanted to let me know that they were hoping to have their own lawyer represent—"

"NO WAY," Kat snapped, cutting me off as she growled in frustration. "THAT'S SO TYPICAL OF HER."

"I take it you don't approve?"

"*No*, I certainly don't. She's *always* trying to control my life," she snarled through gritted teeth.

"Listen, I get you're angry, but there's something I need you to do."

I managed to calm Kat down enough for her to listen to me. She did well despite her anger, and I went about explaining the issue I faced with them meddling around. What I needed was for her to film a video for me and send it through. In it, I needed Kat to clearly explain that she didn't want them helping her and that I would effectively remain her lawyer. I also explained that I would deliver the video to them the very next day.

That last part was kind of true, although I think we all knew I wouldn't need to deliver anything to anybody. I expected nothing less than for her parents to find out their daughter had been bailed and then make a beeline back to my office. When that happened, I would simply play the video for them and, if need be, have the couple escorted from the premises. I made a mental note to remind myself that I also needed to forewarn Dwight about my plan so that he'd be ready for any repercussions. I didn't know how hard the Wrights would kick back, and Lois had already shown just how seriously she took having control.

Kat agreed, and once I had explained what I needed, I asked to speak with Grace again, who also confirmed she understood. Less than an hour later, the video came through, and when I watched it the first time, I considered it a perfect production. All I needed then was to share the creation with Kat's parents and await the fireworks.

The moment I closed my laptop and set it next to me on the couch, all the energy I thought I still had faded away in an instant. Exhaustion washed over me, and every muscle in my body felt fatigued. The eyelids, which hadn't made their presence known up until then, suddenly came alive, their weight increasing with each passing second. I swear I felt like my body had suddenly decided to shut down right there and then, and I pushed myself off the couch in a moment of panic.

My left leg pinged with pain as I stood, the bolt shooting through my calf muscle. I thought I was going to fall and put out my hand to catch the edge of the couch when a second burst of pain bit into my shoulder. At first, I thought I might have accidentally overdosed on painkillers, but then I realized that in my haste to get inside, I'd left the bag from the drugstore in the car. I grinned at my stupidity and immediately regretted the move as that exquisitely sharp needle pushed into my top lip.

"Three for three," I managed to mutter to myself as I grabbed the keys and headed back out to the car.

All I wanted to do was hit the hay, my bed feeling like the best decision at that point in time. If it hadn't been for the same dull ache still throbbing down my side, I might have skipped venturing outdoors again, but if I hadn't, I wouldn't have made the discovery. Halfway across the parking lot was where I spotted it: the same black Buick LaCrosse almost completely hidden in the shadows of the outside street.

The vehicle had been parked directly in between two streetlamps, each some forty feet in opposite directions. The tree hanging directly over the car shielded it from the building it was parked outside of, most of the lights too weak to penetrate the shadows. I froze when I spotted it, two points of contention suddenly at the forefront of my mind. The first was that I was in no shape to run and wasn't carrying like I should have been. The second was that I was definitely being followed, and I wasn't about to back away like a coward.

I considered my options but knew I had limited time. For one, there was every chance that whoever was sitting in the driver's seat could see me, and that meant they knew I was on to them. The other thing I knew was that they weren't there to shoot me, as they would have done it already. My guess was that this person had been instructed to simply follow me, to give updates of my location to their boss. My guess was that they'd use that information when the time came.

Figuring I had nothing to lose either way, I turned for the parking lot's exit before making a concerted effort to get to the car before it had a chance to get away. I wanted to at least get a license plate, something I could use to gain a bit more information about whoever my stalker was. If I could at least get a name, then maybe I had a chance at turning the tables on the threat.

I barely made it to the sidewalk before the brake lights briefly flickered, and the car took off. With its headlights switched off, the license plate remained shrouded in darkness, and by the time the car got close enough to the nearest streetlight to shine some light on the digits, they were too small for me to make out.

"Keep going, asshole," I called after the car, but the painful resistance from the cuts on my lips kept the volume to a minimum. I watched as it barely slowed to the nearest corner and took the turn at speed before disappearing into the night.

If a taxi hadn't driven up behind me at that moment, I might have remained in the middle of the street a while longer, maybe wishing for the stalker to return. I shot the driver a wave, didn't see him return one, and walked over to the sidewalk. The whole experience felt surreal, and if it hadn't been for the continuing throbbing in my ribs, I might have thought of the whole thing as nothing more than a dream. Strangers watching me, hitmen intriguing me, thugs beating on me, drug lords hating on me—how did my life become such a confused mess?

By the time I finally fell into bed some twenty minutes later, I'd just about made up my mind to ease up on the concern for my life. As wild as that sounds, the truth is that I had virtually no control over what Riccardo Costa had planned for me. If he really did have a plan to kill me for defending Katherine Wright, then there wasn't a whole lot I could do about it. My only real choice was to focus all my energy on what I did best, and that was to save my strength for where it mattered most...the courtroom.

12

When I woke the following morning, the first thing I did was to slowly and carefully stretch a smile across my face. When I managed to reach the limits of my lips without feeling the torturous needle pricks that had plagued me the previous day, my eyes joined the smile. Next, I slowly raised one arm above me, felt no real discomfort, and began to gently pivot it around in a circle, feeling for any hint of injury. I did feel a little protest from my shoulder, but only at the very extreme end of my stretch.

Pausing, I considered sitting up. I still hadn't felt any hint of the damage to my ribcage, but I knew that could change in an instant. Instead, I reached over and grabbed both my cell phones off the nightstand to check on what I had missed while passed out. The first, the one Linda had given me, showed nothing, which hopefully meant Grace and Kat had had a restful night. There were no text messages waiting for me on my main phone either, which was a good thing. The emails I watched drop into my inbox amounted to little more than spam, and as for the news, there was nothing that involved my part of the world aside from an ongoing carjacking spree that had been going on for a couple of months.

When I closed the apps again, I met the gaze of my wife staring back at me from a better time, a time right before the news of our pregnancy and the...event that would ultimately claim her life. I had taken that photo during a random Sunday afternoon while the two of us had set up a kind of backyard picnic on the lawn. We'd finished eating the platter Naomi had thrown together from things in the pantry and just kind of fell on each other for some cloud-watching. I could still feel her hair across my neck as she lay with her head on my chest.

Closing my eyes, I imagined lying in that very same spot, wanting to feel that same hair shifting across my skin in the gentle breeze. I could almost smell the sweet scent of her perfume, the hint of peach and vanilla mingling with the smells of our garden. I moved my hand over to the other pillows, hoping...no, *praying* to feel the warmth of where she had lain just moments before.

"I miss you so much," I whispered into the room, my eyes remaining closed as I felt the onset of grief begin to come forward. A single tear broke free, a token of the pain still bottled up deep inside my soul. I wanted to flick it away, the faint tickle as it tracked down the side of my face feeling more like a screw-you from the universe.

Refusing to let myself give in, I opened my eyes and, ignoring the protesting aches, rolled out of bed. I stood, teeth clamped together as a second tear followed the first.

Heading to the bathroom, the anger suddenly distracted me enough to cause my feet to veer slightly off course, and when my little toe exploded in pain thanks to smashing into the corner of the chest of drawers, I immediately learned how to curse in seven languages.

"DAMN IT," I yelled into the empty room, the silence laughing back at me as the little toe felt broken. Looking down, I saw the nail split in half, a tiny sliver of blood pooling beside one end.

"That's just great," I said and went back to sit on the edge of the bed to inspect the damage. After looking at it for a few seconds and realizing there was nothing I could do about it, I shook my head and made a second attempt to get to the bathroom. "I'll add it to the list," I grumbled along the way, and it really felt like fate had decided to throw me a few more challenges.

After taking care of my toilet needs, I needed something to distract me from my thoughts and put on some music while showering. OK, don't judge me, but sometimes those classic trance anthems just hit the spot, the brain-consuming bass enough to stomp out any unwanted distractions. I even began to move a bit while standing under the stream, my fingers tapping away on my abs in tune with the beat.

By the time I walked out of the building an hour later, I felt like a renewed man, the sunshine adding an extra layer of pleasantness to an already great mood. I did scan the street for any signs of that black LaCrosse, but the only black vehicle I spotted was a pickup. No sign of my assumed stalker brought with it yet another tick on the morning. Even the traffic seemed to give me a break, the fast-flowing tide only occasionally stopping for lights.

I really thought I was on a winner, thinking the day would turn out to be one of those where nothing could possibly go wrong. Those were the days when people bought themselves lottery tickets, thinking their luck might extend to something a little more substantial. How wrong I was. Not thirty seconds after climbing out of my car in the office parking lot, the storm clouds gathered in the form of a voice calling out to me...an *angry* voice and one I immediately recognized.

"You knew she was already out when we came to you yesterday," Lois Wright called out as I walked between Henry Wade's Camry and Jessica's Corolla. I looked over half a dozen cars to see the angry mother coming to intercept me.

"Good morning, Mrs. Wright. So good to see you again," I said with an extra tone of sarcasm for good measure. Just as I knew he would, her husband brought up the rear, walking about a handful of steps behind her and looking more sheepish than ever.

"Cut the crap, Mr. Carter. You deceived us."

"Actually, I didn't. It was you who—"

"Our lawyer will be in touch with you very soon, and when he does..."

Her words barely registered. I stopped as she finally reached me, the woman looking up into my face from her much shorter vantage point. It was comical to see the eyes narrowed down to bare slits as she tried her best to intimidate me. I waited for her to finally take a breath before cutting in.

"I've spoken to Kat, and she's quite adamant about keeping me on as her counsel."

"That's not her decision to make."

"Actually, it is as far as the laws of this state dictate."

"Not if we have her mental stability assessed." That was when she pressed the wrong button with me.

"You want to have your daughter certified crazy because of your own ego?"

"How dare you. Where is she?"

"She's in a safe place until her matter goes before the courts."

"I want to see her." She could have added the word *demand* to her request, which would have sounded more suitable given her tone.

"That, I'm afraid, is impossible." Again, she acted as if my words came with an added slap to the face.

"Who are you to tell me if I can see my child or not?"

"Her lawyer," I said, the words sounding more smug than I intended. "And if you would take a few seconds to breathe, I'll let you see what Kat has prepared for you."

I didn't bother waiting for a reply, instead pulling out my cell phone as I set my briefcase down next to me. Lois took a look behind her at Brad, but he didn't appear to offer any sort of support, avoiding her gaze at all costs. After opening the screen and scrolling through my gallery, I found the video, pressed the play button, and held the phone out. Lois ignored the gesture, but Brad accepted it while I took a few steps away to give them a bit of space.

While I couldn't quite make out the words from the short video, the facial expressions on Lois were enough for me to gauge where in the clip they were up to. I made sure to keep my distance, pretending to watch passing traffic rather than watching them. My only hope was that the woman didn't launch my phone when she heard her daughter effectively telling her to butt out.

When the video finally ended, Lois Wright simply turned and walked away. Just as she had the previous day, she abandoned her husband, leaving him behind to deal with the fallout of her attitude. I could see his discomfort as I walked over to grab the phone, and he barely managed an uncomfortable thanks before rushing to follow his wife.

I stood my ground for a few moments, watching the couple return to their car. When their heads disappeared from view below the roofline of other cars, I waited until their Mercedes rolled past on its way to the road. Neither of the parents paid me the slightest attention, Lois's steely-eyed gaze remaining fixed on the road ahead.

"Gotta give it to a mother looking out for her kid," a voice suddenly said from behind me, and in the micro-second before I spun around in a panic, I expected my thoughts to be the last in this earthly existence.

Leaning against the hood of my car was Riccardo Costa, the same bodyguard as the first time I'd met him standing a few cars down. Costa had a cigarette in one hand, the other in the pocket of his pants as he considered me from a distance. I couldn't see his eyes behind the black Ray-Bans but knew he had me in his sights. The beating in my chest immediately shot up to panic levels, and I think every injury still present throughout my body cried out at the exact same time.

"Riccardo," I said, the word rolling out of me more forced than voluntary.

"In the flesh," Costa said as he pushed himself off my car and slowly made his way toward me. "Nice ride, by the way. I've got one myself, although black has always been my color of choice."

"What do you want?" I said, perhaps the first words that weren't a kneejerk reaction.

"Just wanted to come down and make sure my boys didn't give you too much of a hard time," he said as he waved the hand holding the cigarette back and forth. "I know they can get a little overzealous at times."

He reached a point close enough to inspect the damage left by his thugs and animated his movements, first checking out one side of my face and then the other.

"OK, maybe they went a little overboard, but you can't blame them," Costa finally said. "They're just as upset about my parents as I am, so you'll have to excuse them a bit."

"Why are you here?" I managed to push through my teeth, doing a great job of keeping my temper in check. The guy was close enough for me to hit, and yet I kept both clenched fists down by my side.

"Like I said, just to check on you and make sure the lads didn't go too hard." Again, he looked me up and down. "I don't see any plaster casts, no bandages. Your lips look a bit worn, but then again, it's not like you need them for kissing right now, am I right? Your wife, Naomi, she's dead, isn't she?"

Just hearing her name fall out of his mouth sent a tsunami of rage through me. I felt each of my fingernails dig a little farther into the supple skin of my palms as the clenching became unbearable. Ignoring the pain, I nodded, unable to speak for fear of losing control.

"I'm sorry to hear that. Guess we have something in common."

That was when he took a step closer, took off his sunglasses, and stared directly into my face.

"There's something else we have in common, Counselor. A certain girl. One the boys tell me was responsible for shooting my parents."

"She didn't do it, Riccardo."

"So you say. They say differently. Cops have her tipping the joint, stuffing her scrawny little face with my momma's crostata before stealing her credit card."

"She didn't do it," I repeated but barely heard the final couple of words as they triggered the gangster.

"I SAY SHE DID," he screamed into my face, bits of spittle peppering my nose and cheeks. I flinched but not enough to be noticeable. "I say she did, Carter," he repeated in a much more controlled tone. "And now you're going to tell me where she is."

"That will never happen," I said, feeling the beating in my chest climb to critical levels. "You can shoot me right here and now if you must, but I'm not sacrificing her to ease your pain."

"Hey," someone suddenly yelled out from the side of the building, and when I looked over, I saw Brian Wordell walking toward us. Wordell used to work in the NYPD before moving to our city to be closer to his daughter and now worked as security for the jeweler located right next door to our office.

"There's more than one way to skin a cat, Carter," Costa said without checking to see who it was calling out. His eyes, lacking any hint of humanity, remained fixed on me. "If you won't give up the girl, then I'll just have to go down another path to find her."

As Lois Wright had just a few minutes earlier, Costa turned and walked away without speaking another word. He dismissed me with a simple wave of the hand and led his hired help back to the waiting car. By the time Wordell reached me, the two men had already disappeared.

"What was that about, kid?"

"Just someone needing a shoulder to cry on," I told the old guy as I watched the car rejoin traffic.

I waited until he was gone before thanking Wordell for intervening. He gave me a clap on the shoulder and said just to call him if I needed help. After reaching the sidewalk, we each turned in opposite directions, and that was when I pulled out my cell phone. Finding Linda's number, I pressed the Call button and leaned against the side of the building, waiting for her to answer. It did dawn on me that Costa could be listening, but since I wasn't about to give away specifics, it didn't matter.

"Hey, it's me," she said as I heard her pick up.

"We have a problem," I said, keeping my voice low as a couple of kids walked past. "Costa just paid me a visit at the office."

"Riccardo Costa came to your *office*?" She sounded more shocked than surprised.

"Well, not quite. He caught me in the parking lot, but his message was pretty clear."

"He wants the girl?" Linda read my tone.

"He wants Kat, yes. And not to play checkers with. One sec."

I eyeballed a guy walking his dog and paused. He gave me a couple of glances that I didn't trust, and I waited until he had passed me before continuing the conversation.

"We need to move her," I said, checking the street for anybody else possibly interested in what I was doing.

"Move her where?" Linda asked. "Ben, she's in the safest place possible right now. Other than moving her to the police holding cells, where else would you consider safe?"

My investigator had a point. I didn't know the current place as well as she did, but considering what the previous owners had gotten up to, maybe there was a good reason for it. Fear was what drove me to consider the move, that same lack of control I had when it came to my wife. Unable to control a situation made me vulnerable, and what frightened me the most was losing more people.

"OK, we'll leave her where she is," I finally said, willing to put my spontaneous decision on hold. "But let's meet in the morning and discuss it further."

13

As much as I wanted to move Kat to a different location, Linda insisted that Marlon Shaw's property remained the safest place for her. We met the following morning and discussed the matter over coffee, first ensuring we weren't being watched or listened to by anybody suspicious. I still had a fleeting suspicion about a certain LaCrosse, but since I hadn't seen it in more than a day, put it down to me being overly cautious.

What worried me the most was the fact that if anything did happen out at Marlon's place, it would take me quite some time to reach the property, even with the Mustang at my disposal. It wasn't as if the building stood a block or two down the street. Add to that Kat and Grace's welfare lying completely in my hands, and I had all the makings of an impossible nightmare to live through. What I needed was a bit of a barrier I could put down to keep one side of the case away from the other.

"If it makes you feel easier, I could grab a place down at the trailer park near Marlon's," Linda said when she saw just how stressed I was. "Lord knows I stayed there after his daughter moved in for a few weeks. Ebony stayed in the cabin while she and her husband were going through a rough patch."

"What I really need is two of you right now," I said, kind of cradling the cup of coffee between my hands. "One to watch over Kat and one to help me with the investigation."

"Grace is a lot more capable than you give her credit for," Linda said.

"How so?"

"Well, aside from the fact she packs a pretty decent caliber weapon, regularly attends the shooting range, and took self-defense classes as recent as last year, I think she'd make a formidable opponent."

"Formidable enough to defend against the likes of Riccardo Costa?"

"Maybe not for hours on end, but I think she'd be OK defending the girl until the cavalry arrived."

"And what if that cavalry doesn't show up in time?"

"Look, Ben," Linda said as she reached out and squeezed my wrist. "You can't keep trying to save the world. I know how hard it must have been for you losing Naomi the way you did, but the fact is, people die. Be it through accidents, disease, natural causes, or by the hand of assholes like Riccardo Costa, all we can do is try to put up the best fight we can. You need to have faith in the people supporting you. We have a few weeks to get this case in order, and once you get into that courtroom, I know you'll work it the best you can. All we have to do is outsmart them until then."

"Easier said than done," I said, feeling a pinch in my gut at hearing Naomi's name for the second time in as many days.

"Yeah, it is, but do you know what? We're all in the same boat with you."

I smiled at her, returning the wrist squeeze before each of us picked up our cup and took a mouthful. Once we finished our beverages, we headed back outside, agreed to catch up again that evening for dinner, and climbed into our respective vehicles. After a final wave, I watched Linda drive out onto the road and disappear into the morning traffic. It should have been my cue to do likewise and head to the office, but I just couldn't bring myself to put the car into gear. Instead, I pulled out my phone and stared at the wallpaper, my wife looking back at me with that eternal smile I'd imprinted in my brain.

It took barely a microsecond for me to know what I needed to do next, and it didn't involve me heading to the office. What I really needed was to go to a place where two of my biggest worlds collided, a place with the power to put things into perspective while reminding me of who I really was.

The drive to the cemetery turned out to be just as somber as it was every other time. The moment I realized where I was heading, my entire demeanor changed, the mood taking a definite downturn. I've said it before. Grief is a curious emotion. The pain never really goes away. It just becomes easier to live with as time passes us by. Those who have lost loved ones can attest to that. It's those little triggers that sometimes come along that remind us of just how powerful the pain inside us still is.

An uncomfortable tightening grew inside me the closer I got to the place where my wife lay at rest. Each passing mile proved more difficult than the previous, and when I eventually turned the car onto the street where the entrance to the cemetery sat, that nervous uneasiness inside me shifted just as it always did. Call it familiarity or anticipation, but something about actually seeing that open driveway always set my mind at ease.

After parking the car and climbing out, I walked along the main path to where the specific row peeled off. Passing familiar graves, I looked at some of the headstones, almost nodding to a couple with a kind of acknowledging gesture.

Hi, Pam, how are you enjoying the sunshine, the nod seemed to imply to one, with other similar greetings for a few more. Not until I reached Naomi's did I pause in silence.

It pained me to see her grave in the state it was in, with leaves strewn over the grass and an empty soda can lying nearby. Even her headstone seemed to have this dusty, dirty blanket of water spots over it, the scene looking completely unloved.

"Hey, babe," I said as I took my jacket and began to rub the blanket of dust away. I always carried a small water bottle with me and used some of it for the more stubborn patches. The soda can I set next to the spot where I would sit during the visit, and the leaves I kind of raked away until her entire plot looked a little more appreciated.

"Sorry to leave you in that state," I said as I finally took my seat at the foot of her plot and faced the much cleaner headstone.

Seeing her face staring back at me from the small photo always brought with it the reality of her death. No dream, no weird hallucination lasting several years, just the coldness of a reality I still felt betrayed by. I smiled, resisting the urge to give in to the mind-numbing grief lingering just beneath the surface.

"I see you got a new neighbor," I said, noting a plot three spots down that had remained empty for the duration of my visits and was now finally occupied. "Hopefully, they keep the noise down for you."

What followed was a long moment of silence, one that felt awfully familiar to me. It was the kind of silence that looked peaceful from the outside but felt like a war of emotions on the inside. The struggle to control my emotions wasn't new to me, of course, but it still presented a significant challenge when trying to maintain a certain posture. I wasn't exactly alone, with other visitors discreetly passing back and forth between the rows. Yes, I know that grieving in a cemetery is perhaps the most logical of places, but to me, the grief was something I still considered private. I wasn't one to let it all go in full view of the public, be it in front of total strangers or not.

I must have sat there caught in that internal conflict for close to a half hour before I managed to speak again. Naomi didn't mind, waiting patiently for my words to begin flowing. Once they did, there was no stopping me as I began to spill about everything that had been happening to me, including the latest cases I'd worked on.

When I came to share the difficulties I faced with Katherine Wright or, more so, Riccardo Costa, I didn't hold back.

"You're probably wondering about my newly decorated face," I said, lowering my voice on account of another couple passing by close behind me. I waited for them to get out of earshot before continuing. "Call it a health and safety issue. Comes with the job." I grinned, imagining Naomi not being impressed with my joke. "Sorry, babe. I know it's not anything to kid around about. These are serious people, and I just don't know whether I'm going to have the strength to protect this girl."

I looked up to where I heard more voices, listened as they faded away again, and turned my attention back to the photo.

"If there's one thing you were always able to do, it was to see through my bullshit." I shook my head in frustration. "I'm scared, Nay...really scared and not just for myself. There are people who believe in me, people who trust me to get them through this, and I don't know if I can do that." That was when the threat of tears rose again, my voice close to breaking. "I couldn't protect you." The lump in my throat felt big enough to choke me. "I failed you. I wasn't there when you needed me most."

It was Linda's voice that I heard speak up inside me, sounding almost as clear as if she was standing right there beside me.

"Control the things you can and let others focus on those you can't," her voice told me, the imaginary face behind it stern yet empathetic. She was right, of course, her wisdom giving me exactly what I needed.

You might think that someone like me, who'd success-fully fought and won some of the toughest court cases imag-inable, should have the confidence to handle a situation like the one I found myself in, and I guess, to a certain extent, you're right. The problem I had was that life didn't play out inside a courtroom, and it was those unexpected twists and turns that I feared the most. Riccardo Costa was one of those twists.

His unpredictability presented me with a problem I felt powerless against. I didn't know his reach and didn't under-stand the lengths he was capable of going to to achieve his goal. Midnight assassinations, car bombs, hitmen, random beatings...all the hallmarks of a mobster dishing out mob justice. How far was he prepared to go to get to Kat? Or, more importantly, how long until he sent one of his cronies to pick me up, drive me to some abandoned warehouse, and begin pulling toenails until I gave up my client?

It might sound strange, but I saw Costa as a kind of judge, putting Kat and myself on trial for his loss, his only method of retribution being the same one used against his parents. In a way, this wasn't just a trial about murder...it felt like we were in a trial *controlled* by murder. An eye for an eye, with no care about whose eye paid the ultimate price just as long as *someone* did.

"Ben, hey, sorry to interrupt you," a familiar voice suddenly said, and I looked up into the face of Walt Henry, the husband of Dorothy Henry, Naomi's fourth-to-the-right neighbor.

"Walt, lovely day to come and see your beloved."

"That it is. Gotta take the opportunity with this sunshine."

Walt was a good guy. Not only that, he was also one of the few who understood the unwritten rules around engaging someone visiting a loved one. Walt came and went just as fast as our conversation began and ended, with a few passing words to make the exchange a little more comfortable. I didn't watch him walk the rest of the way to his wife's resting place, nor watch the man as he set himself up for some alone time. Instead, I turned my attention back to the image of my wife and continued our chat as if never interrupted.

Have you ever attended an appointment with a counselor before? I have, perhaps not as often as I should have, but definitely enough times to understand the process. For me, sitting in front of my wife's headstone and speaking to an image of her felt a little like those counseling sessions. I drove the conversation, and the more questions I myself brought up, the more the silence guided me to find the answers.

When I left the cemetery a couple of hours after arriving, I might not have been given the answers I'd come looking for the way a person might when asking questions of another. What I did find was a certain sense of clarity about the confusion I'd carried into the place. It's amazing just how many answers one might find within silence itself; the power of the mind is truly one of life's mysteries.

14

THE DAYS EVENTUALLY TURNED INTO WEEKS, AND WHILE I STILL expected to find a bomb under my car or a shooter waiting for me inside the foyer of my building, life continued on just as Linda had predicted. Riccardo Costa did show up once, but it was only in passing when we crossed paths downtown near the courthouse. He drove past me in a car and, after lowering his window, pretended to shoot an imaginary gun in my direction.

On the morning of July 11, 2022, the game changed forever. What had been an uneven playing field for the previous seven or so weeks would finally level out as the case returned to the courts. It was time for me to put on my imaginary armor, grab my weapons, and ride into battle in the one place I understood above all else. Was I prepared? Maybe not as much as I would have liked. We still hadn't found a better suspect for the murders nor a motive that might have driven someone to commit the heinous crime, but then again, that wasn't my job, so to speak.

The prosecutor's job wasn't to hold my client for ransom and demand I prove someone else guilty. That wasn't how the courts operated. Innocent until proven guilty, remember? It was up to Xavier Bartell to prove Kat's guilt, not the other way around. My job also didn't require me to prove someone else's guilt, although it would have made the task so much easier if we had found something significant. It was my job to disprove the prosecutor's attempts to prove my client's guilt.

During the previous three to four weeks of our investigation, Linda and I had focused our efforts on Riccardo Costa and his dealings with Solomon Malak, an often fraught and dangerous relationship. Drugs, gambling houses, brothels, people smuggling—if there was an opportunity to make a buck, these guys wanted a piece of it, and it was because of their greed that territorial boundaries often overlapped. You might call it a turf war, if you will, each gang trying to remove the other and claim bragging rights.

When we began tracking the movements of Mansur Diab, the man proved to be a worthy opponent for us. We could barely find a trace of him, and trying to build a picture of his time in Pittsburgh did throw up several challenges until he made one curious move. We think the rental he'd been using suffered some sort of malfunction, and to keep to whatever schedule he had, he had caught an Uber a half hour before the shooting to a spot less than two blocks from the victims' home. What's more, the Uber driver, a man named Mufadal Singh, also vanished that night; his burnt-out car was eventually found just over state lines near Steubenville.

Call it a coincidence, but something was definitely amiss, and I would have put money on it that Diab was the killer we'd been hunting. The problem was, with no murder weapon, no evidence, no witnesses, no confession, and not even any contact with the man, the chances of me proving so in court sat somewhere fractionally above zero. My only choice was to try and throw as much circumstantial evidence at the jurors to make them see that someone else had definitely pulled the trigger.

The problem I faced in the latter part of the investigation was being held up by the jury selection. Dwight assigned Helena Moore to help with assisting me while Grace remained with Kat. I needed somebody I could trust to remain with my client. Despite not hearing from Riccardo Costa, I had no doubt he continued trying to find ways of locating them, but I remembered what he'd said to me about there being other ways to skin a cat. I often wondered whether he would simply bide his time until he knew she'd have to show up at a specific time and place...at her trial.

I woke up that morning with an extra spring in my step, not because I was excited, but because of finally getting a chance to use my own talents in the matter. The investigation was good and all, but I felt more like a sidekick to Linda's talent while she took the lead searching for leads and then following them up. Now that it was time to step into the courtroom, I was the main event, and I could steer the ship with a new sense of determination.

The first thing I did after jumping out of the shower was

to check in with Linda about a lead she'd been following up on the previous day. She'd been working her way through the homes situated across the street from the Costas, speaking with the owners and tenants to try and find any hint of evidence. Witnesses proved hard to come by, the majority not home at the time or just inside and unaware of what had transpired so close to their homes. Only two of the homes appeared to have security cameras, but neither of them had their lenses pointed up far enough to see the other side of the street. Three homes sat empty, three more with their occupants out of state, two out of the country. It was those still out of the country Linda had been trying to get in contact with.

After Linda confirmed that she still hadn't heard from either of our overseas possibilities, I hung up and grabbed the other cell phone. Grace answered on the third ring and confirmed that they were ready to head to the courthouse. Both me and my investigator would be waiting for them in the parking lot to walk Kat inside. If Riccardo Costa did try anything untoward, we would be ready.

I didn't expect him to do anything, not right then, anyway. In fact, I assumed that he might have had a change of heart and had decided to wait and find out the truth. It wasn't as if he had to rush to kill Kat. The girl still had an entire trial ahead of her, and with her attendance mandatory, it wasn't as if we could keep her hidden. Either that or his suspicions had changed. If that was the case, I would have paid money to know what information he had found out to change his mind about my client.

Once I finished with the phone calls, I went about grabbing myself a strong black coffee to really blast the final remnants of brain fog from my head. I needed to be clear for the day ahead, and fatigue would only hinder my concentration. With the cup in my hand, I returned to the bedroom, set it down on the nightstand, and finished getting myself dressed.

One plain white shirt, mint green tie, and dark ash pinstripe later, I sat on the edge of the bed, slipped into my black shoes, and finished the easy stuff. I took a careful check in the mirror to make sure I hadn't missed any unwanted wrinkles, rogue ear hairs, or unsavory flappers in the nasal passages, straightened my tie, and gave myself a tick. With the defense attorney finally presentable, it was time to step out into the world and make a difference.

What I didn't do that morning was take my car to the courthouse the way I normally would have, instead ordering myself an Uber for the ride. There were still a lot of questions hanging around the whole Riccardo Costa situation, and while we didn't have an issue arriving at the courthouse, we weren't quite so sure about the leaving part. Who knew what would happen at the end of the day when we had to get Kat to a new safe house?

It had been Linda's idea to move her around to different hotels during the week and then return to Marlon's property during weekends when she had to remain out of sight for three nights instead of just one. Plus, keeping her close to the courthouse would also cut down on driving time for all involved and make guarding the girl that much easier. Again, we only assumed that Costa had temporarily paused his hunt, although we couldn't be sure.

The drive into the city proved to be a lot quicker than I anticipated, with the morning traffic barely noticeable. I thought the laminated notice my Uber guy had fixed to the back of the passenger headrest deserved a grin of bemusement. It read...

Hi, my name is Larry, and I'll be your driver today. I get that different passengers have different needs, so allow me to give you a simple way of making this the perfect ride for you. Just choose a number from the options below and I'll be sure to stick to the rules.

1. Silence. I won't bother you, and you don't bother me. We'll get through it in our own little bubbles.

2. Small talk and a little music on low volume.

3. Screw the small talk. I want to know everything about you, so feel free to chew my ear off.

4. Just the tunes. I'd like something to distract me while we cruise through the traffic.

Clever is what I thought, and when I finished reading the list, I asked Larry for a Number 4 ride. He gave me a nod of appreciation and asked whether I preferred any particular style. I said I was happy listening to whatever he had, and a few seconds later, I found myself listening to the voice of Harry Connick, Jr. Not my first choice, but I had given him the option.

The only time we slowed was for a couple of lights and one broken vehicle stopped in the very middle of an intersection. All up, the half hour or so whizzed by, and while pulling up in front of the courthouse, I remember hoping the rest of the day would pass by as smoothly.

"Thanks, Larry," I said to the driver and, just before I

climbed out, handed him a ten. I much preferred tipping drivers with cash to ensure they received all of the tip instead of a percentage going to the rideshare app.

A few seconds after climbing out, I found Linda already walking toward me, and we headed off to the side, away from the main entrance.

"Grace just texted to say she's about five minutes away," Linda said while scanning the parking lot for any possible threats.

"Are we expecting anybody to crash the party?"

"I've got eyes on Costa's main guy," she told me. "One of my guys is watching his house, and he hasn't moved since arriving home late last night. Riccardo is still in LA, so unless they organized someone ahead of time, we might just be free for the time being."

"Let's hope so," I said and as a precaution, checked a couple of the high-rises nearby, taking note of any open windows.

When Grace eventually showed up a short time later, the drop-off happened in a matter of seconds. She pulled up right beside the side entrance down the alley, and Linda immediately walked Kat inside the courthouse while I closed the rear door of the car. Grace continued on toward the parking lot, and I watched her disappear around the corner before I followed the girls inside.

We all ended up in one of the meeting rooms off the main corridor, Grace joining us about five minutes after I'd lost sight of her. Kat had already taken a seat at the conference table, and it was the first time I'd gotten a good look at her in a couple of weeks. She had lost weight, not exactly a considerable amount, but definitely enough for me to notice. The other thing I noticed was the way one of her hands kept fidgeting with itself, the fingers constantly moving by either tapping them on something or just flexing and relaxing.

Sitting opposite her, I set my briefcase down on the chair beside me. Interlacing my fingers together, I leaned forward and rested my hands on the desk before getting Kat's attention.

"I get you're nervous," I said, "but believe me when I tell you that this is the easy part. All you have to do is sit next to me and try not to react to what you hear being said on the stand." I looked up at Grace, and she gave me a nod of confirmation. "And you already know the process. First, the prosecution will call their witnesses, which I then cross-examine, and then we call ours."

"Yes, but who will go up there and talk on my behalf? Certainly not my parents."

"No, not your parents, although I believe they will be in the gallery watching."

"Why?"

It was a good question and one that I would have loved to answer, but after the way our previous meeting had ended, I didn't think asking the Wrights would have given me the answers.

"You just focus on you and let me worry about the rest." Kat looked up at Grace.

"And you'll be there too, right? You promised."

"Yes, I'll be there as well. Right behind you."

Checking my watch, I saw that we had just minutes

before the official start time. I gave Linda the nod, and she walked to the door.

"It's time to go in," I said and initiated our next move by rising to my feet.

Kat first took a deep breath, gave Grace another look, and then followed my lead. Linda opened the door, and together, the four of us made our way down to Courtroom 6, where the doors stood open and a small flow of foot traffic was already making its way inside.

"Stay behind me," I said as I took the lead, briefly slowed to let an elderly woman inside, and then followed close behind.

Bartell was already sitting at his desk, and surprisingly, I saw none other than District Attorney Arthur Clements sitting immediately behind the prosecutor, all three hundred pounds of him trying to balance on a single chair. He saw me approach, made a comment to the woman sitting beside him, and shook his head while muttering something under his breath.

When I reached our table, I stepped a little to the side and waved Kat ahead of me. Only after giving Grace yet another glance did she walk past and take her seat, my assistant taking the one immediately behind her. The fidgeting from Kat intensified almost immediately, one of her legs bobbing up and down while one hand tapped away on the table.

Standing next to Kat and seeing her in that state actually pained me somewhat. The girl I had met when I'd first taken on the case appeared a shadow of her former self, looking almost gaunt under the bright fluorescent lights. Her hair appeared stringy, unkempt, barely long enough to be tied back into a short ponytail. Even her complexion had suffered, acne breakouts dotting both sides of her nose and the visible patch of skin above her brows. If she had raised what bangs she had, I would have seen more evidence of a girl suffering internally.

Sitting beside her, I opened my briefcase, took out the single file I had inside, and placed it on the desk. Closing the briefcase, I set it down beside the desk leg, paused while considering the file, and leaned a little closer to Kat.

"If you think you have it bad, see the district attorney sitting on the other side there?" She snuck a look past me but didn't say anything. "You see how he's trying to sit with his weight all on one of his butt cheeks?" Again, she looked but didn't speak. "He's trying hard not to sit with his weight evenly distributed because he has a bad case of piles." Kat looked at me, confused. "Hemorrhoids?"

That was when the frown broke just enough to let the grin through, the faintest bit of lip curling in an upward trajectory. I had to build on the breakthrough. "I'd say it might be the size of a thumb and definitely causing him a bit of grief. See how he struggles to keep himself leaning?"

She giggled, clapped a hand over her mouth, and closed her eyes. I could see the girl struggling to contain the emotion but not to suppress it.

"Imagine him trying to wi—"

"Stop, stop, please," she hissed, looking around nervously to make sure nobody else heard. The bailiff cut in before I had a chance to continue, but I'd achieved my goal... or at least part of it.

"Now just relax and pretend you're watching a movie minus the popcorn," I whispered as I stood and waved for her to join me.

The bailiff brought the courtroom to order, and after a few seconds of silent waiting, Judge Edward Becker shuffled in looking just as annoyed as every other time I'd seen him. I think he must have been born with a permanent frown, an annoyance that seemed to consume every ounce of his being.

"Good morning," he managed to mutter just before reaching his chair, giving the crowd a quick glance over the top of his wireframed glasses. Once the bailiff gave the all-clear for the room to resume their seats, a muffled shuffle rolled over the crowd as each person sat in unison.

It took the judge a few minutes to get himself ready before calling for the jury to be brought out. This was where I considered the real game to start, the one I had now taken over from Linda. This was my domain, and while many considered a lawyer to be nothing more than a glorified arguer, the process went a lot deeper than that. I once heard someone describe the courtroom process for a lawyer to be an art form, and I tend to agree.

Think about the kind of trial I was about to undertake: a murder case with me defending the accused. The only real people who mattered to me were the jury, the people I'd painstakingly chosen over several days for the job. They would be the ones to determine Kat's innocence or guilt, which meant it was them I needed to convince. Not the judge, not the prosecutor, and certainly not those looking on from the public gallery. No, this was a show specifically tailored to the twelve people sitting in judgment. If I failed with them, I failed the case and, ultimately, my client.

As each member of the jury entered the room, I watched them with intrigue, remembering the questions I'd put to each of them in turn. Dorothy Dunn, the grandmother with twelve grandchildren who insisted on knitting each of them a sweater each and every Christmas. Or Belinda Hodgson, the widow of an Iraqi soldier who often spent her evenings watching true crime shows while solving Sudoku puzzles. There was Cole Malone, a mechanic, Hugh Franklin, the accountant, and Cynthia Schmidt, a single mother of two.

Each person brought with them the kind of life experience I needed to help me win the case, hoping that they saw the evidence objectively enough to understand that it might not paint the right image. I needed them to use common sense and logic, to see my client for the child she was and the circumstances that had put her inside that house.

When Becker handed the floor to the prosecutor to deliver his opening statement, Xavier Bartell almost jumped out of his chair with a little too much enthusiasm. One of his feet caught the leg of the chair, and he had to grab the edge of the desk to keep himself from faceplanting into the floor tiles.

"Oh, excuse me, Your Honor," he managed once he had regained his balance, pausing long enough to take a deep breath.

"It's just the opening statement, Mr. Bartell. Nothing to break your neck over."

A reserved chuckle rose from the gallery, and I looked over to see the color rising in the prosecutor's face.

"Yes, of course, Your Honor," Bartell said and continued as he walked over to face those selected to sit in judgment. "Ladies and gentlemen of the jury," he began before taking a long pause.

To add to his theatrics, he took a quick look back in my direction to try and make eye contact with Kat. Like a true soldier, she never looked away, holding his gaze without reaction.

"Members of the jury, the defense attorney is about to tell you all how his client is nothing more than a little girl who found herself in the wrong place at the wrong time. He will hope to convince you that the same girl has been living rough on the streets, abandoned by family...abandoned by friends. That this girl couldn't possibly be the heartless killer who gunned down two innocent victims inside their own home. That she couldn't possibly have taken a gun and fired bullets into the bodies of two elderly citizens of this city and then calmly grabbed some food from the kitchen before stealing a credit card to go shopping."

Bartell looked at the floor as he slowly began to walk along the front of the jury, pretending to consider his words, words I knew he would have practiced multiple times before walking into the courtroom.

"Ladies and gentlemen, we will show you the facts of the case, how Katherine Wright walked into a random home, found the occupants home alone, and subsequently seized an opportunity for the smallest of gains. We will show how two people, a loving couple married for more than forty years died for the sake of just $27." He shook his head in disgust to add to the role-play. "You have been selected to decide whether this woman is guilty of murder, but I think you have been selected to ensure justice for Amadore and Ersilia Costa."

Bartell held the jury's gaze for a few moments, making eye contact with nearly half of them before slowly walking back to his chair. You could hear a pin drop in the courtroom, the silence screaming out for more.

"Mr. Carter, your opening statement, if you will?"

"Thank you, Your Honor," I said as I carefully pushed my chair back enough to give me safe passage and avoid a similar spectacle as the prosecutor's.

I walked briskly to the same spot where Bartell had stood just moments before, adjusting one of my sleeves along the way until I faced the twelve people who I had the job of convincing of Kat's innocence.

"That was a fine speech by the prosecutor," I said as I began to slowly walk back and forth before the jury. "But unfortunately for you, there was a lot of factual information he conveniently left out so as not to distract you from the verdict he hopes for you to come together and agree on."

I stopped in the very center of the jury and turned to face them front-on with my arms hanging by my side. I didn't want my hands to distract them, to appear like I was somehow shielding myself. Liars needed to shield themselves. Truthtellers allowed their arms to hang, to open themselves up to any and all judging.

"The fact is, the victims weren't just any random elderly couple, as you might have been led to believe, but instead, the parents of a known high-level criminal of this city. The fact is, this known criminal has substantial enemies walking around the city and has been fighting a turf war with rivals for years. The fact is, my team and I have been tracking a known hitman hired by a known rival of Riccardo Costa and will show this man practically drive to the house of the victims just minutes before the shooting."

I looked back over my shoulder at the prosecutor, playing my own version of theatrics for the jury.

"Mr. Bartell doesn't want me to use words like *wrong place, wrong time* because that would require him to look beyond the weak circumstantial evidence he's put together in the hope of turning this into a fast open-and-shut case for him." I stopped to take a quick look back at Kat. "No...I cannot allow that to happen," I said as I began meeting the eyes of each member sitting before me. "And neither can you. You're better than that. Katherine Wright deserves to have a fair trial where *all* the evidence is presented, not just the parts that follow someone else's agenda. Thank you."

15

WITH THE OPENING STATEMENTS OUT OF THE WAY, IT WAS TIME for the real part to begin, the part where Bartell and I donned our imaginary weapons and climbed into the arena together. It was time for the actual case to begin and for me to finally work on getting Kat freed. If only things would have played out the way I had envisioned, then maybe all of the subsequent craziness could have been avoided.

After we finished with our opening statements, Becker called a brief recess, more so for himself, I think. He was one of the few who actually left the courtroom. He was only gone three or four minutes, just enough time for him to empty that old man's bladder of his and get back into the seat to continue the trial. Once Becker returned, he handed the floor over to the prosecutor, who called his first witness, Officer Vincent Davison.

While the cop walked to the witness stand and was sworn in by the bailiff, I leaned in a little closer to Kat and reminded her to just ignore what she heard. If I had some headphones she could have used, I would have gladly handed them to her, maybe put on some music to distract her. The thing was, I could feel her nerves from where I was sitting, one leg still bouncing up and down under the table while she wrestled her fingers in her lap.

"Officer Davison," Bartell began. "Could you share with the court your experience as a policeman in this city?"

Davison spent a few minutes telling the prosecutor the places he'd worked and the neighborhoods he served before Bartell finally asked the question most people had been waiting for, the one pertaining to the moment he found the victims.

"And, Officer Davison, you and your partner were the first to arrive on the scene, is that correct?"

"Yes, we were. Officer Neville Jordan and me."

"Could you tell us what you found?"

"Well, one of the neighbors alerted us to hearing some sort of banging from inside. She'd phoned 9-1-1 but was still waiting for someone to respond."

"And you just happened to be there?"

"Yes, that's right," Davison continued. "Jordan was thinking that we should wait until—"

"Objection, Your Honor, hearsay," I called out. Next to me, Kat flinched just a bit, me catching her by surprise, but I had to ignore it.

"Sustained," Becker said.

"Sorry, Your Honor," the cop said and continued. "We decided to go into the house, and I said I'd take upstairs while Officer Jordan checked out the downstairs area."

"And what did you find?"

"I found a distinct smell of gunsmoke in the air as I climbed the stairs, so I pulled my service weapon. Once I reached the main room at the top of the stairs, I found two bodies lying almost next to each other."

"What happened next?"

"I first called for backup and then called down to my partner to secure the home as we had a possible homicide. I knelt down and checked for a pulse on each victim but found them both to be deceased."

"Officer Davison, did you happen to find a murder weapon?"

"No, I did not, and none was found during the subsequent search of the home."

"What about witnesses? Did they see anything?"

"Once the scene was secured and backup arrived, I went back to the woman who'd first alerted us to the home, and she told me about seeing a suspicious girl matching the defendant's description."

"Objection, Your Honor," I said, and again, the judge sustained it.

The officer explained what little else he could about the scene, but having spent the majority of the time at the house, only his initial evidence proved helpful. Bartell kept him on the stand for as long as he could before handing him over for me to cross-examine.

"Thank you, Your Honor," I said once Becker called me to question the witness. I got out of my chair and walked closer to the witness stand, beginning my questioning once I neared the officer. "Officer Davison, when you reached the home, did you find the door open or closed?"

"The front door was closed."

"And once inside, did you happen to notice the back door standing open or closed?"

"I didn't take notice, but my partner—"

"That's OK; I'll ask your partner when he takes the stand," I said. "What about windows? Find any of those open?"

"Objection, Your Honor," Bartell called from behind me. "Relevance?"

"It's very relevant," I said in an instant. "The initial officer in the building just told this court that he smelled gunsmoke in the air. I think it's highly relevant to know just how long gunsmoke remains detectable in an enclosed space once fired."

"Overruled," Becker said after not a lot of consideration.

Officer Davison turned out to be just one of three who Bartell called to the stand that opening day, each of the first two painting a picture of a loving couple brutally gunned down inside their home. The third officer went through the arrest process, which sounded like nothing more than routine, given that Kat didn't resist in the least. I only threw in a single objection for the final officer, but nothing worth writing about.

It was the final witness of the day that ended up throwing the entire case on its head and not one I saw coming. Bartell first gave me a bit of a sideways glance as if he already knew what to expect, but I honestly don't think even he could have predicted what was to come.

"The prosecution calls Ivan Maxwell to the stand," Bartell said once the judge asked him to call his next witness.

The man who walked into the courtroom clearly wasn't someone who spent the majority of his life in a suit. From his unkempt hair to the crookedly worn tie around his neck, Maxwell looked more uncomfortable than Kat did. During the short walk through the middle of the gallery, he nervously eyed both sides of the aisle while trying to look down, doing his best to avoid eye contact with those looking on.

What I expected was for Maxwell to perhaps describe seeing Kat use the credit card or maybe walking into or out of the home. I expected him to give evidence that would link her to the killing in some way but definitely not in the sense that he did. From the moment the bailiff finished swearing him in, Ivan Maxwell became a key tool for the case. Unfortunately it wasn't to benefit me *or* the prosecutor but someone else entirely.

"Thank you for coming here today, Mr. Maxwell," Bartell said as I leaned a little closer to Kat.

"Do you know him?"

She shook her head. "Never seen him before," she said, and I straightened back up.

"Could you tell this court how you came to know the defendant?"

Maxwell continued staring down at his hands as he looked more uncomfortable than any witness in living memory for me. He kind of squirmed in a way that only seemed to amplify his nerves, his bad complexion of acne growing redder by the second. He mumbled something completely unintelligible, and Bartlett had to intervene.

"Louder, please, if you will, Mr. Maxwell."

"I was a client of hers," he repeated as the first hints of warning took hold in my middle.

"A client? A client for what?"

"For sex," Maxwell managed to blurt out before the entire courtroom exploded into complete chaos.

The crowd, which had been sitting in silence for the majority of the session, suddenly unleashed cackles of laughter and cheers, the majority almost drowned out by several people shouting insults in Kat's direction. I looked at my client as she first sat in stunned silence before unleashing her own tirade back at the crowd, eventually turning her anger to the witness.

"LIAR...YOU'RE A DAMN LIAR," she screamed.

Up on the bench, Becker fumbled for his little hammer and began slamming it down again and again, all the while calling for the room to come to order. It was obvious nobody was listening, least of all Kat, whose bright red cheeks looked close to bursting into flames from her rage. Only when he knew he wasn't going to regain control did the judge call in his officers to take over, and it took them a few minutes to finally calm the masses. Unfortunately, it was me who Becker ultimately came down hard on.

"Control your client, Mr. Carter, or I will control her for you," he said as he turned his attention to the rest of the audience. He looked beyond pissed, the tips of his ears a bright red that almost glowed. "And if there's another outburst such as we just witnessed, I will order my officers to clear the courtroom."

The silence did eventually return, but it failed to push aside the energy in the room. You could feel the tension in the air, a kind of electricity remaining close by that would need little to set it off again.

"Calm yourself," I whispered to Kat.

"But he's lying," she snapped, not bothering to quieten herself. Becker immediately turned to stare in our direction.

"I warn you, Miss Wright. This court will not tolerate—"

"BUT HE'S LYING," she yelled, the emotions proving too hard for her to control.

"MISS WRIGHT, THAT IS ENOUGH," Becker boomed. Kat flinched hard enough to hit the back of her chair. "One more outburst, and I will hold you in contempt of court."

"Kat, please," I whispered. She looked at me, and I could see her top lip trembling from the adrenaline coursing through her system. I shook my head at her, mouthing for her to stop before looking up at the judge. "Your Honor, if I may request a recess to get—"

"Request denied, Counselor," Becker shot back in a heart-beat. "This court doesn't schedule itself around your client's moods." Behind us, someone chuckled. I swear I recognized the voice but at the time, couldn't make the connection to a name.

"But Your Honor, I—"

"DENIED," Becker yelled and turned to the prosecutor. "Continue your questioning, Mr. Bartell."

"Yes, Your Honor," the prosecutor said as he stood and walked out from behind the desk while turning his focus to the witness stand. "My apologies for the outburst, Mr. Maxwell. Could you please clarify what you meant by your previous answer?"

"I-I'm a c-c-client of hers," the witness said, and I wasn't sure whether he was a regular stutterer or just when under pressure on a witness stand.

"For sex, yes, we heard that," Bartell said. "Are you telling us that Katherine Wright is a prostitute?"

"Y-y-yes," he said, but that was as far as he got before something next to me exploded.

"LYING SNAKE," Kat screamed as she launched herself from the chair. I tried to pull her back but only managed to catch the edge of her shirt, which slid effortlessly through my fingers. "YOU LYING PIECE OF—"

"MISS WRIGHT, I DEMAND—" Becker began, but whatever else he yelled got lost as the crowd again lost control almost as much as my client. The deafening uproar completely took over the room as people fought to see the spectacle. Court security came rushing over, and it took three of them to wrestle the girl under control as she writhed around, screaming, underneath them.

"Kat, just stop..." I tried calling to her, but there was no way she could have heard me. The screams of defiance continued as she was cuffed, and my own voice became nothing more than background noise.

"YOU'RE NOW IN CONTEMPT, YOUNG LADY," Becker just about screamed as the crowd's noise finally began to subside enough for the judge's voice to be heard. His face had turned a furious purple, and given his facial expression, I wondered if he was caught in the throes of a stroke. "Your bail is revoked" was how he finished, the words rolling off his tongue on their own as his energy finally ran out. The old guy managed to slam home his gavel one final time, sealing Kat's fate to whatever now waited for her behind bars.

For a moment, I just sat in my chair, unable to move, the scene before me playing out like some kind of weirdly realistic movie. The only thing missing from the jury were the buckets of popcorn, their own expressions eerily similar to each other as they took in the show from their prime positions. Kat tried her best to fight off those tasked with controlling her, and when they finally brought the girl to her feet, Becker simply waved her away. I watched her dragged from the courtroom, the only part still out of control continuing to shout out her defiance.

I thought the day would be over after that horrendous episode, but as it turned out, Becker had other ideas. The judge immediately called for the rest of the courtroom to be cleared while the jury, the prosecutor, and I watched from our respective places. Bartlett exchanged a brief look with me, and there was no denying the satisfaction in his eyes. He really thought he'd won that particular round, and he was probably right.

Once the court was clear, Becker reminded the witness that he remained under oath and subsequently directed the prosecutor to continue his questioning, which he did. Unfortunately, the damage had already been done. Whatever purpose Maxwell was to serve, he played his part to perfection. He claimed to have had a prearranged appointment with her just a block away, and when he saw her walking along the street a couple of hours later, he said that she told him she didn't need his money. She had enough and wouldn't be available again for a long time. He also claimed that she flashed him the credit card, although when I questioned him about the appearance of said card, he couldn't recall what it looked like.

"He was paid to testify" was what I told Linda after my third straight shot of bourbon at a bar later that day.

I felt cooked, used up, a complete failure, if you will. I wasn't sure how my mood could ever recover, let alone my confidence in the case. I felt like one of the leading ice skaters who fell within sight of the finish line to allow Australia's Steven Bradbury through for a win, and if you don't know who he is, google the name. That guy skating through the finish line with his arms raised was how I pictured Xavier Bartell after the first day of the trial, claiming victory long before the race had even finished.

"Even if he was, he certainly gave whoever paid him their money's worth."

"That he did," I agreed as I held up the latest shot glass. "And then some," I said and downed another. "Oh, man." I groaned, digging a thumb into each temple and pressing just hard enough for it to feel uncomfortable. "Somebody tell me that was just a nightmare."

"If you think *that* was a nightmare, then you've got issues, Ben Carter," Linda said as she downed her own shot, stewed on the taste with a grimace like she always did, and then set down the glass with an audible pop. When the bartender looked over, she indicated another refill.

"I suppose you have a worse one," I said nonchalantly,

not really expecting her to reply, but the silence I heard in return answered for her. When I looked over at her, Linda had this kind of...stare... a gaze that didn't go anywhere except into the dead space between her and the back of the bar.

We must have sat in silence for at least three or four minutes, if I recall the moment. Time has a funny way of distorting after a few drinks. It might have been longer, but I can definitely remember the bartender having enough time to pour us another round. I wasn't sure whether to try and delve a little deeper into what she'd said, but as it turned out, I didn't have to.

"If you could only see what I saw, Ben Carter," Linda near-whispered as she held the next drink in her hand, her eyes still fixed on that same focal point. "Then you might understand what a *real* nightmare is."

The thing about Linda that I may not have mentioned yet is that she's fiercely private. The references she brought with her to the job interview when I needed someone to help me highlighted some truly impressive credentials, which immediately made my decision easy. What her resume and those references didn't mention was a past that remained shrouded in secrecy until that night in the bar.

I could have asked her what she meant, of course, but sitting there caught up in the moment, I knew what the conversation really needed was patience. Linda continued cradling that glass, rolling it back and forth between her hands and looking as if she was rubbing them together in glee. Her eyes remained fixed, staring off into the past that lay somewhere within three feet ahead of her.

"I've never told you about my days in the Bureau," she finally said as the conversation turned down an unforeseen path. I knew she was law enforcement but not the federal kind. "I guess there's a reason behind it. Maybe some secrets are best left lying alone where they fell."

Her gaze turned from the nonspecific point to the glass as she paused rolling it between her palms. The amber fluid quit moving, the minuscule waves making way for a flat top. That was when she looked at me. What I saw in those eyes was the kind of grief I myself had felt within me, the kind of grief that shattered lives.

"I killed a kid during my second month on the job," she whispered with trembling words.

"What? Linda, my God."

"Not on purpose, of course, but who the hell cares about specifics, right?"

"What happened?"

"A bank robbery," she said as her attention turned back to the glass. "We'd been tracking a gang for a few weeks." She grinned as a new memory surfaced. "My first real case, you might say. We got word that they were set to hit a branch that morning, and so we lay in wait for them. Four teams. Three outside, and my team waiting inside the bank. As it turned out, we'd staked out the wrong bank; the actual target was two blocks down. When the alarm sounded, we ran as fast as we could, but the getaway car was already moving toward us. My partner began shooting at the car, as did a couple of others. The car was already too close to us by the time I took aim and managed to squeeze off a single round."

Linda paused, and I almost asked her to continue, but I

knew she wouldn't need prodding. What began as my own self-pity session had turned into hers, and I knew she wouldn't stop until this story had been shared in full.

"None of us knew there was a kid in the car. It…it all happened so fast. They grabbed a mother and her son on their way out and bundled them into the car. Somebody apparently called it, but with all the chatter going on, nobody heard anything." Linda swallowed hard as I watched her top lip begin trembling, the emotional juggernaut making its presence felt. "Forensics ran the bullet that killed the boy and…and it turned out to have come from my gun." She shook her head in disbelief. "One single bullet was all I ever fired during my time out in the field for the Bureau, and that one bullet took the life of an innocent child."

"Aw shit, Linda," I said as I tried to imagine the level of grief she must have gone through. "I'm so sorry."

"So was I. Of course, they tried to help me through it. They always do, you know? Lots of advice and appointments and talk of support, but it's not long before you see through the bullshit and find out what it's really all about." She turned to look at me again. "Ass-covering. Their own, and definitely not mine. All the offers of help were just ways for them to ensure nothing could come back on them." Shaking her head, Linda finally swallowed the drink, set the glass down, and ordered another. "I quit not long after. Once the matter had been ruled accidental, I put in my resignation and ended up in Marlon's back cabin, where I found the bottom of too many bourbon bottles. It was he that finally convinced me to get back on the horse, and after too many lost months hating myself, I worked my way back into society."

When the bartender poured another drink, Linda didn't take it, instead sliding the glass over to me.

"The girl ending up back inside doesn't change anything," she said. "There's still a court case to fight, and as long as we keep doing what we have been, we'll eventually find the evidence we need and, with it, win her freedom."

After giving me a clap on the shoulder, Linda got up, kissed the top of my head, and wished me a good night before walking out of the bar. I stared at that glass for a long time, trying to picture the hell she must have gone through to get to where she was now. She'd been right, of course. I hadn't yet lived a nightmare the way she had, and perhaps that was a good thing. What I did know is that it was because of that nightmare that she was the person I knew.

I didn't take that final drink. It felt wrong in a weird way, and I ended up leaving it sitting on the bar. What I really wanted was to go home, get a decent night's sleep, and prepare for another day in court, one where I could hope-fully turn the tide back in our favor after the shit storm that had erupted just a few hours earlier. If I couldn't, then Kat might have effectively sealed her own fate by playing into someone's hands. The only question was whose.

16

A MAN ON A MISSION IS HOW I'D DESCRIBE MY MOOD THE following morning after a restful night's sleep. A few nerves remained floating around, of course, not entirely unexpected after the events from the previous day's session, but I expected them. I planned to use those nerves to fuel my morning while doing my best to get the train back on the tracks, so to speak. Show the jury that not everything they saw was factual.

Now that we'd essentially lost the ability to personally guard Kat for ourselves, it freed up Grace to get back to doing what she did best, which was to help me in any way she could. When she texted me a good morning just after seven, I asked if she could set her sights on finding what she could on Ivan Maxwell...after wishing her a good morning in return, of course. I needed to know what Maxwell's motive was for taking the stand. His demeanor alone was enough to tell me it wasn't his idea, and Linda's assessment that he'd been paid was exactly what I believed as well.

Grace texted back her reply just a few seconds after I sent mine, saying she would get right on it as soon as she got to the office. That meant I could continue focusing on whatever curveballs Bartell still had in store for me. Linda would continue delving through the shadows of the underworld crowd, searching through names like Riccardo Costa, Mansur Diab, and Solomon Malak. We still hadn't found a possible connection between Diab and the victims, and other than him catching an Uber to a nearby location on the day of the murders, it wasn't enough for us to conclude he was our killer.

When I reached the courthouse just before nine that morning, my first few minutes were spent fronting the media pack lying in wait for me. They pounced the moment they saw me, attacking me with a wall of questions. As it turned out, Kat's wild outburst had drawn significant attention to the case, surprising since the double homicide had almost vanished from the newspapers completely.

The most common question asked of me was whether I thought Kat was guilty of the murders, and when I made it abundantly clear that it wasn't my role to determine her guilt, the questions turned to her background, with some of the reporters asking how often she'd been arrested for other crimes. I did my best to try and answer as many of their questions as possible and felt almost relieved when they turned their attention to the approaching prosecutor. I shot Bartell a wink when he found himself suddenly surrounded before heading inside. It was just after entering that I felt my cell phone vibrate.

It took me two attempts to make sense of the message someone had sent me, the private number the first indication that this wasn't a friendly hello. Whoever sent it wanted me to know who it was without making it obvious to anybody who might want to trace it back to its source.

I guess now I know exactly where she'll be when I need to find her, the message read, and I didn't need a second guess at who the sender was. I did look around me to see whether Costa might have employed someone to watch for my reaction, but I couldn't see anybody fitting the bill. After shutting the phone and dropping it back in my pocket, I decided to ignore it and get on with my day.

My first port of call was the courthouse's ground floor bathroom to take care of the two cups of coffee I had already consumed by then. My second was Kat, whom I found in the holding area. The on-duty guard walked her through to one of the interview rooms for me, and it was there I finally had a chance to talk to her for the first time since the aforementioned shit-storm.

"Crazy afternoon," I said once we'd both taken a seat.

"That son of a bitch lied," she said, repeating the final words I heard her scream the previous afternoon.

"And something we could have proven if given the chance," I said. "Something we now aren't able to do the way I had hoped. Kat, you didn't do yourself any favors by reacting that way."

"What was I supposed to do?" she spat at me defensively. "Sit there and be called a whore?"

"Yes, that is exactly what you need to do," I said. "I already told you that there will be things said that you might take offense to. The prosecutor is looking for those kinds of reactions because it doesn't paint you in a very good light."

"Then the prosecutor is a son of a bitch too."

"Yes, he might be, but he's also the one that's going to ensure you spend the rest of your life behind bars, and he won't even bat an eyelid doing it."

"I don't care."

"Yes, you do care," I said, knowing I needed to lower my tone if I was going to get through to her. "Kat, I'm here to make sure that you get to leave this place free. Whatever you do after that is up to you, but I'd like to think that you will see it as an opportunity for a fresh start."

Kat didn't answer me, but I could see that she had taken in my words regardless. I didn't need her to respond, just to ponder the words and see that all hope wasn't yet lost.

"I do need to ask you about something, though," I said, changing the subject. "When you left the Costas' home, do you remember if you closed the door or not?"

Kat first looked at me and then up at the ceiling as she considered the question. I watched her try and recall the moment.

"Definitely left it open," she eventually said. "I left it open because that was how I found it. Why?"

"Just curious, that's all," I said. "In cases like this, details matter."

Checking the time, I suggested we'd better get her back to the holding area, and once I effectively handed my client back to the security staff, I made my way around to the courtroom, where the public gallery was already beginning to fill. From the looks of it, the previous day's antics had done more than just stir interest within the media. It appeared as if a lot more people had come to watch the show, all of them anxious for a repeat.

"Carter," Bartell said to me when I passed him by, and I returned his blunt greeting with a head nod and not much else. The district attorney who'd been sitting behind him the day before was nowhere to be seen, and from the looks of it, I could see the similarities between the prosecutor and myself, each of us alone to fight the next battle.

"As long as we win the war," I mumbled under my breath as I went to take my seat.

Just before I did, I ran my eyes across the public gallery to see if I could spot any familiar faces. I still had a feeling that Riccardo Costa might still show up, but it wasn't his face I found staring back at me from among the dozens sitting on the far right side of the aisle. The face staring back at me and looking almost sheepish was none other than Lois Wright herself, the former headstrong woman sitting alone and appearing embarrassed at being spotted.

I like to think that it was the motherly side of her who came that day to watch her daughter's trial continue, perhaps hoping that she would be found not guilty and released through some small miracle. Unfortunately, the cynical side of me put forth another reason, that being the mother coming to watch me fail so that she could pounce and install her own lawyer in my place. I sometimes think that it was the latter that reflected the real soul living behind the face of that woman, someone who preyed on the misery of others so as to appear like the savior.

"All rise," the bailiff suddenly called out from behind me, drawing my attention back to the moment, and I set down my briefcase beside the table leg before standing upright again. A few seconds later, Judge Becker entered the room, and the new day officially began.

I expected the judge to make some sort of comment to Kat when she was brought out from the door leading to the holding area, but surprisingly, Becker kept quiet, instead moving right along to the next part of the process. Once all the pieces had again been set up, he called for Bartell to call his first witness of the day, acting as if nothing significant had changed.

The man brought to the stand first that morning was none other than Dr. Peter Watts, a forensic specialist dealing with blood splatters. He looked like a natural walking into the courtroom, the attention not bothering him in the slightest. The man went through the motions as if alone in a room and calmly turned to the prosecutor once he'd been sworn in by the bailiff.

"Thank you for your time this morning, Doctor," Bartell began. "Could you tell the court the kind of experience you bring to the case?"

"Yes, of course," Watts said. "Twenty-three years in my current role, seven in my previous as an assistant technician for Rolster's Industries."

"You've been assisting law enforcement with forensic analysis for quite some time, Doctor. I'm curious to know, how many murder cases such as this current one would you say you've helped with?"

"If I had to guess, I'd say close to two hundred."

"And is there anything you'd say strikes you as similar in all of those cases?"

"The science behind the evidence," Watts said without hesitation. "It's perhaps the one thing that never seems to change." Bartlett nodded his head as he walked a little closer to the witness stand.

"And what did the blood splatters from this particular crime scene tell you?"

"After examining all the crime scene photos, I can safely say that both victims had been upright when shot, each standing a minimum of seven feet four inches from the wall behind them. It was also clear that given the lack of gunsmoke residue found on the victims, the shooter must have been more than seven feet from each victim."

Bartell continued questioning the doctor for a few more minutes, but the problem for me was that the man spoke in facts, not something I could really cross-examine. If he had thrown in an opinion or two or maybe tried to explain a theory proving why the shooter could only have been Katherine Wright, then I might have had an opportunity to throw in the odd objection or two. Unfortunately, it wasn't to be, and when Becker passed the witness over to me, I declined, stating I had no questions for the witness at this time.

The morning flew by, and after the prosecutor and I worked our way through three witnesses, Becker called for the lunch break and closed the morning session with a single rap of his hammer. I packed up my file and asked Kat if she was OK before watching her get escorted out through the side door. Only once she disappeared from view did I grab my briefcase and head out of the courtroom.

Grace phoned me not two minutes later just as I lined up at the courthouse café to grab a bite, and after the initial pleasantries were out of the way, she told me what she'd found out about Ivan Maxwell.

"He went to the same high school as your client," she said just as I reached the front of the line. The revelation was enough for me to step to the side and forgo my turn.

"But she told me she didn't recognize him," I whispered. "Why would she lie?"

"Maybe she just forgot," Grace said. "I mean, she did drop out shortly after starting high school, and who knows? Maybe she had a lot going on at the time and just...forgot about him."

"Or she really does know him, and what he said is true," I said while leaving the café and heading for the corridor leading to the holding area.

"How are you going to find out the truth?"

"By asking her," I said and then stopped and pulled out my phone. "Or maybe somebody knew his relationship to Kat and decided to manipulate the situation," I said as I held up the phone to show Grace the message. I watched her eyes dart across the screen.

"He certainly got what he wanted."

While I didn't exactly think Kat was a hooker, I couldn't dismiss the idea totally on account of the lifestyle she'd led. Living on the streets was hard. I didn't know this personally, of course, but I'd represented enough people who did, and through them, I had a fair idea about the hardships they faced. A lack of food was perhaps the most obvious, and while a lot of them did resort to stealing some, they told me that there were always times where they inevitably went without. Hunger proved a significant driving force and often drove people to do things they normally wouldn't. Did I think Kat was a prostitute? Perhaps as a last resort. It was a question only she could answer.

When the guard led me around the corner to the cell she was sitting in, Kat had a half-eaten sandwich in one hand and an empty wrapper in the other. A bottle of water sat on the bench next to her and still appeared sealed.

"Your lawyer wants to talk to you," the guard said and opened the cell door.

I could have questioned her right there and then, of course, but I figured with such a sensitive topic to discuss, an interview room was the wiser decision. After asking the guard to make it so, he walked Kat through to where we'd talked earlier in the day, and once inside the room with the door shut, I didn't bother sugarcoating the matter.

"You told me you didn't know who Ivan Maxwell was, and today I find out that the two of you went to the same high school together." Imagine my surprise when she didn't react in the slightest.

"What's the difference if I knew him or not?" she said. "He's still a liar."

"Liar or not, I need to know *everything* about you there is to know, do you understand?" When she didn't answer, frustration got the better of me. I stepped toward the table and slammed my fist down, causing her to jump in surprise. "Damn it, Kat, I feel like I'm fighting *two* battles here."

"Nobody asked you to help me," she snapped back, the defensiveness in her voice piqued to the maximum.

"I'm trying to keep you out of jail, and you're doing everything possible to keep yourself in there."

I dropped my briefcase on the floor and took a seat, leaning forward over the table to get her attention.

"I don't think you've seen just how bad the inside of the prison really is for someone like you."

"Someone like me?"

"Someone young and vulnerable. They'll use you for whatever they can until there's nothing left to abuse."

"Kind of sounds like home," she muttered under her breath, sending my temper even further into the red.

"Damn it, girl." I felt my insides twist into a lead weight, my eye twitching uncontrollably.

"Don't say those words to me," Kat said while staring at me, her voice suddenly calm and controlled. "Not ever. My father used to say those exact words to me."

Fearing my temper wouldn't serve any worthwhile purpose, I took a couple of deep breaths in the hope of bringing the temperature in the room down several degrees. Only when I was sure I could speak calmly again did I try once more.

"I'm not trying to offend you," I said with a lowered voice. "I'm trying to *help* you." She didn't look up at first. "I warned you there would be things said that may hurt you, and it's imperative you ignore them." I leaned a little closer. "And yes, that includes being called a whore."

That was when she did look up at me, her eyes barely able to focus on me with the anger raging behind them.

"It hurt hearing him say those words."

"I'm sure they did, but if you understand the game being played, you'd know why I'm forewarning you."

"I thought I was supposed to be innocent until proven guilty."

"That's only in textbooks and B-grade movies," I said with a bemused grin. "Out here in the real world, every man and his dog wants to judge you, and it's up to your lawyer to set things straight." The grin that broke across her face was enough to tell me she'd returned to my side of the field. From that moment on, I knew we were traveling in the same direction and, ultimately, would arrive at the same destination.

17

ONCE BACK IN THE COURTROOM, BARTELL WASTED LITTLE TIME getting back into the swing of things by calling another witness who supposedly knew Kat. This time, the witness wasn't a man claiming to be some sex client but instead a woman claiming to have regularly seen the defendant buying drugs from a local dealer.

"Was this a regular occurrence you witnessed, Miss Humphries?" Bartell made sure to turn slightly after asking the question so he could look at my client, an added bit of theatrics he liked to occasionally throw in.

"At least once a week but sometimes every other day." The girl shifted uncomfortably in her chair as Bartell thanked her and advised the judge that he had no further questions.

"Your witness, Mr. Carter," Becker called to me, and I thanked him before rising to my feet and crossing the floor to a closer spot.

"Miss Humphries, what drug are we talking about here?"

"Excuse me?"

"The drug," I repeated. "Which specific drug was Miss Wright buying from this dealer? Are we talking heroin, cocaine, crystal meth?"

"Heroin, I think, but I'm not too sure." I nodded to show I heard her.

"And this dealer, could you describe him? I assume it's a him?"

"Yes, it's a him," Humphries said. "Oh, I don't know. Average height, average build."

"White or Black?"

"Black."

"Clothing?"

"Yes, he was wearing some." A brief chuckle rolled through the crowd of onlookers, but one look from Becker ended it quickly.

"Describe it."

"Jeans, T-shirt. There wasn't really anything specific about him." She began to sound frustrated, but I ignored it.

"And if you saw this man again, you'd recognize him?"

"Yes, of course. I've seen him enough times."

Again, I nodded to indicate I understood, but instead of standing my ground, I returned to my desk and grabbed a couple of things off the top of the open file. With one photo in hand, I returned to the witness stand and held it out to the witness.

"Is this the man you claim to have seen selling drugs, Miss Humphries?" She took the photo and studied it for a few seconds before holding it out to me.

"Yes, that's him."

"That's the man you claim was selling drugs...*heroin*...to Miss Wright every other day?"

"Yes, I'm sure of it."

"And what about this man?" I said as I held out the second photograph to her.

This time, Humphries took longer studying the image but didn't look as sure as previously.

"Well, Miss Humphries?"

"I'm...I'm not sure."

"I can confirm that the man in both images is the same, Miss Humphries, Reverend Thomas Saunders," I said as I turned to the jury. "Reverend Saunders hands out food parcels most days along Smithfield Street. I doubt anybody could possibly mistake a wrapped sandwich and bottle of water for drugs." I turned back to the witness. "Miss Humphries, who paid you to come here and lie?"

"Objection, Your Honor," Bartell called out in an instant, but I didn't stop.

"Who paid you to come to this court and attempt to discredit my client with blatant lies?"

"Your Honor, obj—"

"Who was it?" I continued, refusing to let the prosecutor save the witness. I watched as her cheeks flushed, her lips trembling while trying to form words that failed to send.

"Sustained," Becker finally cut in. "Mr. Carter, that's enough."

"I apologize, Your Honor," I managed. "No further questions."

When I got back to the table and took my seat, I felt my

hands shaking with anger, more mad at myself for giving in to the frustration. I looked at Kat, who stared back at me with a stunned expression, and I shot her a wink.

"It's all good," I whispered as Bartell called his next witness.

The next witness Bartell called to the stand brought proceedings back down to a reasonable pace, giving me a chance to ground myself. I couldn't let go of the idea that someone was in the background paying witnesses to come in and lie, but I knew I had to focus on the present so I could put up a good fight.

"State calls Fiona Heath to the stand," Bartell said as he moved things along.

I watched from my vantage point as a woman using a single crutch entered the courtroom and took her seat on the stand. The bailiff processed her as any other witness and, when finished, retook his own seat as Bartell took over.

"Thank you for coming today, Ms. Heath. And I apologize for making you come down here after your traffic accident."

"That's quite all right," the woman said with a jovial smile. "It's just a bruised ankle. Nothing broken."

"That's good to hear," Bartell said as he took up his spot in the middle of the floor. "Can you confirm your role for the court?"

"I'm a crime scene investigator for the city of Pittsburgh," she said.

"And you attended the crime scene at 4551 West Wiltshire Avenue on the afternoon of May 5th, is that correct?"

"Yes, that's right."

"And can you describe what you found?"

"Police had cordoned off the property. Two victims were located upstairs, both shot in the main sitting room. I mainly processed the home for fingerprints."

"And you found some, I take it?" The woman grinned at Bartell's dry attempt at humor.

"Yes, I managed to find just a few. Seven people in total."

"And was the defendant one of those seven?"

"She was, yes."

"And can you tell the court where you found Miss Wright's fingerprints?"

"Mainly in the downstairs area, mostly the kitchen."

"So none upstairs near the bodies?"

"No."

"What about the handrailing by the stairs leading to the second floor?"

"No."

"But you did say mainly in the kitchen. Did you find Miss Wright's prints anywhere else?"

"Yes, on a glass."

"And where was this glass located?"

"On the upstairs table beside the bodies." A subdued hum rolled over the crowd but didn't last more than a few seconds before Bartell continued. As he did, I took out a couple of the crime scene photos I'd been carrying around with me and gave them another glance. Beside me, Kat began twitching again.

I barely heard the prosecutor continue his questioning of the witness, too caught up in the photo. If there had been an opportunity for me to throw in an objection, I'd never know as something odd suddenly struck me, odd enough to steal my attention until...

"Mr. Carter, do you intend to cross-examine the witness or not?"

I looked up to find the courtroom staring at me from multiple angles, in front of focus, the judge. I immediately stood and apologized.

"I'm sorry, Your Honor, yes, I do."

With the crime scene photo in hand, I walked around the table and out to the floor, my bootheels the only sound as I made my way to the witness stand.

"Ms. Heath, I'm wondering if you could clarify something for me," I said as I held out the photo. "You recognize this as being the room where you saw the bodies of the victims?"

"Yes, that's it," the witness said.

"Your Honor, I'd like to direct the court's attention to Item 2B." I waited for the court projector to show the image on the screen for the jury's benefit. "And can you tell us about the items located beside the table there? The coffee table?"

"Yes, there appears to be several pieces of broken crockery."

"A small plate and a cup are what I believe they were found to have been before shattering onto the floor, would you agree?"

"Yes, I believe so."

"You will also note the angle of the table in conjunction with the rest of the room. Doesn't it strike you as odd?"

"Odd how?"

"Odd as in having been moved from its original position."

"Yes, I would also tend to agree."

"And looking at the position of Mrs. Costa, do you think it's fair to say that she might have struck the table on the way down and knocked the cup and plate onto the floor?"

"Another fair assessment," Heath said.

"And yet the glass remained on the table?"

"That's where I found it."

"Objection, Your Honor. What is the relevance here?"

"Overruled," Becker said, but then added, "If you have a point to make, get to it."

"Yes, Your Honor, of course." I turned back to the witness. "Ms. Heath, do you think it possible that someone else might have placed that glass on the table after the victims had been shot to make it appear as if the defendant was upstairs even though she hadn't been?"

"Objection, Your Honor."

"Sustained."

"I'll rephrase the question," I said. "Ms. Heath, do you think it possible that the glass could have been placed on the table after the victims had been shot?"

"Yes, it's possible, although I only found the defendant's prints on the glass."

"Thank you, no further questions."

The witnesses continued into the middle of the afternoon, at which time the judge called a premature end to the session. Bartell and I exchanged a look of confusion as we had been on somewhat of a roll, but with Becker in charge, who were we to question the man? I learned later that the judge had made a last-minute doctor's appointment, and I guess he really needed to attend.

It was just after four when I eventually walked out of the courthouse, and instead of heading home, I dropped by the office first. There were a couple of files I wanted to add to my collection, namely one about a girl who I planned to call to the stand, a former friend of Kat's. It was a girl Grace had found out about and someone who I hadn't yet told my client about. Knowing how touchy she was about anything to do with her past, I had to find the right time to tell her.

When I walked into the office, I found several of the desks empty, and the majority of people had already gone home. Grace was in the lunchroom making herself a coffee while chatting with Jessica, the receptionist, and Martin Pike, one of the other lawyers.

"Court finished already?" I nodded at Pike as we shook hands, having not seen each other in a few days. "Becker must be taking it easy on you guys."

"I wish," I said. "Heard he had a doctor's appointment."

"Did you get the file I left on your desk?" Grace asked. "Reagan Byrd was not easy to track down."

"Not yet, but you definitely hit a home run with her."

"You need to pay this lady more," Pike joked.

"I would, but she pays me," I joked back, and Grace let out an uncomfortable chuckle.

"Any plans for the rest of the afternoon then?"

"To get ready for this dinner at Caesar's," I said.

"That new Italian joint?" Grace looked jealous. "What's the occasion?"

"Paul Garroway's fortieth."

"Garroway is forty?" Pike looked genuinely shocked. "Man, time really does suck," he said and gave me a clap on the shoulder as he headed for the door. "Have a drink for me."

"I will," I said and gave him a wave.

"You know, I heard that Paul's wife kicked him out a few days ago. Something about him getting a little too frisky with his secretary?"

"Yes, I heard the same," I said as I grabbed a quick drink of water. "I offered him a room, but apparently, he's moving in with said secretary."

"Really? Talk about spontaneity."

Once I thanked Grace again and grabbed the files from my office, I headed back out into the late afternoon and went home, where, after a quick shower and change of clothes, I sat down to take a quick look through the files. Reagan Byrd lived just an hour out of Pittsburgh, and I made a mental note to visit her just as soon as I could. Grace had already prepped the girl to meet with me, and all I needed was to set a time and place.

I was still thinking about whether the upcoming Saturday would be a good day to meet the potential witness when I pulled into Caesar's parking lot an hour later. When I saw the man of the moment walking by the front of my car with his new girlfriend hanging off his arm, I pushed the Byrd girl aside as I tapped on the horn. Garroway flinched, saw me, and flashed his usual grin at me.

"Scared the shit out of me," he said and whispered something to his girl, who smiled at me before continuing on to the restaurant's front door. My friend looked after her and sighed. "You know, *you* could get yourself one of those," he whispered, tilting his head a little as he stared at his girlfriend's butt.

"I don't think I'd have the stamina," I joked and gave him a hug. "Happy birthday, young man."

"Thanks. Just another year around the sun."

I'd met Paul Garroway during law school, both of us sharing a room on campus at one point. We'd also interned at the same law firm before Paul left to take up a role in Reading, near Philadelphia. He only returned to Pittsburgh the previous year to head his firm's new office here in town. He'd dropped me a note on the day of his arrival.

It was good seeing my friend, and for the next couple of hours, I got to hang out with what I saw as a small piece of my past. There were only eight of us at the table, and six of them were Paul's current colleagues. I was the only one not involved directly with where he worked, so the conversation tended to fly over my head for most of it. Paul would throw in the occasional joke that only the two of us would laugh at, but they were limited.

After checking the time at just before ten, I politely leaned across the table and whispered my intention to leave. The day felt like a particularly long one, given I'd spent the majority of it in court, and with another extensive one ahead of me, I knew I'd need a decent night's sleep if I was going to have my wits about me.

"No, you can't leave," Paul said without bothering to lower his voice. "We're headed to Kenny's after this," he added, indicating a trip to a nearby bar.

"As much as I want to, old buddy, I've got court in the

morning," I said, and while I did feel bad, I knew I had to stick to my guns.

"Hey, who are you calling old?" He tried to look wounded, but the grin gave him away.

"You," I said, wiped my mouth with the napkin, and dropped it on the plate before holding a hand out to him.

"I'll walk you out," Paul said, and while I asked him not to bother, he insisted.

I made sure to give each of the others a handshake, including his girlfriend, then followed my friend out into a warm night breeze. Paul stopped when we reached the edge of the parking lot, and after peering in through one of the windows to where his girl sat at the table, he turned back to me.

"Thanks for coming tonight, man," he said. "I know you've got a lot going on with the trial, so I do really appreciate the effort."

"No effort at all," I said. "It was actually great to catch up again. It's been too long." I paused as a passing car briefly lit us up with its lights. "And if you need any help with moving your things, I'm more than happy to pitch in," I decided to add.

"Nah, there's not much to move," he said. "I only have a few personal items, and everything else I'm leaving for—" was as far as he got before his head suddenly snapped to the left. A weird mist sprayed my face, and I remember thinking at the time that there had been no rain forecast for that entire week. It felt warm, *too* warm to come from the sky, and then a blood-curdling scream suddenly broke through the night.

Somewhere in the distance, I heard tires squealing as a car sped away, the screaming woman taking a deep breath before letting go a second time. Someone ran up from behind and knelt beside me, and when I looked down, I saw my friend crumpled in a heap before me. Blood streamed out from the side of his head, pooling into an ever-growing puddle that slowly worked its way along the concrete path. When the newcomer rolled the body over, the eyes staring up at me lacked any hint of life. A crowd began to encircle us, some coming from the parking lot but the majority from the restaurant. And when Paul Garroway's girlfriend launched her own scream, and it broke through the panicked cries, I wondered whether the bullet had been meant for me.

18

When I agreed to attend my friend's fortieth birthday dinner, the last thing I expected was to be caught up in his murder investigation. The parking lot quickly filled with all manner of emergency vehicles as law enforcement took control of the situation. Several officers began to interview witnesses, while others cordoned off the area and processed the crime scene.

What I didn't realize at the time was just how much in shock I really was. My friend had just been shot, had his brains blown out right in front of me, to be exact, and I stood there like a lamppost unable to put more than two words together. Staring at the others being interviewed, I could barely answer the cop's questions until he snapped a couple of fingers in front of my face to wake me up.

"Sorry, I'm here," I said, feeling like a rank amateur among the others.

"You were in a conversation with the deceased?"

"Yes, he was a friend of mine. We'd known each other since law school," I said, not sure whether the volume of my voice was enough to reach him.

"I'll take it from here, Officer," a new voice suddenly said, and I looked up to see Jack Barnes standing next to me.

"All yours, Detective," the cop said and moved off to find someone else to question.

"I told you to keep an eye over your shoulder," Jack said once he was sure nobody was within earshot of our whispers.

"You think that bullet was meant for me too, huh?"

"Maybe not specifically for you, but perhaps as a warning?"

"Really think Costa would go this far?" Just asking the question sent goosebumps racing down my arms.

"He's a nutjob, remember? Who the hell knows what goes on in that fried brain of his."

What transpired over the next few hours lives in my mind as brief flashes of memories. The coroner inspecting the body, the crime scene analysts pouring over the parking lot, the crowds lining the perimeter behind the police tape. At some point, the TV crews began to assemble, the lenses from their cameras appearing like peering eyes in the shadows while the reporters searched for any possible leads they could muster.

I must have lain awake in my bed for most of the night thinking about the finer details of those hours, wondering if I was actually a part of it or just a viewer watching events unfold on some massive screen. I do remember the girl-friend getting loaded up into the back of an ambulance after collapsing. The rest of Paul's colleagues stood in a group near the very edge of the scene while sharing what they knew with the cop assigned to take their statements. There was no missing the repeated glances they sent my way, the looks of suspicion more than evident.

I did eventually fall asleep...I *think*...but the dream I experienced felt like more of the same, the assassination playing over and over again as the same mist of warmth slapped across my face. When I eventually woke up, the final scream hung in the air like an unwanted soul, its echo reaching back at me from the corners of the room. The bedsheet stuck to my drenched skin as I desperately tried to fill my lungs, the horror already fading back into the shadows of my mind where they would undoubtedly wait until the next time I closed my eyes.

When the alarm suddenly began to scream next to me, I jumped and almost fell out of bed, the sheet wrapped tightly enough around my ankles to hold me in place. I slapped my phone, but instead of ending the mindnumbing whirring, I only managed to send the device cartwheeling across the room.

"OK, calm down," I muttered to myself while trying to untangle my legs and eventually managed to climb out of bed to kill the noise.

With the silence finally back in the room, I sat myself on the edge of the bed and closed my eyes as the reality of the previous night came flooding back. A friend had been shot dead right in front of me, the man's life stolen by an assassin's bullet. I pinched my leg hard, letting the pain confirm my consciousness and ensure it wasn't another vivid dream.

Opening my eyes again, I looked down at the red patch of skin on my leg, two neat finger marks brightening up the area.

"I'm sorry, man," I whispered, recalling the grin Paul had during those final few moments. He'd been happy, about to start a new chapter of his life, when bam...he snuck over into my neck of the woods and paid the ultimate price.

Standing in the shower that morning felt way too familiar to me, with flashbacks to Naomi's death bombarding me. While the grief itself wasn't even in the same ballpark (sorry, Paul), it did have that certain similarity about it, so much so that the same heavy lead weight sat firmly in my middle. I must have stood under the stream of water for a decent twenty minutes just staring into space before I realized the time.

I was still in the process of fixing my tie when a knock on the door interrupted my morning. It must have been my feeling on edge that caused me to stop by the cabinet near the hallway on my way to the front door and pull out my Glock. I held it behind my back as I opened it and breathed a subdued sigh of relief when I saw Linda standing there.

"Why didn't you call me last night?" she said with an air of frustration as I held the door open a little wider for her.

"Had my hands full," I said as I closed the door and followed her into the kitchen. When she saw me put the gun down on the table, Linda gave me a kind of unsurprised look.

"Yes, and I see that you're obviously feeling safe and well."

"Just a precaution."

"From what? Damn it, Ben, we're a team. Somebody took a shot at you, and you didn't phone me?"

"I honestly don't even know if that bullet was meant for me," I said, sounding about as confident as a kid caught stealing candy. Linda's reaction confirmed my lack of conviction.

"Don't give me that crap. You and I both know Costa has been looking for an opportunity."

"How does killing me solve anything for him?"

"I don't know, but that's not the point," she said, clearly pissed.

"Then what is the point?"

For a moment, we just stood there staring at each other, the object of the conversation briefly lost before Linda came around for a second go.

"I've looked into your friend, and there's nothing to indicate that he was the target. That bullet was either meant for you, and the shooter just didn't aim properly, or they aimed perfectly and managed to send a message."

"What message?"

"For you to lose the case and make sure Kat remains in jail where Costa can take his time making her life a total misery."

"Don't have to be in prison for that," I mumbled under my breath, and when Linda asked me to repeat myself, I waved the comment away.

"I have to keep getting ready," I said. "Talk to me while I finish getting dressed."

Linda followed me down to the bedroom while asking about my history with Paul. It was while asking about how somebody might have known about me being at the restaurant that I stopped and stared at my reflection in the mirror.

"Ben, what is it?"

"Nothing," I said, ignoring the lightbulb moment and continuing to fix my tie.

We chatted while I prepared for another day in court, and by the time we walked out of my apartment, Linda had agreed to follow up on the previous night's shooting to try and find any possible leads she could. We already had an insider working the case, so access to evidence would be easy, but Linda had a way of seeing things in a different light and always managed to find something the cops couldn't.

"I'll keep you posted," she called over her shoulder as she headed back to her car. I called thanks after her and felt my cell phone vibrating against the side of my leg.

"Grace, good morning," I said after answering it and briefly stopped while watching Linda climb into her car.

"I heard about the shooting. Are you OK? Do you need anything?'

"No, I'm fine, honest," I said as I began slowly walking toward my car. I'd barely walked three steps before Linda passed by. She gave me a brief tap of the horn and a wave before disappearing down the street. If I hadn't kept watching her drive off, I might have never noticed the black LaCrosse parked about three hundred yards down the street. I think the only reason I noticed it was because the sun reflected a beam off its windshield directly into my eye at just the right moment.

My first thought was to turn and head back inside, phone Linda, and have her approach the car from the other way, maybe even box it in. Continuing to walk slowly, I barely heard Grace telling me that she could request an adjournment from Becker if I needed the day to recover.

"No, that's fine," I replied, reaching the halfway point between my building's front door and my car.

"I'm sure he won't mind after what happened."

"No, honest," I said. "The case is more important, and besides, tomorrow is the weekend, and I'll have two days to deal with the fallout."

"OK, suit yourself. I'll see you at the courthouse then."

"Yes, see you then," I said, but instead of hanging up, I kept the phone pressed to my ear. I heard the connection between Grace and me end with a moment of silence before I started speaking random gibberish while watching the LaCrosse through my dark sunglasses.

With the vehicle sitting way too far down the street, I couldn't make out any of the finer details. For one, I didn't even know if it was the same one that had been stalking me, the license plate still evading me. Plus, with the angle of the sun reflecting off the windshield, I couldn't get a look at the car's interior to confirm that someone was actually sitting inside it. The only thing I did have were my instincts.

"OK, you slimeball," I whispered into the phone as I reached the Mustang. "Let's see what you've got."

Once inside the car, I pulled the Glock from my briefcase and set it on the passenger seat while starting the engine. I still kept all of my movements calm and controlled in case I was being watched through binoculars. Who knew just how prepared this guy was? I also didn't take off like a crazed lunatic once I began rolling, instead driving just as I always did, idling my way to the parking lot exit and then slowly turning right in the direction of downtown.

A hundred yards from the LaCrosse, I finally managed to get a look at the person sitting behind the wheel, the mass matching what I had seen previously. At the sixty-yard mark, the baseball cap came into view, and thirty yards later, I saw the shoulders sink down ever so slightly to try and keep from being seen.

"Too late, asshole," I snapped as I hit the brakes and came to a hard stop directly next to the car. With the Glock already in my hand, I yanked the door open, slid out from behind the wheel, and aimed the gun directly at the driver's side window.

"GET OUT SLOWLY," I called out, the pounding in my chest feeling like a bass drum. "NOW," I added when it looked as if nothing was going to happen.

When the door finally opened, I tensed up even more, the grip on the pistol almost enough to cramp my fingers.

"Slowly," I called out when I saw one empty hand appear above the top of the door. When an object appeared in the second hand, I pushed my gun forward a few inches. "I SAID SLOW."

It wasn't a gun in the guy's hand but a cell phone, and when his face finally appeared, rising up above the door line, I could see he was just as nervous as I was.

"Take it easy, man," he said while holding his leading hand up, palm facing me. "Don't go doing anything stupid."

"Why are you following me? Who sent you? Costa?"

"The answer you're looking for is right here," he said as he held up the cell phone. "Just take it."

For a second, I thought he was trying to distract me. Maybe throw the phone at me and then pull a gun and shoot my dumb ass while I was trying to catch the thing.

"Is Costa on there? What game are you playing?"

"No game," the guy said and slowly took a step toward his side of my car. "I promise, just listen."

When it looked as if he was going to put the phone on the roof of my car and then push it across, I held up a hand to stop him. OK, so that may not have been the time to get all protective about my car's paint job, but I had a protective streak.

"Hand it over," I said and leaned across the roof enough for my hand to reach the halfway point. With the other guy standing at least four inches taller than me, he easily reached the same point and dropped the phone into my hand. "OK, now back away," I said, thrusting the barrel of the Glock back and forth at him.

Looking at the screen of the phone, I could see an active call, the timer indicating it had been going for about a minute and a half. That put it at around the same time as me pulling up, and I figured he'd made the call while I was shouting for him to come out.

"Just speak to him, man," the guy said while watching me, and figuring I had no other choice, I pressed the phone to my ear.

"Who is this?" I asked just as a droplet of sweat ran from my brow and down into the gap between the top of the phone and my ear. It tickled as it worked its way down, but the sensation immediately disappeared when a voice suddenly spoke. To be honest, I expected to hear laughter, thick, disrespectful laughter from a man whom I'd met outside the prison that first morning when I had gone to visit Kat. Imagine my surprise when the voice turned out to belong to someone a lot closer to home.

"Ben, what the hell are you trying to do to my guy?" Dwight Tanner said with a tone of frustration.

"Dwight?"

"Of course, Dwight. Who were you expecting? Charles Manson?"

"What the hell is going on?" I looked over at the guy, and he shrugged his shoulders apologetically at me.

"Sorry, kid, I know I should have probably told you, but I knew you'd just knock the offer back. Jimmy there is a guy I hired to watch your back after that little beating you copped. I use him myself from time to time, although I don't really need him so much these days."

"A *bodyguard*?"

"Sure, if that works for you."

"What the hell do I need a bodyguard for?" It felt like my mouth had grown a mind of its own as my real one struggled to make sense of the situation, throwing out random words I didn't know I was going to speak.

"Look, just let him follow you around. You won't even know he's there. If something happens, he'll back you up."

"Like last night?"

"Yeah, well, sorry about that. He had a thing on with his kid and couldn't be there for that," Dwight said as his tone changed. "Sorry to hear about your friend."

"I have to get to the courthouse," I managed to say, and while I did thank Dwight, I don't remember actually meaning to say it, my mouth pushing the words out for me.

The odd thing was I recognized the face staring back at me from the other side of the car. Not only that, but I felt a certain sense of familiarity about the name as well, although I couldn't quite place it.

"I'm heading to the courthouse now," I said after considering my options. "I guess if Dwight is paying you to watch me, then...then who am I to turn him down?"

I'd never had a bodyguard before, and while this guy didn't actually protect me in the same way as one, I did feel a little better knowing he was mingling somewhere in the background. What I wondered while driving the rest of the way to the courthouse was just how different things would have turned out if he had been watching me the previous night.

19

GRACE MET ME ON THE STEPS OF THE COURTHOUSE TWENTY minutes later, and when I looked over my shoulder, I saw my new tail pulled into a parking space just a few rows behind mine.

"Did you know about this guy?" The look on her face confirmed her answer long before the words did.

"Dwight made me promise not to say anything," she said as we turned for the door. "Said you'd turn the help down if he'd asked you."

"I probably would have," I confirmed and forced a smile as the first of the reporters began to surround us.

While a few of the questions thrown at me during the course of that gathering were about the case, the majority turned out to be about the previous night's shooting, something I hadn't even considered. The first question caught me completely off guard, but I quickly managed to find my feet again. It was only when one of the reporters asked whether I believed that I might have been the intended target, given the identity of the victims my client was accused of killing, that I hesitated.

"Thank you for your time," I eventually said, dismissing the question with a smile that remained until I had safely walked through the doors.

"You handled that extremely well," Grace whispered to me once we'd walked far enough into the building to mingle with the rest of the crowd.

"Thank you," I said, but I had already shifted my thinking. "Listen, I need you to do something for me."

"Of course."

"Could you head back to the office and look up anything you can on Paul? I need to know if he's had gambling debts, an unknown drug addiction, whatever you can find. I also need records from his wife's cell phone and any social media messaging services she might be using. And ask Linda to help you."

"Are you thinking he might have been the real target after all?"

"No," I said. "But I do need to try and rule out the possibility."

Grace and I parted ways halfway through the foyer, and I was still trying to remember key things about my friend when the bailiff brought me to my feet a short time later. What I remembered most about Paul Garroway was the way he lived a clean life. I know it doesn't sound like it, given the affair and everything, but when I heard about it, that might have been the first time ever that I had known him to do anything deceitful. The man had been clean for as long as I could remember. No smoking, no drugs, no gambling. His alcohol intake only ever involved beer, and even then, he limited himself to two bottles of Corona.

It was only when Becker finally handed the floor to the prosecutor that I returned to the moment. By then, the jury was already seated, and Kat had taken her place by my side. I must have greeted her on auto-pilot, my mouth continuing to operate on its very own frequency.

"The state calls Officer Dyllan Nash to the stand," Bartell called out and effectively started the new day's session.

Nash, as it turned out, wasn't just someone associated with the case but actually had somewhat of a history with Kat. He'd arrested her on three separate occasions, once needing to call for backup when she resisted.

"She had quite a temper during the times I crossed paths with her," Nash said when Bartell asked him to describe their interactions. "I once confronted her in a corner store where she'd been accused of shoplifting, and when I came to question her, she began throwing things at my partner and me."

"Would you describe her temper as volatile, Officer Nash?"

"Volatile is a good word for it. Not surprised those good people died."

"Objection, Your Honor," I called out, and it came as no surprise when the judge sustained it.

"Just answer the question if you could, Officer Nash," Bartell said, but I could see from his expression that he appreciated the comment. He'd do anything to further stack the deck against me. "You also saw the defendant a few hours before the shooting, did you not?"

"I did, yes. Down at the 7/11 on the corner of Western and Allegheny."

"Did you happen to converse with the defendant?"

"No, not in the beginning. It was more of an eye-contact thing at the start. She appeared to be watching my partner and me pretty intently, and I thought she might have been attempting to shoplift something."

"What gave you that impression?"

"Just the way she kept her hands hidden behind her and watched our every move."

"What about her mood?" Bartell asked. "Did you notice anything particular about her that morning?"

"The only thing I did notice was that she looked ill. Her face lacked any real color, and if I had to guess, I'd say she looked hungry."

"Hungry?"

"I ended up buying my coffee and donut and bought an extra one, which I handed to her."

"Did she take it?"

"At first, she looked like she might but then changed her mind and ran out of the store."

"Thank you, Officer. No further questions."

"Your witness, Mr. Carter," Becker said to me, and I thanked him before rising from my chair.

"Officer Nash, I'm curious as to how you would describe the relationship you have with the neighborhood you serve?"

"I'd say it's a fairly good one. I try to help folks as much as I can."

"So you understand the needs of the people, is that what you're saying?"

"Yeah, that's right."

"If you saw a woman with a flat tire, for instance, you'd pitch in and help?"

"Yes, of course. Who wouldn't?"

"What about a lost child?"

"Yes, I'd help them find their way home."

"Objection, Your Honor. What is the relevance here?"

"I'm beginning to ask the same thing myself, Mr. Carter," Becker said.

"The relevance is, Your Honor, I'm trying to understand how a police officer such as Officer Nash might be viewed by the people he serves. Just because you see a uniform doesn't always mean help to people. This officer just explained how he saw a sick girl who appeared malnourished, and the best he could do was hold out a donut to her." I turned back to the officer before Becker could respond. "Is that how you would treat a starving child, Officer Nash? With a donut?"

"Your Honor, objection."

"Sustained."

"I have no further questions, Your Honor," I said, and after giving the cop an appropriate glare, I returned to my chair.

"The witness is excused." Becker checked his watch and called a ten-minute recess.

Nash did give me a sideways glance when he walked past me, but I mostly ignored it, turning my attention to Linda, who had taken a seat behind me during the previous session.

"Got some footage of the shooting from last night," she whispered to me. "And we have the car."

"Manage to get anything from it?"

"Unfortunately not," she said while watching Bartell walk from the courtroom. "The shooter dumped the car and torched it."

"And incinerated any possible evidence."

"We're running the plates and numbers but nothing as yet." She looked around. "How are things here?"

"Not going the best," I said. "Bartell is building a pretty credible case, and unless I can throw something in his way, I don't see how I can win this."

"We'll find something soon, I promise. I'm still waiting for a couple of neighbors to get back to me. The one who flew to Paris is due back next week."

"They don't have phones in Paris?"

"He's some sort of student and taken a momentary...what do you call it? Taken a vow of silence?"

"He's a Buddhist?"

"Not sure if he's an actual monk but something to do with it. I'm not sure. Religion has never been my forte."

"Well, let me know the second you find something."

"Count on it," Linda said and left me standing alone as I looked down at the pile of paperwork.

When the following session eventually began again, Bartell's next witness was a forensic pathologist who took the jury through a detailed explanation of the crime scene. The problem for me when it came to those kinds of witnesses was that they spoke in facts, and it's very difficult to change course when dealing with specifics. It's not like I can change the angle of a chair to prove my client's innocence.

The afternoon session proved to be much the same, with Bartell again bringing in the experts to explain blood spatter patterns, blood *splatter* patterns, bullet trajectories, and so many more factors. I could see several members of the jury begin to do that head-bobbing thing while trying to keep both awake and alert to what was being described for them. It actually made me feel a little like I was back in elementary school, in Mr. Neiborg's history classes. Talk about a borefest. The man had the uncanny ability to turn any exciting subject into an endless drone of slides he'd shuffle through that ancient overhead projector he insisted on using. The current witness's voice sounded eerily similar to old Neiborg.

Thankfully, Becker eventually spared everyone's sanity by bringing the session to an end just after four that afternoon, and after spending a few final minutes chatting with Kat to make sure she was doing OK, I headed back to the office. I wanted to grab an extra fistful of business cards and catch up with Dwight about my newly adopted tail that insisted on following me just about everywhere. The other thing I needed to know was whether Grace had uncovered any possible motive for Paul's shooting. While he might have appeared to be clean, I knew those with the darkest secrets often appeared as the cleanest of all.

"Becker let you out early, did he?" Grace asked as I walked into the office.

"He was feeling generous," I said with a grin. "How did you go with Paul?"

"Just as expected. Aside from what he had going on with his new girlfriend, the man could put a priest to shame with how honest he was. His work appears impeccable, no gambling habits that I could find, nothing shady, I'm afraid." She looked up at me with a renewed seriousness. "What if the shooter really *had* been aiming for you?"

"Maybe they were," I said without much emotion. I gave Martin Pike a head nod as he walked past. "Going for a drink after I have a quick chat with Dwight," I told Grace. "Is he in?"

"Yes, he should be free."

"Wanna come?"

"Where? To see my husband?"

"No, for the drink."

"I'll pass. Got my sister's birthday dinner to get ready for."

"Oh, sounds fun," I said and continued on to Dwight's office.

"Where you headed for a drink?" Pike asked, his own office just two down from Dwight's.

"Thinking Ed's," I said, the bar just four blocks from the office and almost directly on my way home.

"Maybe I'll drop by. Just got to finish this opening statement for Monday."

"Might see you there then," I said and knocked on the boss's door.

"Come on in," Dwight called out, and when I walked in, I found him lying face up on the floor.

For a split second, I thought the man had fallen, and my arrival had been perfect timing to help him back up, but when I saw the hands clasped together across his stomach and his feet jiggling back and forth in rapid succession, I breathed a little easier.

"Are you still using that weird contraption?" I walked around his feet and the machine they rested on, grabbed one of the chairs, and pulled it out before sitting backward on it. Using the backrest to support my front, I watched my boss try to ignore me, his eyes closed as the Zen machine continued working its purported health benefits.

"You're just jealous that it's not you lying here," Dwight eventually said, his voice breaking the silence after me waiting patiently for a couple of minutes.

"If this is me being jealous, I'll take it," I said, still unable to fathom the purpose of the device. "How does that thing shaking the crap out of you fix anything?"

"Magic," Dwight whispered as he opened his eyes, grabbed the remotely wired control, and shut the machine off.

I waited until he managed to get himself back onto his feet, slip into his shoes, and take his usual seat behind the desk. Two seconds later, leaning back in his chair, he rolled a cigar across his top lip, pretending to smell it.

"How's your bodyguard doing?"

"Great, I guess. Don't you think it's a little over the top?"

"After last night?" He sounded surprised as he leaned forward and dropped the cigar on his desk.

"You had him following me long before last night," I said

and shared the first encounter I'd had with the man. "Who is he anyway?"

"You mean to tell me you don't know who Jimmy Waters is?" Dwight shook his head in disgust.

Again, I felt a hint of familiarity with the name and still found myself unable to find the right file in my brain. Dwight gave me a clue when he put up his fists as if preparing to fight me. That was when the penny dropped.

"That man is *Jimmy Waters*? *THE* Jimmy Waters?"

"The one and only," Dwight said, looking a little too pleased with himself.

"Why the hell would Jimmy Waters be following me around like a—"

"Careful how you speak of that man," Dwight interrupted, holding his palm out to stop me.

I should have recognized the name the second I first heard it, given my previous interest in the man, but then again, it had been a good twenty years since I'd last heard it. He'd been one of the greatest boxing personalities in the state, often stopping by local schools to give talks in between bouts. My school happened to be one of the ones he stopped at just after winning his last world title fight back in '03. It was during that particular visit that I managed to sneak a poster in for an autograph, a poster I still kept bound up in my collectibles drawer.

"He can't rely on his past forever and chooses to offer limited protection work from time to time," Dwight said. "I just happened to get in contact with him at the right time, and now...well, he's watching your ass."

"I appreciate the ass-watching," I said, unsure of what else to say. "Thanks."

"You're welcome," Dwight said with a smirk as he picked up his cigar again. "Now get out of here and leave me to get some work done."

I did as he asked, and after grabbing my briefcase, I thanked Grace for her work on my way to the door. She sent me a wave, and once I was back at my car, I threw the briefcase onto the passenger seat, took off my jacket, and sent it after the piece of luggage. Loosening the tie, I dropped into the driver's seat, started the engine, and lowered the window after slamming the door shut.

There's something about rolling out of the parking lot at the end of the working day knowing the only destination ahead of you is one where you can relax with a cold beer and a lack of attention. It felt good sitting in traffic for a change, the music turned up just enough to drown out the other vehicles, with the cool breeze blowing in through the open window. Every now and then, I'd check the rearview mirror to see the familiar black front of the LaCrosse sitting a few cars back and pictured the legend sitting at the wheel.

When I reached the parking lot of Ed's, I waited in the car until Jimmy grabbed a spot of his own, as usual keeping his distance. This time, I wanted to make sure Dwight hadn't just been yanking my chain, so I approached the car to confirm his identity for myself. This time, when the man climbed out, it took me barely a second to recognize that distinctive glint in his eyes, the shoulders still wide enough to eclipse the sun.

"Mr. Waters, I understand you've been asked to watch my back, but I really think—"

"Save it, kid," Jimmy said, doing his best to maintain a polite tone. "Mr. Tanner was very specific in his instructions."

"Yes, but if we're—"

"Not interrupting, am I?" A new voice spoke from directly behind me, and I didn't need to turn to know who it belonged to. My bodyguard immediately reached into his jacket but kept the gun out of sight.

I turned to find Riccardo Costa standing a dozen feet away, his usual accomplice about the same distance behind his boss.

"What do you want?" I asked, my patience growing thinner by the second.

"Just to say hi and to see how the case is going," Costa said, completely unfazed by my hired help.

"If you'd bother to come down to the court once in a while, you might know how the court case is going."

"Aw, Benny, don't be like that. I have my connections update me occasionally, but it's never as exciting as being there, am I right?"

"If you say so."

"So who's your friend?" Costa asked as he took a couple of steps closer. Behind me, I heard Jimmy shift and imagined him taking the pistol out of its holster.

"Just someone watching my back," I said.

"Oh, is this about the shooting? I'm genuinely sorry for your loss." His voice mocked me with each syllable. I could see that Costa enjoyed the moment but couldn't bring myself to react the way he might have hoped.

"Look, I've had a long day, so if there's something specific you're after…"

"I'm actually not playing," Costa said, and for the first time, I actually believed him. "Your friend wasn't shot by any of my associates. I'm only telling you this because I want you to concentrate on this case. While I do still have my suspicions about this client of yours, I also want to make the right person pay for what they did to my family."

His words took me by surprise, and if he hadn't turned around at that moment, who knew just how long the silence would have hung between us. I stood my ground, watching Costa return to his waiting car, and once he was gone, I turned back to my bodyguard.

"Look, I know what instructions Dwight would have given you, but since he's not here and I'm technically in control of where we go, I say you need to follow me into that bar and have a cold beer with me."

"I never drink on the job," Jimmy Waters said as he stuffed the pistol back into the holster.

"Neither do I," I said, gesturing to the bar's entrance. "Which is why now is the right time for us to have a drink."

20

WHILE I COULDN'T CONVINCE JIMMY TO HAVE A BEER WITH ME, I did manage to convince him to enjoy a club soda, and that was enough for me to begin a conversation that lasted a couple of hours. He ended up relaxing by the third glass and eventually filled me in on what he'd been up to since walking away from the world of boxing some fifteen years earlier. The biggest surprise came when he remembered who I was after I shared my story about the poster. You should have seen his face light up at the memory.

I was still thinking about that moment several hours later while I was lying in bed with one arm curled up under my head and the other resting on my chest. Dark shadows danced across the ceiling as I thought about the day, each moment taking just a few seconds to work through. The part I struggled with the most was the distinct lack of conviction on my part. I didn't think I was building enough of a case with Bartell's witnesses, which meant that when the time came for me to begin calling my own, I'd be far behind the starting line. In a way, I felt like I'd stalled and was waiting for the spark to send me racing down the track.

When I reached the part of the night when I thought through the latest run-in with Costa, I felt a nagging tightening in my middle, his endless reminders about watching me taking their toll. This time, however, he'd surprised me with a revelation I wasn't sure I believed. If Costa was telling the truth and he really wasn't behind the shooting, then who was? I had seen the killing of Paul Garroway as purely accidental and that I had been the intended target, but if Costa wasn't responsible for sending the assassin, then who would have taken the shot?

I rolled onto my side in the darkness and closed my eyes, replaying those frightening few seconds back through my mind. The scene played out both in silence and slow motion, each frame lasting a few seconds as my brain tried to evaluate every minute detail. The bullet hitting him, the spray of blood across my face, the squeal of tires from somewhere out on the road, the screams, the...the beating in my chest that seemed to drown out everything else.

Frustrated at not seeing the answer in front of me, I rolled over and faced the wall, keeping my eyes closed as the darkness felt a little comfortable. I'm not sure at which point I finally drifted off, but what I do know is that the dream that followed continued the nightmare on repeat, playing out again and again like a warped version of *Groundhog Day*. It was only my alarm that woke me the following morning and finally brought me back to reality, breaking up another monotonous cycle.

While I could have slept in, given it was the weekend, I still had plenty of things on my plate. For one, I wanted to get to the office early so I could work through the case's latest updates with Linda and Grace. They'd both agreed to meet me at nine, although Grace did make it clear she could only stay until noon due to other commitments. I also wanted to pay Kat a visit to see how she was coping with being back inside. I had spoken to her before each court session, of course, but the environment alone tended to keep her closed off. Yes, I know prison wouldn't have felt any easier, but I hoped just turning up in jeans and a T-shirt would help ease the officialness of the chat.

There was also something else I hoped to address, although I wasn't sure if the other party would show up. I don't know how much attention you've been devoting to this story so far, but I had become somewhat suspicious about a matter I'd been keeping in the back of my head since the very beginning. I hoped to make today the day that I finally got to the bottom of it.

After doing the shower thing and getting myself looking presentable enough to go out among the general public, I skipped the whole morning coffee and breakfast thing and headed straight for the door. Halfway to the office, I stopped by a nearby café and grabbed half a dozen coffees plus a bag filled with different kinds of pastries. Not knowing who would be in the office, I wanted to make sure I had a wide enough selection for the skeleton crew.

We didn't have a receptionist on the weekend, so the first person I ran into was Julio, the end-of-week janitor, who gave the place a thorough, deep clean on Saturdays. After a very brief exchange, I left him with a cappuccino to sip on while polishing the foyer. Next, I found Liza Mallory sitting at her desk outside Erin Basking's office. She opted for a flat white, passing on one for her boss, who remained hidden behind a closed door on a conference call that would continue for more than an hour.

I found Grace at her desk while chatting with Linda and dropped the bag of pastries in front of her. They each grabbed a drink before I set down one for myself and continued on to palm off the last one. I found Martin Pike in his office alone, tapping away on his keyboard. I offered to read the opening statement he'd been working on, but he declined, saying he'd rather finish it alone. He did take the final cup out of the tray, though, and promised to bring in the next round, something he'd often said and never followed through with.

Once I was back at my office, I asked Grace and Linda to follow me in, and after taking our respective seats, I began by sharing my latest run-in with Riccardo Costa and how he insisted that the shooting wasn't one that he'd arranged.

"But he's the only one that makes sense," Grace said before taking a sip and giving a nod of appreciation. "Oh, yeah, that's good."

"What about any past cases?" Linda asked. "Anybody come to mind who might want to get some revenge?"

"Take your pick," I said, thinking of at least half a dozen off the top of my head. "Plenty of those in the old filing cabinet." I thought about it while sampling my own beverage but barely tasted it. "It just doesn't feel like some random person coming out of the woodwork to take a potshot at me. Why now?"

"To try and blend in with your current case?" I looked at Linda, but again, I couldn't see the connection. Something inside me...my instinctual subconsciousness, if you will, was telling me that the shooting had *everything* to do with the current case. I just didn't know how.

"It's connected," I said. "I don't know how or why, but that shooting is because of this case."

"So you suspect that Costa is lying?" Another look at Linda. She offered some valuable input, and I considered each comment in turn.

"I wish I knew," I said, remembering back to the tone he'd used while telling me.

"He doesn't strike me as someone who'd hide the fact he'd shot a friend of yours," Grace said. "I mean, if he tried to cover the fact and was actually the one behind it, what would be the point?"

"What do you mean?"

"Well, if he shot Paul to send a message to you, why then try to make you believe he wasn't the one behind it?"

I smiled when she finished, a genuine grin that I found powerless to hold back. Linda also looked at Grace and did the same.

"And that right there is why I love you so much," I said. "You just answered the question for me. You're absolutely right."

In the blink of an eye, Grace had managed to clear up the one part eluding me, the pivotal piece that brought light to the dilemma. It was in that instant that I realized Costa wasn't behind the shooting after all, which meant somebody out there had acted alone. The only question I still had that needed answering was whether the bullet had found its intended target or whether it had been aimed at me all along. That was when Linda added something to the conversation that immediately changed the course of the day.

"Is Ed's a bar Riccardo Costa is known to frequent?" Both Grace and I looked over at her before looking at each other. What I found looking back at me was the face of a person asking the very same question we'd held in the back of our minds for weeks. "What did I say?"

It took me all of half a second to suddenly see the answer right in front of me, and I think I saw the moment the penny dropped for Grace as well. That was when I knew I had to act and rose out of my chair.

"Linda, you carrying?" I didn't need to ask the question, but I did anyway. She patted the side of her chest.

"Always, why?"

"Just follow me and be ready," I said, and after a quick nod to Grace, I headed out through the door.

Walking down the corridor, I could feel the tension already building inside me, the purpose in my stride accentuating with each step. I heard the two women following, one set of high heels clip-clopping on the tiles. When we reached a particular lawyer's office, I didn't slow down and walked in unannounced.

Martin Pike was in the middle of reading whatever he'd written, squinting at the screen with an obsessive expression. He turned to see who the new arrival was, and his eyes subsequently grew wider as each new person came in behind me.

"Ben? What's up?" he asked, looking from one of us to the next. He appeared genuinely surprised and sat upright as we stopped directly in front of his desk.

"Unlock your cell phone and give it to me," I said, my tone flat and direct.

"My phone?" Again, he looked at Linda and Grace before shaking his head at me. "Why would I do that?"

"Because I think you're the one who's been feeding Riccardo Costa information," I said and leaned across his desk. "Now give me your phone."

For a second, I could see his mind ticking, a virtual avalanche of thoughts all dropping at the same moment. He was looking for a way out, confirmation that he'd been busted, and a worthy alibi that would release him.

"Have you gone crazy?" He looked at Grace. "Tell me he's joking," he said before returning his focus to me. "I'm one of the senior lawyers for this firm. Why on earth would I need to bother with Riccardo Costa?"

"Because you have an insatiable gambling habit, and my guess is you're in quite deep with one of his crew. Now give me the phone."

I didn't expect him to give in so easily, but after giving me a nod of submission, he reached for his cell phone, used the Face ID to unlock it, and handed it to me.

"I'm going to need an official apology after this," he said as he leaned back in his chair.

I scrolled through the texts but found nothing indicating he'd ever communicated with Costa. I worked my way through the contacts, looking for a name I might recognize, all of the messages, and opened the email app. Still nothing.

"Now I'm going to need you to move aside," I said as I went to step around the side of the desk.

That was when Pike suddenly lunged for his top drawer and managed to pull out a revolver, but I heard a distinctive click from directly beside me that froze the lawyer in place.

"I wouldn't," Linda said and took a step forward, the barrel of her weapon aimed directly into his face. I stepped closer, reached for the gun, and pulled it free.

"Dumb move," I said and held it out for Linda. "On both counts."

This time, when I gestured for Pike to move, he did so by walking to the end of his office, where Linda kept him covered. I could see the defeat in his eyes, and I knew it was just a matter of time until I found what I needed. When he broke eye contact and stared down at his feet as I opened the bottom drawer of his desk, I knew I had him.

Lying underneath a pile of files, I found a small, cheap-looking cell phone, the kind Linda and I liked to call burners. It's the sort of phone you might find on display next to the register at a gas station or in the impulse-buy display at the grocery store. I picked it up, held it up for Pike to see, and gave it a shake.

"This it?" He sighed and as he looked down at his feet again, he gave a surrendering nod. "Unlock it," I said as I walked closer and held it out to him. "Try to break it, and you follow close behind."

He didn't try to break it, nor did he resist helping us. I think the second Pike saw me pull the phone out, he knew he was toast, and his best bet was to play ball in the hope of saving his ass. After handing it back to me, I began searching through the messaging app and quickly found the ongoing exchange he'd had with Costa.

"He told me he'd give me more time to pay what I owed," Pike whispered when he could see me reading through several of the specific texts.

When Dwight suddenly walked into the office, the entire mood swung south as Pike understood the finality of his actions.

"What the hell is going on?" Dwight asked, looking from Linda to Pike and finally to me.

"We found our spy," I said and handed Dwight the phone. He took his time working through several exchanges.

While he had a heap of options open to him, Dwight took the simplest course of action, just as anybody who knew him would expect. The man wasn't one to beat around the bush and certainly didn't sugarcoat things. While he could have stretched the confrontation out and highlighted all the ways he was going to make Pike pay, Dwight kept it short and simple.

"You're fired," he grunted with an extra dose of pissed-off under his breath. "Pack your shit and get out."

Pike nodded, his silence enough answer for Dwight, who handed me back the phone and walked out. Grace exchanged a look with me before following her husband out into the corridor. The thing to understand is that Martin Pike wasn't just any lawyer. He and Dwight went back a long way and had worked together on some truly epic cases. I think my boss saw him as the brother he'd never had and would have done anything for him. Unfortunately, this level of deception wasn't something that could be forgiven.

Linda and I ended up escorting Pike from the premises shortly afterward. He never spoke a word, the final look he gave me while walking through the front doors of the building one of shame. I waited until he walked out of sight before turning to Linda.

"Thank you," I said. "That's one less thing to worry about."

"It will only mean that Costa assigns someone else to track you, you know."

"As long as they stay out of my way and let me work this case," I said and gestured for us to head back to the office. While I had effectively resolved one issue, there were still plenty that needed my attention.

21

I DIDN'T END UP GETTING TIME TO SEE KAT AT THE PRISON ON that Saturday, but I did manage to go and see her early afternoon the following day. She looked a lot better than I expected, and when we were finally alone, she explained that she'd managed to make a friend inside the unit, a woman the other inmates referred to as Mama Hen. According to Kat, this particular inmate ran the unit and had taken a special liking to her, who she referred to as Madam Bitch.

"I refused to hand over my tater tots to another girl, and when she threatened to beat me up, I stood my ground and just glared at her," Kat explained to me. "Mama Hen called out when a couple of other girls looked like they were going to step in and help this girl, and I didn't mean to, but I glared at her as well."

"Sounds like you're making a name for yourself," I said with a hint of pride. I didn't want her in prison, of course, but if I knew she was finally learning to look after herself, maybe we had a shot at getting out the other side intact.

It was during the conversation that I asked Kat about anybody she might know who could testify on her behalf. Maybe share a story or two about why she ended up on the street, how difficult her home life was…anything I could use to paint her in a better light than she had been by the other side. It was then that she mentioned the girl named Reagan Byrd, a friend she'd had since age five. According to Kat, this girl knew her better than anybody and would definitely help if given the chance. I could have mentioned that my assistant had already tracked her down but knowing how sensitive Kat was about her past, I decided to hold back. Easier for her to share the details with me.

Once I was back out in the prison parking lot, I phoned Linda and asked if she could perform a more thorough background check of the girl for me. Given how efficient my investigator was, I didn't think she'd take very long.

"Send through what you can and I'll arrange for Grace to go and talk with this girl."

"You don't think I have that maternal streak in me?"

"You're good with the other things," I need. "Convincing young ladies to attend court is more up Grace's alley." Linda chuckled before hanging, leaving me standing next to my car, wondering about the next move.

The thing I loved about my team was just how efficient they were when left alone to follow the tasks they excelled at. Take Linda, for example. She knew how to find people, had access to any number of databases by way of secret contacts and fake log-in details, plus knew her way around a city by way of the internet. If she needed to investigate a business, person, or other kind of entity, she was your go-to girl.

Grace, on the other hand, knew how to talk to people. When not in the office working on any number of things a lawyer's assistant needed to do, I could count on her to use that empathic soul of hers to convince people to do things they wouldn't normally do. She just had that kind of presence about her, that inner warmth people gravitated towards. I felt it that very first morning we met after Dwight assigned her to me and I've known exactly how to use it ever since.

By one that afternoon, Linda had a file for me, including a business address where the girl worked a part-time job. She served hungry diners at a Burger King in between classes she attended at the University of Pittsburgh, where she was studying nursing. From what I was told, she was in her second year with exemplary grades. Linda also told me that Reagan Byrd lived alone near campus in a flat she herself paid for with her earnings from the job, as well as a small trust fund left to her by her grandmother.

Grace messaged me at three to say that she had made contact with the Byrd girl and was meeting her at four after her shift finished. At five, Grace phoned to say that the girl agreed to testify on her friend's behalf, although she felt that there might have been some sort of friction between the two friends. Grace said that when she mentioned Kat needing a friend due to her parents not testifying on their daughter's behalf, she became somewhat fidgety and mentioned Kat not always agreeing with what people said about her.

By seven that evening, I added Reagan Byrd's name to the list I'd been keeping, making her what I considered the fourth quality witness I intended to use for the case. Staring down at the names, I already knew it wouldn't be enough to ensure a win, but then again, some cases had a way of swinging back the other way on the back of just a single good witness. Any one of the four I already had could hold the key to ensuring Kat's freedom. I just had to know which questions to ask to give them the opportunity to provide the right answer.

If there was one way I used to feel where a case was at, I'd have to say it was when I lay in my bed at night trying to go to sleep. The ease with which I tumbled beneath the top level of consciousness was as good a guide as any and one I'd come to rely on for quite some time. Some nights, I'd toss and turn as my brain raced through a multitude of thoughts at a thousand miles per hour, sleep feeling like a virtual impossibility. Other times, I'd slide beneath the veil of sleep the second my head touched the pillow, the rest that followed reserved for a man on top of his game.

So where did I feel myself sitting with the Katherine Wright case? I'd say somewhere in between. I lay in the dark, staring up at the ceiling while trying to picture Kat in her cell. Brief flashes of the case quickly followed, such as moments in the courtroom, interviews with potential witnesses, and exchanges between the prosecutor and me. But then other thoughts crept in, like my run-ins with Riccardo Costa and Martin Pike. As morbid as it sounds, I even thought about Paul Garroway lying on a tray in some morgue's freezer, his corpse waiting patiently to be buried beside his mother.

It was while thinking about Paul that I did finally manage to fall asleep. The dream that followed wasn't exactly a nightmare per se, but I did find myself talking to Paul's corpse several times as he seemed to follow me around my apartment, asking why I would have him shot when he only ever wanted to be my friend. The dream felt a little too similar to something Stephen King might write, and I did spend a few minutes after waking the next morning trying to figure out if I had indeed read a story by the author describing what I had dreamt.

"I'm pretty sure a corpse followed the main guy around in *Pet Sematary*," Linda told me the next morning during my drive to the courthouse. I'd phoned her to see if she had any updates on Garroway's shooting but got distracted by the dream.

"That was the ghost of a student, if I remember correctly," I said as I pulled up at a traffic light.

"Damn, looked like a corpse with his brains hanging out like that," she said with disgust. "Don't think I could ever forgive Marlon for making me watch it."

There was no update, of course. Despite having access to quite a number of security feeds from the area, the shooter had taken care to avoid streets housing some and managed to slip into the night. This alone told me that whoever had pulled the trigger had also taken care to do their homework.

"Keep me updated," I said, and after wishing me good luck with the upcoming court session, Linda ended the call.

When I walked into the courthouse foyer less than a half

hour later after spending a few minutes speaking with the media mob, I briefly paused at the sight of the people. It doesn't happen often these days, but sometimes, I still get a sense of someone being there for more than just a case.

I remembered back to when I first stepped into the same building on my very first case, an overwhelming sense of purpose driving me through that crowd. Most of those people were there for whatever cases they had to attend, to find out whether a loved one was going to prison or to find out what punishment the judge was handing down for their latest infraction. Me? I was there to save a life, to help a client avoid losing their freedom for the rest of their days. My purpose for being there just *felt* more than what I imagined others would feel, a real sense of responsibility to my client. Either that or the smell of the place was just screwing with my brain, causing me to ramble.

Do you know who doesn't walk with a sense of purpose? A judge, or at least the one who walked into the courtroom after the bailiff brought everybody to their feet. The man just kind of...strolled into the place, looking more like he'd rather be out on his boat fishing or something. Becker gave the place a brief gaze over the rim of his glasses, mumbled something unintelligible that may have been a good morning, and took his seat.

Kat, on the other hand, walked out with a certain sense of dread hanging about her and one I could totally understand. Each member of the jury, however, emerged from their holding area like a soldier marching in tandem with the one before them, each taking almost the same number of steps minus one to get to their place. Once seated, they joined the rest of the crowd in staring at the judge to get things moving.

"The State calls Officer Hailey Butters to the stand," Bartell called out once Becker finally handed the prosecutor the floor. Beside me, Kat shifted her weight uncomfortably, and I recalled her telling me about the relationship she had with the forthcoming witness.

"Relax," I whispered to her as a tall, slender woman entered the courtroom. "Just breathe."

When the woman took the stand and sat down, the first person she looked at was sitting beside me. Kat did not meet her gaze, instead looking down at her fingers, which she continued wrestling against each other. I also felt a certain energy coming off her, a kind of tension not entirely foreign to me. It didn't concern me as such, but I did get a bad vibe from it.

Bartell began his questions by asking the woman the usual ones he put forth to most experts. The agency worked for, position held, how long for, general experience, things like that. Butters answered each in turn with an air of confidence. I got the feeling that she had a reason for wanting to be there. What I mean is, unlike most experts who come because they've been asked to offer their professional opinion, Hailey Butters seemed to be someone who wasn't asked to appear but had instead offered. She had something to say and made sure she could.

"Ms. Butters, how do you know the defendant?"

"I was assigned to her case back when Katherine first became known to the State. She left home quite young, and with nowhere to go, we tried to make sure she had a safe place to stay."

"And did she accept your help?"

"No, she did not, or at least not in the beginning."

"How old was Miss Wright when you were first made aware of her?"

"Thirteen," Butters said, her answer sending a subdued murmur across the gallery.

"That's quite young to be out on the street," Bartell said.

"We've had younger, but they usually accept our offer."

"And Miss Wright didn't?"

"No, she did not."

"There was another reason you became aware of the child, isn't that true?"

"Yes."

"Could you tell the court what that reason was?"

Butters again hesitated to answer as she looked across the floor to where Kat was sitting. If her reason for the delay was for dramatic effect, she certainly knew how to play the game.

"According to the friend who phoned us, she was pregnant."

This time, the outbursts from the gallery were enough for Becker to rap his little gavel on the bench a couple of times while calling for order. Yes, sir, the people loved gossip.

"You were told that Katherine Wright was pregnant at the age of thirteen?"

"Yes, I was."

"And did you investigate the matter?"

"I did, yes. It took me a bit to finally track her down, but when I did, she eventually agreed to come into the office for a talk. I needed her to understand that there was help available for her. All she had to do was be open to it."

"And was she?"

"Not exactly," Butters said, sending another look in Kat's direction. Inside, I felt something tighten, sure that the woman had something she *really* wanted to share. "It was during that first meeting that she told me that nobody needed to worry about her or the baby because she had already gotten an abortion."

As you can imagine, chaos ensued. The crowd reacted just the way I expected, and all I could was sit there as Becker again went to work on bringing the courtroom back into order. I did sneak a look back over my shoulder and, halfway up the aisle, saw Lois Wright sitting quietly alone. She didn't see me looking, mirroring her daughter's uncomfortableness by staring down at her hands.

It took Becker a couple of minutes to calm the crowd again, this time threatening to clear the courtroom if he heard another outburst. Having already followed through a previous time, people knew to take him seriously, and they quickly came to order. Once Becker was satisfied the courtroom was back to normal, he gave the prosecutor the go-ahead to continue.

"Ms. Butters, I take it you offered the girl some counseling? It can't have been easy for her."

"It wasn't, and yes, I offered her quite a number of services which could help her, including a family willing to take her in."

"You mean foster care?"

"Yes."

"Did she accept?"

"No, she did not."

"You also did a little investigating, did you not? About this abortion?"

"Yes, I did. Katherine told me where she went to have the pregnancy terminated, and given that the place was more of a backroom kind of set-up, they weren't exactly known for keeping to the letter of the law."

"You asked the place about this termination?" Beside me, Kat shifted her weight again.

"I did, yes. As it turned out, there was no pregnancy."

The outcry from the gallery rose up in an instant, most of the shouting directed in Kat's direction. Butters looked over again, and I could see the satisfaction in her eyes. Kat sank a little deeper into her seat as her cheeks turned crimson. I did happen to look over my shoulder again and just saw the back of Lois Wright as she walked out of the room. It was those final couple of steps she took that told me she wasn't leaving to answer nature's call or to grab a coffee. She was leaving with no intention of ever returning.

22

XAVIER BARTELL KNEW HOW TO PLAY HIS HAND SO HE COULD end on the best possible high, and calling Hailey Butters for his final witness proved to be the ace up his sleeve. After presenting his case, the jury would have found the defendant to be manipulative, a liar, and a possible prostitute, the exact opposite of how *I* saw Kat. To me, she was just a kid wound up in a nightmare situation, caught in the wrong place at the wrong time and handed the responsibility of clearing her name.

"The prosecution rests, Your Honor," was how Bartell finally ended his case, and Becker immediately called a recess for lunch.

Grace met me out in the foyer, and a few minutes after we sat down so I could eat, Linda joined us. We had a lot to go over, and one turkey and ham on rye later, I had my list of witnesses arranged into a specific order and a few minutes left before I'd be calling the first of them to the stand.

"Guess it's finally time to show our hand," I said after the last swallow of soda. "I'm still hoping to see if there's any information from our monk guy."

"He's due back shortly," Linda said. "I left messages for him at both his hotel and the airport, but nothing yet."

"And Reagan Byrd? She's definitely confirmed?"

"She assured me she'll be here first thing tomorrow," Grace said.

"If only I had a couple more people like her," I said, thinking about the length of my list of witnesses. "The people I have now just don't feel like enough."

"All it takes is one," Grace said, reciting my own words that I had spoken many times before back to me.

"You're right," I said. "All it takes is one."

I looked down at the list I'd written on the napkin for the sake of visualizing the names and saw a very limited bunch.

"The girl just doesn't have many friends, no real job history, and the only people who really know her are the agencies and, well, we saw how that turned out with the prosecution's last witness," Grace said.

"Nope, these will do for now," I said, checking the time and rising to my feet. "Thank you for all your help, ladies."

"I'll leave you to it," Linda said. "Got a bit on my plate. Might have a lead on something that could help explain how your first witness might have managed to beat her brother by paying for the bar."

"Sophia Cafaro?"

"I'll keep you posted," Linda said with a nod, shot Grace a wink, and headed for the door.

"I'll be interested to see what she finds," I whispered as Grace also stood.

"Same," she said and, after pushing her chair back under the table, followed me back to the courtroom.

It was my first intended witness and her husband, who I found standing near the open doors, and when they saw me approach, Sophia gave me a subdued wave.

"I'll meet you inside," I said to Grace.

"I can't tell you how nervous I am," Sophia said once I led her a little farther down the corridor. "I honestly didn't think there was anything I feared in this world."

"Neither did I," Savio said. "This woman's strength puts me to shame."

"Yes, a court can certainly feel overwhelming, but the trick is to ignore everyone else," I said. "Just pretend it's you and the person asking you the questions, and you'll be fine."

"Easier said than done."

"I won't be straying too far from the questions we've already gone through," I said. "And a lot of what you're here to describe is just the standard stuff between you and your brother."

She looked up at her husband. "Don't you dare leave me," she insisted to him.

"I won't," he said with a big grin.

I felt a smattering of nerves myself once the bailiff called the courtroom to order, the indelible tightening that always came forth whenever I was about to start a fresh case by calling the very first witness. I say indelible because it always felt the same, a permanent sensation that felt more like a preprogrammed alarm at that particular moment in a case.

"Mr. Carter, you may call your first witness," Becker eventually called to me, and I rose to my feet; it was time to take control of the train.

"Thank you, Your Honor. The defense calls Sophia Cafaro to the stand."

The woman who I watched enter the courtroom and make her way to the witness stand was not the same one I'd met out in the corridor just moments before. The one walking toward me, shooting a brief smile in my direction and then continuing on to where the bailiff stood waiting was the woman I'd first met in her bar several weeks earlier. It was the confident business owner, the bar manager, who had skirted the very edge of bankruptcy and beaten a hostile takeover.

Sophia took her seat and immediately turned to face the bailiff, her posture upright and straight. She had the kind of poker face that I saw as concentration rather than fear; the woman focused on the task at hand rather than fearing it.

I didn't ask my first question until I got out of my chair and walked all twenty-three steps from my table to the witness stand, coming to a halt maybe six feet from where Sophia was sitting. I made sure to pass her a little just so that when I turned back to face her, I also had a view of the jury.

I'm not sure how versed you are with theatrics, but I once read an article about movie-making. It was there that I found out about the focus of every shot needing to be captured by a central point, the camera lens. Every scene's purpose was to play through that lens, every bit of dialog, action, and drama needing to be captured for the sake of the audience who would see the piece from that viewpoint.

The jury was the courtroom's camera lens. Every bit of testimony, questioning, and evidence presentation...all of it had to be delivered in such a way that the courtroom's unique camera lens captured it. Only when I was sure I was standing in the perfect spot did I begin asking my questions.

"Thank you for coming here today, Mrs. Cafaro, and my condolences for the recent loss of your brother and his wife. I'm wondering if you could describe your brother, Amadore, for the court."

"He was a very headstrong man," Sophia began. "My mother used to say that he was as pigheaded as his father, but I saw it as a pride thing."

"You went into business with him, is that correct?"

"Yes, we decided to purchase a bar together."

"How did that work out?"

"Not good. Amadore liked to control the finances and make all the decisions, and so we fought a lot."

"Fought over what?"

"My brother was a proud man, Mr. Carter, but that didn't make him smart. He wasn't the best businessman, and it wasn't long before we found ourselves back in the red and sinking fast."

"Did you know why the business was failing?"

"Amadore insisted on using his own contacts for supplying the bar because he had known them for many years. Despite me sourcing much cheaper suppliers, he refused to use them."

"But why? It makes sense to use suppliers offering cheaper goods."

"He didn't want to lose face with his people."

"The business your brother ran with you wasn't the only one he was involved in, is that correct?"

"Yes, he ran several other businesses, but most weren't exactly legitimate," Sophia said as she looked past me at the crowd. I saw Savio sitting among them and watching his wife.

"Not legitimate how?"

"Mostly illegal. Reselling stolen goods, drugs, luxury vehicle rackets. Those kinds of things."

"Mrs. Cafaro, did your brother have any enemies?"

"He had many, yes, some through my nephew."

"By your nephew, I assume you mean Riccardo Costa; is that correct?"

"Yes, that's right."

"Was your brother attached to any *business* operated by your nephew that you know of?" Someone in the gallery suddenly coughed hard. I noticed Sophia look over to the sound and shift uncomfortably in her chair. "Mrs. Cafaro?"

"Not that I know of. All I know is that Amadore took his interests seriously and managed to make a few enemies along the way."

"Enemies that would murder him?"

"Possibly."

"Objection, Your Honor, hearsay."

"Sustained."

"I'll rephrase the question," I said, not wanting to lose such a critical point. "Mrs. Cafaro, have you ever heard your brother mention somebody threatening to kill him?"

"Yes, I have, and I witnessed it once, as well."

"You personally witnessed such a threat being made against your brother?"

"Yes, I did, about three months ago. One of my nephew's rivals came into the bar and got into a heated argument with Amadore. Told him to convince my nephew to abandon the northeast side of the city or there would be hell to pay."

"Mrs. Cafaro, did you recognize the man making the threats?"

"I did, yes. Solomon Malak."

"You mean Solomon Malak, the head of the Jesters Gang?"

"Yes, that's him."

"The same Jesters gang responsible for multiple homicides and countless drug arrests within the city of Pittsburgh?"

"I believe so, yes."

I continued for another few minutes, and while the prosecutor did throw out another objection, I don't think he managed to obstruct the core purpose of the witness. Not even when he cross-examined Sophia did I sense any change in the overall feeling from the jury. I honestly believe that for the first time since the start of the trial, the people sitting in judgment of my client had become aware of other possible suspects who might have carried out the killings, and it was that kind of doubt those thoughts promoted that I wanted to build on.

"The defense calls Dr. Bryce Gibney to the stand," I said once Becker asked me to call my next witness.

The man who walked into the courtroom next did so with the aid of a cane, one he seemed to rely on more than the manufacturer might have intended. Gibney wasn't a small man but did find height a bit of a challenge. He couldn't have been much taller than Kat but made up for his lack of height with considerable weight, weight that seemed to accentuate the pressure on his knees. From the looks of it, his left seemed to be where the aid of a cane helped.

Gibney's other shortcoming came in the way of his eyes, the thick horn-rimmed glasses magnifying them considerably. He reminded me of a *Star Wars* character, the way his eyes widened whenever he tried to engage someone in conversation. But whatever he might have lacked in other areas, the man was a genius when it came to forensic analysis. His specialty? Shooting homicides. If a bullet was involved, this man could read the scene like a regular Nella Jones, able to pinpoint specific angles and trajectories, and God knows what else. I'd worked with Gibney on a previous case, and his evidence alone had ended up turning the tables on the entire investigation. When Grace said that all it took was one witness to win a case, Gibney would always rank among the most likely.

I began questioning the man with the usual introduction by having him share his experience both within his field and current position. Nobody could deny that forty years in any profession is exceptional and would gift a person with incredible experience, but throw in twenty-six of those years in the same role, and you know you have talent.

"Dr. Gibney, could I turn your attention to the screen?" I began and pointed to where the bailiff had already set up the projection where an image of Amadore and Ersilia lying dead in their upstairs sitting room stared back at us. "Do you recognize this crime scene?"

"I do, yes," Gibney said with his usual nasally speech. He sounded as if he had a permanent cold but never so much as sniffed.

"And have you had a chance to analyze it?"

"I have, yes," the doctor said as he turned his attention back to me. "I took careful measurements of the distances between the victims, their eventual positioning, the damage to the walls caused by the bullets, plus several other crucial points."

"And after putting together all of these measurements, sir, what did you happen to find?"

"That it is highly unlikely that your client could have pulled the trigger that killed these people."

A murmur spread across the gallery but not nearly as intense as previous outbursts. Becker merely looked at the crowd, and the silence quickly returned. Gibney's tone alone sounded like facts, the man even giving a confirmatory head nod when he finished to add more weight.

"And how did you happen to come to this assumption, Doctor?"

"It's not an assumption, young man," he said with an air of annoyance.

"I didn't mean any disrespect."

"None taken," he snapped and continued without hesitation. "Based on assuming both victims had been standing at the time of the shooting, it would appear that a person much taller than the accused would have been responsible. The blood splatters alone show the victims had been upright, so this evidence is enough to corroborate my theory."

"And how tall are we talking here, Dr. Gibney?"

"Katherine Wright stands five feet five inches tall, and her hand, if held at the usual positioning of a gun about to be fired, would place the barrel of the gun between approximately four feet two inches and four feet six inches from the floor." He stood and acted out both a stomach-high shot as well as a chin-high shot. "However, after taking into consideration the angle of approach and the triangulation of all the trajectories, I surmise that the shooter must have been at least six foot three in height to bring the barrel up to a height of between five-eight and five-eleven."

"Let me see if I understand what you're saying, Doctor," I said as I stopped pacing and faced him front-on. "You're telling the court that it is unlikely the defendant, Katherine Wright, would have held the gun up here to fire," I said as I animated the actions and held my hand up a lot higher than I would have if shooting a gun, also turning my fingers into a pretend pistol.

"That is correct," the doctor said. "Based on all the possible measurements, I'd say we're looking at a shooter much taller than the accused."

"And can you show the jury how you came to this conclusion?"

Rather than walk to the screen, I handed the witness a laser pointer, and after a few seconds of trying to figure out how to use it, Gibney began to indicate certain areas on the screen and explained specific angles. I stood back, giving the man the space he needed to build my case and gifting me some of the best testimony money couldn't buy. I shot a couple of quick glances over at Bartell and could see his brain desperately trying to figure out where to throw in an objection. When Gibney eventually finished his analysis, I knew I had a much better standing than before his arrival.

"Thank you, Doctor; no further questions."

Just as I found cross-examination of expert testimony almost impossible, so did the prosecutor, and while he did try to ask Gibney a couple of questions in an attempt to tarnish the testimony, he might have saved himself the effort. The experienced doctor easily sidestepped Bartell's question about the couple perhaps jumping in the air or maybe even standing on the coffee table at the moment of being shot.

By the end of the day, I considered the case to be leaning back in our direction ever so slightly. Still not unquestionably leading the charge but a lot less in the prosecution's court. Maybe 70/30 still in their favor, if that's a better way of putting it. While I might have still been losing, I felt that Bartell had lost some of the momentum he'd built up during the previous few days, and if I could keep things going, who knew where the case might end?

23

THAT NIGHT, I WENT TO BED WITH RENEWED HOPE, NOT ONLY from the witnesses I'd called that day but because of who I still had on the list to come. As a defense attorney, I often analyze witnesses based on what they can offer the case. I know it sounds strange, but consider this. A person who has known a defendant for twenty years but hasn't really been involved in their life isn't as valuable as a witness who might have only known a client for a month but during that time had spent a considerable amount of time with them.

That moment between dropping my head on the pillow and when my soul dropped into whatever plane of existence it went to during the sleep cycle was when I took inventory, so to speak. It was there while lying in the dark with one hand underneath the back of my head that I watched the shadows dancing across my ceiling while thinking about the balance sheet. The winners, the losers, the points gained, the points lost. I considered what had already been presented to the jury and what I still had left in the gas tank. I was just trying to work out where, in the rank of things, I'd put Reagan Byrd, the next witness on my list, when an enormous explosion suddenly rocked the whole building.

My first thought as I jumped out of my bed was an earthquake, but that quickly subsided when I saw the sudden flickering of light on the bedroom ceiling. I raced across the floor, almost tripped over a rogue shoe, and reached the window, looking out across the city. Five floors down and three rows into the parking lot, I saw the source of the explosion, the remaining wreck engulfed in flames that encapsulated both vehicles parked on either side of it.

What I didn't need to do was count the number of cars from the end to know the ball of flame was my Mustang. Despite not a single panel appearing familiar, that sickening feeling inside me was confirmation enough. For those first few seconds, or perhaps even minutes, all I could do was stand in that window staring down at my pride and joy, the one piece of me I would have called my most prized possession. When the first sirens began to wail in the distant darkness, I knew I had to head down to confirm my worst fears.

That elevator ride to the ground floor must have been one of the longest of my life. I even questioned riding it down at all, wondering if I wouldn't have been better off racing down the stairs. I barely slowed through the lobby, running at full speed out into the night. By the time I reached the edge of the parking lot, the first fire crews were just arriving. Moments later, a police cruiser pulled up, and a few seconds after that, another.

A total of four fire trucks and five police vehicles encircled the area within ten minutes, each officer working effortlessly on predefined tasks. It took them a while to extinguish the flames, and I remember exactly where I was and what I was doing when I heard that distinctive shout above the rest of the noise.

The cop interviewing me had just asked whether I might have had any known enemies willing to do that to my car, and I was about to tell him about Riccardo Costa when that shocked voice called out.

"Chief, we got a body over here." We exchanged a look with each other before the cop turned and took a couple of steps toward the remains of my mangled wreck. The twisted lump of metal and molten plastic stood in the very center of a group that continued growing in depth as more units came to confirm what everyone else had heard.

I stood near the back, not sure whether it was a dream I found myself unable to wake from or a nightmare that continued growing in depth the more I thought I was awake. I could just make out a couple of firefighters leaning down around the back of the car when I saw one of them give another officer standing farther back that defining nod, the one that confirmed everybody's worst fear.

If you think losing my car under such circumstances was enough, imagine what followed as I began a night filled with interviews. At one point, someone decided it more appropriate for me to be questioned down at the station, and during the short drive to one, I actually wondered whether this could end with me being charged for the murder of whoever had been caught in the blast.

I don't know how long I spent in an interview room alone, waiting for the investigating officers to come and question me, but what I can tell you is that your brain feeds on such stressful times. The number of scenarios playing out in my head must have run in the dozens at least, perhaps even hundreds. The one that stood out the most was me standing in the crowd with that God-awful smell in my nostrils, the one that I knew to be the burning flesh of the mystery victim.

By six the following morning, Dwight had come down to the station himself and managed to get some answers for me. No, I wasn't under suspicion of either the blast or the death of the victim, who still remained unidentified. I also wasn't suspected of any ill deeds, such as trying to claim some insurance payout. The detective told me that they needed to ask all the questions to effectively close all the doors.

At seven, the first theory came forth, and it came as a complete shock when Dwight relayed it to me while we were waiting for the official clearance that would let us leave the station.

"They think the guy was trying to fix the bomb to your car when it exploded prematurely," he whispered while leaning in close. I pulled back just enough to stare into his eyes and confirm he wasn't messing with me. A quick head nod from him confirmed the story to be true.

Do you know what it does to a man to believe that he's had two attempts on his life? With Paul Garroway's shooting and now my Mustang blown up by some car bomb, I was beginning to rethink my position. Just how serious was whoever was doing this to try and kill me? Two attempts, two people dead, and me still around asking questions. While this second attempt did confirm, for me at least, that I might have been the target all along, I still didn't know to who.

Linda phoned me shortly after Dwight confirmed the bomber getting trapped under the car, and I filled her in just as fast. She said that she was already working on gaining access to the security feeds covering the parking lot in an attempt to identify those responsible. My investigator certainly wasn't someone to sit on the sidelines, and I knew it wouldn't be long before she had something for me.

Detective Robert Tyson came and saw me a final time around seven-thirty that morning to confirm that the initial investigations pointed to someone trying to fix a bomb on my car that ultimately triggered an unexpected explosion. They also found some sort of metal plate on a chain around the victim's neck that appeared to hold a passcode to something, but investigations would continue throughout the morning.

When we finally managed to make our way to the police station's parking lot, Dwight insisted on driving me home so I could get some sleep. I expected him to argue with me when I refused, asking instead for him to wait for me and take me to court.

"But you've had no sleep, and no offense, kid, but you look like shit."

"I *feel* like shit, so I guess it just confirms it then. In any case, I'm still going to court, boss."

"Don't call me that, you know how much I hate it. But as your boss, I insist."

"You can insist all you want, but I'm still going to attend this morning's session." I locked eyes on his across the roof of his BMW. "I'm not about to put a halt on this case just as I've gotten some momentum going."

Dwight held my gaze for a long time before he finally admitted the reality to himself. We could either stand there arguing the point, which would end with me simply ordering myself an Uber and doing things my way, or he could help. He eventually opted for the latter.

"Get in," he said with a sigh and climbed in ahead of me.

The whole process of getting back to my apartment, showering, and getting dressed and back downstairs to my waiting ride took less than an hour. It's amazing how fast a person can get themselves ready when serious about needing to meet a deadline. Dwight was still shaking his head when I reemerged from the building but didn't say anything once I climbed in. He did wish me luck once we pulled up out the front of the courthouse, and with just minutes to spare, I thanked him and made a dash for the front doors. The media pack did try to stop me but quickly moved aside when they saw that I wasn't about to slow down for them.

I made it to the courtroom in the nick of time, Grace waiting patiently for me in the front row. She gave me a stern look and a shake of the head, but I knew it was just for show.

"Dodging bullets and bombs, Ben Carter," she whispered when I neared her, and I gave her the most mischievous grin

I could muster. It seemed to say, *Who me?* She gave me a playful slap on the shoulder, but that was when the bailiff brought the room to order.

"I commend you on being here this morning, Mr. Carter," Becker said once he had taken his seat. "I heard about the incident and am more than prepared to adjourn the matter until tomorrow." The offer surprised me but still didn't convince me to accept it.

"Thank you, Your Honor, but I'll be fine. I'd much rather proceed."

"As you wish," Becker said and continued with the routine of bringing out all the interested parties before handing the floor to me once everybody had taken their seats.

I had initially planned to start the day with Kat's friend, Reagan, but due to her running late, I instead called Professor Hans Reuter to the stand. Another forensics expert, this one covered an area not often needed in many crime scenes but one I saw as crucial considering the situation. Plus, he came highly recommended by my previous expert, Dr. Bryce Gibney.

Unlike the man who'd recommended him, Reuter bounced into the courtroom like a man late for a tennis club meeting. The only thing the two men shared was that they were almost the same age. While one needed a cane to get around, the other moved like a man in his thirties. He reminded me of one of those old guys who drove around in convertibles with the tops down just so those in the traffic could see him with his arm around the shoulders of a girl less than half his age. Even answering questions, Reuter spoke like a man ordering lunch at the club, impressed that the prawn cocktails hadn't yet sold out. Once the bailiff finished swearing him in, Reuter looked at me as if expecting a compliment.

I started by getting the usual details, getting him to high-light his credentials so others knew he was the real thing. Only once I established his authority did I dive into the purpose of his being there.

"Professor Reuter, I'm curious as to the specifics of the actual discharge of the firearm in a home the size of the one in question. You studied the home, is that correct?"

"Yes, that's right."

"And what can you tell us about that?"

"I took the time to visit the premises myself to ensure I could take measurements personally and took various details. I studied the size of each room, the positioning of doors and windows and which had been opened and closed at the time of the shooting, the number of times the weapon was discharged, as well as the available ventilation vents throughout the home."

"And what conclusion did you come up with?"

"That the gunsmoke would have been detectable by the human nose in every part of that house within just five minutes of the shooting, and as long as none of the doors or windows were opened, would remain detectable for a period of up to three hours."

"And yet we find the defendant walking in and unable to smell the gunsmoke from her location in the kitchen," I said, more as a statement than a question. It was a comment more meant for me than everyone else, but it slipped out so fast that I had little chance of catching it. The prosecutor wasn't about to let it slide.

"Objection, Your Honor. Speculation."

"I withdraw the comment, Your Honor," I said and continued down a different path.

While the comment may have been speculation to the prosecutor and the rest of the court, it wasn't to Kat and me because it was a question I had asked her only recently. When I posed the question to her, I remember Kat looking up and to the left for a long time as she tried to recall the moment. When she eventually answered, she was adamant she would have noticed the smell in the air because of how nervous she was about going into the house in the first place. Anything out of the ordinary, like that smell, would have stood out to her, and I tended to agree.

I think Reuter helped our case considerably, but while he may have added more weight to our defense, I didn't think it would be as much as the next witness I called to the stand, somebody who had a direct connection to the girl on trial. When Reagan Byrd finally took her seat on the stand, Kat whispered something to me under her breath that I will never forget.

"Please don't be too hard on her" was what she said, and when I looked at her, I saw something in those eyes I hadn't seen before. There was a genuine fear there, but more than that, it was a fear for someone else. What did you call that kind of fear? Was it a nervous kind?

"I won't," I whispered back just as the bailiff finished swearing Reagan in.

While I wasn't expecting Reagan Byrd to break the case wide open with her testimony, I felt that she held more weight than the rest because of her connection to the defendant. Sure, there were aspects of the case we couldn't ignore, but the Byrd girl offered an insight into the person many still saw as a cold-hearted killer. I needed them to see the other side of her, the side that had been living the streets in a constant state of survival. I needed them to see the lonely girl hiding in the shadows.

I stood as per usual and crossed the floor the way I did when trying to get close to a witness. A renewed silence hung over the room that felt quite foreboding, and I could see the apprehension in the girl's eyes similar to what Kat showed.

"Thank you for coming here today, Miss Byrd. You've known the defendant for quite some time, have you not?"

She nodded instead of answering, and I had to point out that the court needed words. Her cheeks flushed almost immediately, the color rising all the way to the tips of her ears.

"Yes, since we were six years old," she managed, the last couple of words louder than the rest as she tested her voice.

"And since knowing her, have you ever known Katherine Wright to be violent?"

"No, never."

"Angry?"

"Angry, yes, a few times, maybe. She didn't have a temper back when we were kids."

"What about now?"

"Since leaving home, yes, although I haven't seen her as often as I'd like."

"How often, would you say?"

"Maybe every couple of months."

"And what would you guys talk about during those occasional visits?"

"Just how she's trying to find a job, wanting to build a home for herself. She talked about traveling to New York and making a fresh start. Go to dance school."

"Dance school," I said. "She's a dancer?"

"We did ballet back when we were younger, but Kat always said she wanted to try and get into music videos."

"Your friend didn't have an easy home life, did she?"

Reagan looked down at her fingers and shifted her weight uncomfortably. "No, she didn't. She had issues with her mother."

"What kind of issues?"

"Her mother, she always..." Reagan paused and looked up at the gallery. I followed her eyes and saw where Lois and Brad sat in the middle of the crowd, the former's face a crimson shade of red. Seeing her surprised me, of course, but then again, I guess the curiosity got the better of them.

"Yes, go on," I said, turning back to the witness.

"Her mother never let Kat do anything. She had to be home twenty minutes after school let out; Kat had to stay home during the weekends and do homework even though we had none; Kat had to do chores nonstop, like washing walls and floors. She had no freedom whatsoever."

"Just floors and walls?"

"No, there was more. She had to wash dishes, wash

windows, and then there was the endless Bible study. School was about the only time that Kat could get away for some freedom. And then…then there was the beatings."

I heard a subdued commotion behind me and looked back to see Brad trying to calm his wife down. Becker also looked over, and it was enough for the woman to calm herself. I thought she might get up and leave, but Lois remained in her seat.

"Beatings?"

"Yeah, every now and then, Kat would show up with fresh bruises. I'd ask her about them, but she never told me how she got them. She'd always try and cover them up, but I saw them." She looked over at the Wrights. "I knew it was her beating her daughter."

"Objection, Your Honor, speculation."

"Sustained. Just stick to answering the questions with what you know, young lady," the judge told the witness.

"Sorry," Reagan managed. She gave me a brief glance and again looked nervously back down at her fingers.

"I'm curious to know about the supposed abortion Kat claimed to have had. Do you know anything about that?"

I knew she did, of course, as the topic had already been brought up with her, but I wanted to continue the dramatics for the jury. One look in their direction was enough to show me their interest. The only thing missing was the popcorn. Reagan nodded again.

"I need a verbal answer," I said with an emphatic tone.

"Yes, I do."

"Can you tell the court why you think Kat faked a pregnancy?"

"She wanted to get away from the house. Knowing how religious her mother was, we figured it might be the best way to make her mother hate her. I know it sounds dumb now, but the way she kept controlling her like that, Kat was sure she would go insane."

"We figured?"

Reagan looked up at me nervously. "Actually, it was my idea for her to lie about the pregnancy and abortion. I wanted to help my friend and have her stay at my house, but then my mom walked out on my father and me, and Kat didn't want to stay with us."

"So she stayed on the street?"

"Yes. I did try to convince her to stay, but...she didn't want to. She said there were places where she could get help, but I don't think she ever did."

"You mean shelters?"

"Yes."

"Reagan, do you think Kat is capable of murdering two people?"

She looked up at me again, her eyes wide with shock. "No, never. She's had it rough, sure, but I know my friend. There's no way she would ever do that. She's helped so many people. Even giving them food when it was the last of hers. She'd rather go without if she knows someone else needs it more."

"And yet she walked into a house that she hadn't been invited into," I said.

"She would have only done so out of sheer desperation, Mr. Carter. And even then, she wouldn't have put up much of a fight if she'd been caught. Kat isn't much of a confrontational person."

"Thank you, Reagan," I said. "No further questions."

To be honest, I walked away from the witness second-guessing myself, wondering if I'd made the right call about bringing her to the stand at all. I wanted to bring some clarity to the courtroom about a girl many saw as the one who'd lashed out when called a whore. I wanted to show that she was just a kid caught in the fight of her life. A quick glance in the direction of the jury and I could see a couple of them looking in the direction of Kat with a certain empathy in their eyes. Had I done enough? I wasn't sure.

"Your witness, Mr. Bartell," Becker said, and the prosecutor immediately got to his feet, picked up a slip of paper from his pile, and began walking across the floor. I was still trying to figure out whether my questions had been enough when the prosecutor woke the courtroom up with his very first.

"Miss Byrd, I'm curious to know whether the defendant's mother ever worked during the time you knew your friend to be living at home?"

"Y-yes, she did. She was a seamstress down at the mall."

"Long hours?"

"Sometimes, I guess."

"And I'm guessing you and some other friends might have gone around to Miss Wright's home to hang out with her?"

"Yes, a few times."

"What about the defendant's father? I've heard you

mention a great deal about her mother but not her father. Was he around?"

"Yes, he was. He didn't work, so he would sometimes bring us in pizza and stuff."

"Did his wife know what he was doing?"

"I'm not sure."

"But he liked his daughter's friends coming over, didn't he? As you said, he'd offer pizza and other things to make you girls feel welcome."

"Yes, I guess so."

That was when Bartell took a couple of steps closer to the witness after giving the jury a sideways glance. I felt a familiar tightening in my middle and suddenly questioned my reasons for asking the girl to testify at all. I watched as the prosecutor held the piece of paper out to the witness.

"Do you recognize this restraining order, Miss Byrd?" The sensation in my middle tightened further, phantom fingers clamping hard.

"Y-y-yes," Reagan said, her whisper barely loud enough to be heard.

"Can you please repeat your answer for the jury?"

"Yes," Reagan said, her face turning deep red as she looked to the floor.

"I'm curious to know why you would take out a restraining order on the defendant's father after just describing how wonderful and welcoming he was to you and your friends."

She didn't answer, or at least not initially. What she did do was steal a look across the courtroom to meet the eyes of my client. I saw Kat's head move just a little before watching a single tear roll down the side of her face. The answer still didn't hit me, but within a few seconds, fireworks exploded in my head as I suddenly realized my mistake.

"I need an answer," Bartell said as he took another look in the direction of the jury for whom he was now directing his act.

"Because he had touched me," Reagan whispered. Not content with the volume, Bartell pushed harder.

"Louder for the jury," he demanded, his own tone growing impatient.

"BECAUSE HE TOUCHED ME," Reagan screamed, the girl bursting into tears as I watched a similar flood rolling down Kat's face. "HE ALWAYS TOUCHED US. WE WERE THERE TO HELP SAVE OUR FRIEND, BUT HE TURNED HIS ATTENTION TO US."

For the first time, the crowd didn't respond the way I pictured, instead sitting in stunned silence. Beside me, Kat began to weep silently into the crook of her elbow while her friend fought to control her anger.

"Kat did nothing wrong other than to try and protect herself. We tried to help, but then her mother banned us from coming, and when there was nobody left to help her, Kat decided it was safer to leave." Reagan took a deep breath and sighed, still looking down at her hands as if searching for a way for them to help. "When my mom left, and it was just my father, she couldn't bring herself to stay with us after what her own father had done, and no matter how hard I tried to convince her he wasn't like that, she didn't believe me."

That was when she looked up at the prosecutor, her eyes

filled with tears. The tone turned more into a plea as she began to beg for her friend.

"Please, she didn't kill anybody. She was just hungry. She doesn't trust many people, and her mother still doesn't want anything to do with her because of the lie we made up. It was only to try and protect her that we did it." She looked over at her friend and mouthed the words *I'm so sorry*, but I don't think Kat saw them. She'd already shut the world out as she continued to sob.

24

AFTER FINDING OUT THAT HER HUSBAND HAD BEEN MOLESTING their child, Lois Wright immediately kicked him out of their home. It wasn't long after that the police arrested him on suspicion of assaulting three other girls from back then, as well as a neighbor's daughter just the previous month. The explosive revelation even hit the front page of most newspapers and was the only thing the reporters asked me about when I left the courthouse that afternoon.

Unfortunately, despite having her deepest and darkest secret exposed to the entire world, the revelation didn't help Kat's case in the slightest. Instead of helping her, it turned around and bit us in the ass...hard. The prosecutor continued questioning her for a few extra minutes as he put forth his theory that the molestation had, in fact, turned the girl into a powder keg, which ultimately exploded when the Costas confronted her in their home. All I could do was watch from the sidelines. While I did call out the conjecture, the damage had already been done.

As for Kat, what could I say? It was yet another secret she'd kept from the guy trying to help her, and all I could do was to try and fix the mess after the fact. She did apologize to me before being led back out of the courtroom, and the lack of defensiveness coming from her told me that this wasn't a small matter. The heaviness in her voice mirrored the pain that lay deep within her soul.

When I walked out of the courthouse that afternoon, the only place I wanted to be was a quiet bar that served something strong enough to dull the shame. The choice of drink didn't bother me, just as long as it helped dampen the thoughts in my head. I would have gladly ordered used engine oil if it did the trick, although I would have preferred something a little tastier.

Imagine my surprise when I found Linda already sitting at the bar when I walked into Crazy Jake's, about the only one I figured I could walk into without getting recognized. I'd been there before, of course, but not enough times for anybody to guess that I might turn up there after a tough day.

"Anybody tell you just how bad you look today?" Linda said when I grabbed the stool next to hers.

"I haven't slept in like thirty-something hours, so I probably ain't looking too hot right now," I said while gesturing for the bartender to give me the same drink as my investigator.

"You need to go home, Ben. Get some sleep."

"I will," I said. "Just as soon as I put out these flames."

"That bad, huh?"

"Yeah, you could say that."

While I dropped the first shot with ease, the second took a bit longer while I shared the details of the last witness of the day with Linda. She listened while holding her own glass and shook her head when I finished the story with how Bartell used the witness to then put forth his theory about what impact the molestation had on her.

"You weren't to know," she said before swallowing the second shot. "And now, I'm driving you home." She slid off the edge of her stool and pointed a finger at me. "No car, right?"

"Don't remind me," I groaned. "Maybe I need a few extra drinks just for my car alone."

"No, no more drinks. Let's go," she demanded while hooking a finger behind my collar. "Let's go, chief."

"Yes, ma'am," I said with a grin that felt wrong.

Linda's cell phone jingled as we neared her car, and when we climbed inside, she paused to read the text. I switched the A/C on after she started the engine, and when she dropped the phone into her lap, she poked two thumbs up into the air.

"I love it when a plan comes together," she said as she slipped the car into gear and rolled out of the parking spot.

"You got good news?"

"No, sir, *we* have good news," she said. "That was Bill Kramer, my tech guy. He's...*found* something that we might find interesting."

"Oh? Something to do with the case?"

"A crypto wallet that paid a large sum of Bitcoin into

another wallet, which was then transferred to an exchange where it was cashed out. Bill happens to do some work for said exchange and managed to find out the details of the account. Thank the Lord for KYC."

"KYC?" I wasn't following.

"Yes, Know Your Customer. The receiver of that sum was none other than Sophia's husband."

"You mean the Bitcoin paid for her to keep the bar?"

"A hundred and seventy-two thousand dollars' worth," Linda said as she rolled to a stop at the first set of lights we came across.

"That's almost the exact sum she paid in order to keep the bar and fight off her brother." I felt the phantom fingers gripping my insides finally release some of the tension. It was a break and one that might help us understand an aspect of the case but by no means a slam-dunk. "We don't happen to know who owns the wallet that sent the funds in the first place?"

That was when Linda turned to me and smiled, a great big toothy grin that distracted her from the light turning green. The car behind us honked its horn and pulled Linda's attention back to the road.

"You know, Bill just happens to be one of the smartest brains I know. One of his great pleasures in life is to try and identify certain wallets on the Blockchain, and that wallet appears to be linked to a certain criminal gang." I wasn't following and felt my face screw up in confusion. Linda saw it and reacted accordingly. "Costa?"

"*Riccardo*?" If I had still been sitting on the bar stool, I would have slid off it.

"No, his brother, although Bill did find several transfers coming from a wallet linked directly to Riccardo," Linda said. "No, the wallet that sent the funds to Sophia and Savio belongs to Franco."

"Think we can go and speak with him?" I wasn't about to waste more time on something as unproductive as sleep.

"What, *now*? Ben, you look like you're about to fall over."

Rather than answer her, I pursed my lips, nodded my head, and opened Linda's glove compartment. After rifling through the bits and pieces, such as her spare gun, extra magazines, bullets, and spy binoculars, I found what I was searching for near the bottom and held up the jar of No-Doze I knew she kept there.

"If they're good enough for you, they're good enough for me," I said, returning my own toothy grin.

While Riccardo was more of a public figure, openly sharing his lavish lifestyle like a regular playboy, his brother Franco practiced more of a private existence. He drove a regular car, lived in a regular suburban apartment, and taught English at a nearby high school, a position he'd held for the better part of five years. During that time, he'd been presented the Teacher of the Year award twice, the students voting for him en masse.

Finding him proved easy, Linda making a single call to one of her contacts who texted the address within a couple of minutes. She turned the car in the direction of Beechview. When she pulled up in front of the building twenty minutes later, we first confirmed the Toyota Camry in the parking lot before heading inside. Linda handed me a piece of gum during the short elevator ride and didn't need to elaborate.

Given my appearance, I didn't think the smell of bourbon on my breath was going to win me any prizes.

When Franco opened the door after our second knock, he did so with the security chain still in place. The eyes checking us out through the narrow gap remained dubious even as Linda introduced herself, but the man did eventually close the door, removed the chain, and pulled it wide to allow us inside.

"Forgive my suspicious nature," Franco said as he led us into the small living room. "But when you have a brother like mine, it pays to be careful."

He offered us a seat and then a drink. We accepted the first and declined the second as I took a look around the place. Linda barely sat before she pointed to a bookshelf in the far corner.

"Oh wow, is that an original Babe Ruth card?"

Franco looked over his shoulder and nodded as Linda walked over to get a closer look.

"Given to me by my grandfather," Franco said before Linda returned to her seat.

"I'm not much into baseball, but I do appreciate the old trading cards."

"It's the only one I have," Franco said with a forced smile. I could see he was trying to be polite.

"We've actually come to ask you about a transaction you made earlier this year," I said, figuring pleasantries weren't going to get us anywhere.

"Transaction?"

"Yes," Linda said, cutting in. "In particular, a Bitcoin transfer you made to your aunt and uncle." When he appeared to try to express confusion, Linda let him in. "We've traced the funds all the way back to your brother, Franco," she said. "And we know that the funds were used to help your aunt pay out the money owed on the bar."

"Which in turn handed the business to your aunt and left your father out in the cold, so to speak," I finished. "He can't have been too happy with you."

"He never found out," Franco said. I expected him to get defensive, but he remained surprisingly calm.

"That asshole should never have had a say in that business. Aunt Soph was the one who ran that place. She worked her butt off to make it what it was, and all my father did was put his hand out for the profits."

"I take it you guys weren't close?"

"No, not with him and certainly not with my brother."

"And yet he was the one who paid that money for the bar."

"Not exactly," Franco said. "I convinced Riccardo that I needed money to fund a new business venture. Stupid twat believed every word and, with a wave of his hand, organized the funds to be transferred to me." He chuckled, but the sound lacked any humor. "It's amazing how ignorant someone that rich is."

"He never found out?"

"No, not even when Aunt Soph paid the outstanding amount the day after he transferred it to me. I had to go through Savio, obviously. He's the one with the crypto knowledge. I guess my brother was too busy rolling around in his wealth to care." He again shook his head. "So I don't mean to be rude, but why are you here? Am I in trouble for making that transfer, or what? Because if it's because of my brother's criminal activities, I had no idea where—"

"Relax, we're not here for that," Linda said. "We're just trying to understand how your aunt got the money. It's about your mom and dad's murder."

"Oh, of course. Trying to find the real killer, huh?" That comment triggered my curiosity.

"You don't think it's the girl?"

"Who in their right mind would think that kid could murder two people like that?" He shook his head again, this time a lot more animated. "Any person with an ounce of common sense would know that the kid had no reason to go upstairs after she spotted the handbag on the kitchen counter."

When I walked out of that apartment later that evening, I was a lot more aware of things than I had been walking in, and I'm not talking about the crypto payments. What Franco said about Kat not needing to go up those stairs stirred something inside me, the off-the-cuff comment opening my eyes. He was right, and I was kicking myself for not thinking of it sooner. Who knew where it would lead?

25

Despite taking one of Linda's No-Doze tablets, I fell asleep the second my head hit the pillow just after seven and didn't wake again until eight the next morning to the sound of my alarm going off. My head felt like lead, the brain inside wrapped in cotton candy. Not only had I slept through the night, but also through two phone calls and three text messages.

I could barely open my eyes enough to see who the calls had been from and had to wipe them more than a few times before they cleared enough to reveal the text. One thought that did cross my mind was how far off my first set of glasses were. As they say, time waits for no man.

The first call was from Grace, her follow-up message asking if I wanted a ride to the courthouse. Just seeing the question immediately pulled the memory of my car burning from the foggy mist in my head. I was still groaning inside when I saw the second call from a private number that I simply swiped away and out of my life. One of the messages came from Linda who asked if I could call her and how I'd fared through the night. Her message had only arrived the previous hour, right before Grace's call.

It was the third and final message that drew my attention, again coming from a private number. You know that weird sensation you get, the one where your insides get grabbed and tortured by some phantom hand? Over the years, I'd come to recognize that feeling as some sort of instinctual cue, and opening the message, I could sense something ominous waiting for me. What I found changed everything.

And now you know were the words I found staring back at me, the short sentence sitting above a very short link. From the looks of it, I assumed it was some hosting site. I know not to click random links on account of scammers trying to phish for my details, but I could tell this wasn't that kind of situation. Whoever had sent the message not only knew me but also wanted to get my attention.

The debate to click the link lasted all of two seconds, and I felt another cramp inside my gut as something opened on my cell phone screen. The clip opened to show a living room, one that I immediately recognized. At first, the person standing before the camera could only be seen from the waist up, but again, I recognized the distinctive brown corduroy pants. It looked as if a couple of people were having a conversation and not exactly a happy one. There was no sound, so I couldn't make out what was being said.

After exactly forty-nine seconds, the camera panned up slightly to show that there must have been two people behind the camera as the owner of the apartment came into view, the man looking far from relaxed. Franco's attention was drawn to somebody standing to the side of the person filming because I could see the occasional hand poking into view as the unknown figure pointed at Franco aggressively.

Unlike the frustration I had seen on Franco's face the previous afternoon, what I saw in that footage couldn't be mistaken for anything but raw fear. He held both hands out in front of him defensively while trying to talk himself out of whatever situation he'd found himself. When the hand pointing at him suddenly disappeared and reemerged, holding a pistol, Franco began to take a couple of steps back but might as well have saved himself the effort.

I watched with my jaw hanging open as four silent shots erupted out of the barrel, the kickback and a brief lick of flame the only cue to the shots. Four neat red spots appeared on Franco's chest at the same time as he first froze and then dropped to his knees. The dots quickly blossomed into dark patches of blood before the man dropped face-first to the floor. Someone's foot appeared shortly after and gave the body a kick to the head to see if there was any life left in it before the video ended.

Instinct told me that the man who'd shot Franco was none other than his brother, Riccardo. Something about the way Franco was trying to negotiate his way out of the argument told me so. I felt sick, not physically, but enough to make me drop the phone on the bed and climb out of it, where I began pacing back and forth, trying to make sense of everything. If the phone hadn't suddenly begun ringing at that very moment, who knew how long I would have continued wearing out my floor? I answered the call without checking the number, almost expecting Riccardo's voice to reach out to me, but it was Grace.

"Are you coming in today?" she asked when I answered. "You're cutting it close, aren't you?"

"Shit, sorry," I said as I realized the time. "I'll be there as quick as I can."

I don't know why I didn't stop to call Linda right then and there, but something about walking late into Judge Becker's courtroom drove everything else from my mind. Despite the aching joints and clouded mind, I managed to tear my butt through the bathroom, shower, and dressing phase in barely a few minutes. I ordered an Uber coming down in the elevator and only had to wait thirty seconds before it pulled up by the sidewalk.

Once in the car, Grace first phoned to make sure I was actually on my way and not still sitting in my apartment, which was then quickly followed by Dwight asking if I needed anything. He even offered to arrange a rental for me while I waited for the insurance to deal with my claim, but I declined.

At the courthouse, I skipped the media pack entirely by getting dropped off around the corner and then mingling as best I could with the crowd. Grace was waiting for me in the foyer, and when she saw me run up, tapped her watch with that fake annoyance she liked to show sometimes.

"Talk about walking the line, Mr. Carter."

"It hasn't started?"

"No, Judge Becker is also running a few minutes behind."

She reached forward and straightened my tie. "Which is lucky for you. Now let's go."

My phone again began to ring when I reached the door, and seeing it was Linda, I stopped to answer.

"Ben, you're going to be late," Grace said as I saw the bailiff call the room to order.

"Linda, I need to speak with you," I whispered. "Franco is dead."

"Yes, I know."

"I can't talk now, court's in session, but I'll call you soon."

"Ben, I really need—"

"Sorry, I have to go," I whispered, instantly feeling bad as I hung up on her. Instead of dropping the phone into my pocket, I handed it to Grace and continued inside.

The first witness I called that morning once Becker officially handed me the reins was a woman named Margaret Schein, who lived half a block down from the Costas. She testified seeing Kat shortly before the supposed shooting when she returned from the store. The girl asked if she had any spare change, but since her purse only contained larger currency notes, she had to decline.

The second witness I called to the stand was a cop who also saw Kat before the shooting walking through a park near the Costas' street. He thought she looked suspicious by the way she kept watching people's unguarded things and was waiting for her to snatch something, but she never did. He said he felt bad for not asking her if she needed help but said if he did that for everybody, he'd be broke.

When Becker called the first recess, Grace handed me my phone back and said I needed to call Linda urgently.

"She's found something," Grace told me, and I didn't hesitate to find a quiet corner to make the call.

"Linda, hey, it's me," I said when she answered me.

"Ben, I think I got something. And if I'm right, I might have the answer we've been searching for all along."

I'm pretty sure my heart skipped a beat when Linda explained what she had for me. Actually, she had two revelations, but the second you don't need to know about just yet. That one blew me away when she told me, and I'm pretty sure you'll feel the same way, but you're just going to have to wait for the right time.

As it turned out, while I'd been busy sleeping my way through the early morning, my investigator had taken it upon herself to follow up on a certain lead waiting for us out at the airport. One particular resident who had been out of the country for quite a few weeks had broken his vow of silence or seclusion or whatever he was on and returned Linda's messages. She'd found out that the guy had left his car parked in the airport parking lot, and when she mentioned the case, he gave her the OK to grab the SD card from his dashcam that might have been active the day of the shooting.

"Do what you have to," I told Linda when Grace came to tell me that the next session was about to get underway. Again, I handed Grace my phone and asked her to keep monitoring it and to interrupt me if Linda called. I still had a strong suspicion that the man responsible for the shooting was Solomon Malak's hitman, and all I needed was to find a way of proving it.

I knew I couldn't stop, and so deciding to ignore most of

what Linda had told me, I called my next witness, a detective who'd been tailing none other than Mansur Diab. Hector Montoya worked for a family in New York whose daughter Diab was suspected of shooting in a contract killing. They hired the private eye to find anything they could on the hitman that might bring him to face justice. The part that interested me was where he followed Diab on the day of the shooting to a block from the Costas' home.

"Can you describe what you saw that day, Mr. Montoya?" I asked once we established who he was and why he was following the hitman.

"I saw Mansur Diab standing on the corner of Sedgwick and Liverpool with another man when a car I later learned was an Uber pulled up alongside the two men."

"Did you happen to recognize the other man?"

"No, I did not. I didn't even realize he'd gotten into the car until I managed to get close enough to them in traffic. A bus stopped between us at just the wrong time, and when the car came back into view, it was already on the move."

"What about when it stopped again? See anything then?"

"Yes, I watched one of the men climb out almost immediately. The one left inside reached out through the window, shook hands with him, and then directed the driver to continue on."

"Mr. Montoya, once the vehicle left, where did Mansur Diab walk next?"

"I think you've got it wrong, Mr. Carter," the witness said, and it was the first time I realized that I was motoring through the questions on auto-pilot. I hadn't had the time to speak with the investigator beforehand. Time had been against us, and the brief five minutes over the phone was enough to tell me he'd followed Diab on the day of the shooting.

"Which part?"

"The part about Diab being the one to get out of the car."

"It wasn't Diab who climbed out?"

"No, sir, it was the other guy. I knew it wasn't Diab because of the way he walked. Diab was the one who continued in the car. I followed it for perhaps another half an hour but eventually lost it in traffic."

"Are you positive it wasn't Diab who climbed out?"

"Objection, Your Honor. Asked and answered."

"Sustained," Becker said, sounding annoyed. "Could you move this along, Mr. Carter?"

His answer threw me. It wasn't what I expected, and the idea that it wasn't Diab walking into that house and shooting the Costas threw everything else out as well.

"I apologize, Your Honor," I said and spotted Grace trying to get my attention. I figured now was a perfect time. "May I ask for a brief recess to confer with my associate?"

"Five minutes," Becker said and made it official with a smack of his hammer.

26

IF IT HADN'T BEEN SOPHIA COMING UP TO ME AFTER I WALKED from the courtroom, I don't think I would have ended up where I did. She and Savio had only just arrived at the courthouse, and she asked whether everything was going OK. She moved faster than her husband, and Savio arrived a few seconds after her.

"Yes, they are," I said as I thought about something Montoya had mentioned. "Excuse me." I held up my phone, and once they continued into the courtroom, I phoned Linda.

That second phone call was the point where I think I started to see the bigger picture, especially when she mentioned more crypto changing hands.

"I asked Bill to go back through some of the other transactions from that wallet that had paid Sophia the Bitcoin, and while he didn't find anything there, he did find something curious in the wallet used by Sophia's husband."

"Tell me," I said, and Linda began to explain a couple of transactions that seemed to have been done with a third wallet her friend recognized.

"While the majority of crypto is supposed to be anonymous, it's easy to track once you know who owns which wallet" was how Linda finished her explanation.

"Can you come down here right now with the footage from the car? I need it urgently."

"Already on my way," Linda said, and I ended the call.

When I walked back into the courtroom, I paused next to the row where Sophia and Savio had taken their seats. I pushed past the first couple of people until I could lean down to whisper to the couple.

"Listen, I know about the crypto payment from Franco," I said ever so quietly before turning my attention to Savio. "I know you took the payment and transferred it into cash before handing it to your wife. I think Franco might have had something to do with what happened to Amadore and Ersilia, but I need to clarify a couple of things about the payment. I know the payment originally came from Riccardo, which is who I need to subpoena. Would you be willing to testify for me?"

Sophia and Savio at first looked at one another before Savio gave me the nod I was hoping for.

"Hang tight," I said. "I'm going to bring you up next."

The thing I couldn't understand was why Riccardo never knew about the payment he made making its way to Sophia, and I think he was going to use that money for something else. I didn't think Franco used the lie he claimed he did, and I needed Savio's input to help prove my theory. What I didn't know was whether I'd survive long enough to bring the Costa crime boss to the stand.

Bartell took his time with Montoya on the stand and asked him almost a dozen questions surrounding what he'd seen on the day of the shooting. He also tried to get a bit more information out of him about the Uber itself; the murder of the driver was still unsolved. When he finally ended his questioning and the judge dismissed the witness, that was when the beating in my chest really took off.

"Call your next witness, Mr. Carter."

"The defense calls Savio Cafaro to the stand."

The good thing about Savio Cafaro was that I had already added him to the witness list ahead of time, as he had direct connections to the family. I knew he handled most of the technical side of the business for Sophia so wanted to save any last-minute headaches in case I found anything I needed answers for.

Savio gave his wife a kiss on the cheek before he shuffled across to the aisle and slowly walked down to the floor. I gave him an appreciative nod as he passed me by, and while the bailiff was swearing him in, I saw Linda finally arrive. We didn't need to exchange words as she handed me a small USB stick, which I immediately dropped into my pocket.

When the bailiff finished his part with the witness, I crossed the floor and stopped a few feet shy from the stand.

"Thank you for agreeing to testify at such short notice. Mr. Cafaro. Could you tell the court your position within the Costa family?"

"I'm married to Amadore's sister, Sophia."

"The same Sophia who had a dispute at a bar with your brother-in-law?"

"That is correct."

"Now as I understand it, Mr. Cafaro, you were the one who first accepted the funds that ultimately paid the debt on the bar your sister co-owned, is that correct? With this crypto wallet address?" I grabbed a sheet of paper from the top of the pile on my desk and walked it back to the witness stand. "A wallet address ending with C5RYZ?"

"That looks about right, yes."

"And can you confirm the third transaction from the top as the one you received from your nephew, which would ultimately be used for the payment to your debtors?"

He scanned the page and nodded. "Yes, that's right."

"May I direct your attention to the transaction two from the bottom for half a Bitcoin, at the time valued at ten thousand dollars."

For a moment, Savio just looked at me curiously as if not understanding the question.

"Two from the bottom, Mr. Cafaro," I repeated.

He looked but began to shake his head as if confused. "OK, I see it."

"Could you tell me to whom you sent that amount?"

"I...it...I'm not sure what you're asking. I think it was for some car repairs."

"Mr. Cafaro, are you aware of a hitman named Mansur Diab?"

"I've heard of him, sure. Who hasn't?"

"But did you know him personally at the time of sending the man that half a Bitcoin?" Again, he looked at me dumbfounded, turned to stare up at the gallery where his wife sat, and then back at me.

"I usually send some Bitcoin to—"

"The wallet address is used by Diab for payments from clients." I handed the USB to the bailiff and asked him to display the first image. "I'd like to direct the jury's attention to the screen, Your Honor." I walked back to the witness stand. "Mr. Cafaro, can you see the transactions from this wallet?"

"I can, yes."

"And can you read out the labels next to the transactions starting from the top?"

"Malak, Malak, Malak, R. Costa, Malak..."

That's where he stopped, one line above where his own name stood out.

"And the next one?"

He hesitated, but I think he knew he had nowhere to go. "Cafaro," he whispered.

"Cafaro, yes," I said with more conviction. "My question to you is, what services did you pay for?"

The truth is, I didn't know what he'd paid the hitman for. The work Bill Kramer did to find the wallet in the first place had proved invaluable, or at least that's what we wanted Cafaro to think. You see, we weren't a hundred percent sure the wallet even belonged to Diab, much less the transactions we claimed to belong to the people listed. I needed a break and decided to take a risk.

Ten thousand dollars wasn't a sum that would have been enough for a hit, that's for sure, especially a double murder involving the parents of a known crime boss. A hundred grand maybe, but ten? Ten grand would have been enough for maybe some information, or guidance...or a gun.

"We know Mansur Diab isn't loyal to any particular client," I continued. "Pay him enough, and he'll come work for you. Mr. Cafaro, I put it to you that the reason for the transfer was to get a gun."

"What?" The silence in the courtroom felt impenetrable, just his voice and mine the only ones echoing back and forth.

"I think you knew him through your nephew and subsequently asked him for help. He gives you the gun, drives you to the location, and gives you some final instructions in the car." I looked up into the gallery to where Montoya was sitting. "Would you like me to recall Mr. Hector Montoya so he can verify that it was you who he saw get out of the car and limp toward your brother-in-law's house?"

"N-n-no, it was—"

"Could you explain this next transaction, Mr. Cafaro?" I asked as I directed the bailiff to move on to the next image. "Another transaction, this one for Bitcoin to the equivalent value of twenty thousand dollars and made just two days before my car blew up."

"B-b-but....b-b—" He stopped and looked to the gallery, scanning for his wife, whom he expected to step in and save him. She didn't.

"Your Honor, with the prosecutor's permission, I'd like to submit the following footage of the Costa house into evidence." By that time, I think even the prosecutor could feel the case turning on a dime and wasn't about to stop the wheels of justice.

The bailiff skipped through the next couple of photos and began the recording Linda had retrieved from the neighbor's car. Dash cams were a funny thing, able to continue in a continuous loop as long as they had access to power. They needed a bump to activate, of course, and thanks to the day of the shooting being quite windy, the camera had recorded several snippets of the view it had from across the street.

Savio Cafaro wasn't a seasoned killer. He was a simple family man who happened to fall into a hole and then didn't know how he could climb out of it again. When he finally broke down, it wasn't the way one might assume. This wasn't a Perry Mason episode where the killer nearly always exploded in a massive rant as they lost control.

Savio Cafaro simply began to weep as he watched himself walking along a suburban street, one hand in his jacket pocket where he held the pistol handed to him by a seasoned killer. I had the bailiff switch the recording off long before the man reached the Costa home, a good thing since the camera never actually captured him walking into the house. I gave him a moment to get his thoughts in order before I continued, still needing the confession that would ultimately free my client.

"It was you who walked into that house to confront them, wasn't it?"

He nodded, one hand trying to wipe the shame from his face.

"He couldn't face the fact that she beat him, and so he threatened to burn the bar down if she didn't pay him half a million dollars." He looked up at his wife, and I could see the same grief on her face, both of them weeping openly.

"And you tried to scare me off the case by shooting me," I continued.

Slowly, he began to nod. "I'm not a very good shot. I still had an old hunting rifle from my younger days and only wanted to send you a warning."

"And instead killed Paul Garroway in the process," I finished. "And my car?"

"I could see you were closing in on the truth, and I thought with you out of the way, things might just disappear."

"You paid someone to put a bomb on my car?"

The nod that followed was enough to add another charge to his ever-growing list of offenses. When I'd walked into the courtroom just a half hour earlier, I wasn't sure how this little act would play out. I knew Cafaro was involved, but I didn't know to what extent. As it turned out, he was the one responsible for the killing of Amadore and Ersilia Costa, my friend Paul Garroway, and the one who tried to kill me by hiring some low-level criminal to fix a bomb on my car.

Court security took Cafaro into custody immediately, and he continued weeping while being walked from the courtroom. Sophia was also taken in, although she eventually ended up avoiding a prison sentence on account of her lawyer pleading the charge of being an accessory after the fact down to failing to report a crime. What I understand is that she visits her husband in prison every other day, her commitment to him never wavering.

27

When Judge Edward Becker formally dismissed the case against Katherine Wright, there was no cheering the way I'd seen several murder trials come to an end. There wasn't any applause from the gallery or even elevated voices. That same silence that had persisted through Cafaro's confession remained. I think for many people, finding the truth ended up feeling somewhat bittersweet, a man trying to protect his wife eventually falling the hardest. I didn't feel the same. He'd killed three people, a fourth indirectly, and almost ended my life. If anybody deserved to go to prison, it was Cafaro.

Kat ended up getting released on the spot, and she gave me a hug once the judge dismissed the case and ended the trial once and for all. I did spot a couple of tears rolling down her face, but she flicked them away just as fast. Grace joined us shortly afterward, also giving Kat a hug.

"We've got some celebrating to do," she whispered to the girl. "I've already got the place booked."

That was when I looked up and saw someone standing behind Grace who I wasn't expecting. I think the reason Lois Wright tried to hide herself from view was because of the shame she continued to carry with her. Once I noticed her, Grace moved aside, and the daughter froze when she saw her mother. For a moment, the two just stood there staring at each other, each unsure of what to do next. It did feel quite uncomfortable for Grace and me, who seemed to be caught in the middle.

"I'll see you outside, Kat." Finally, I managed to grab my briefcase and gesture for Grace to take the lead.

When I reached the doors, I turned back just in time to see the two of them step closer and embrace each other. The location might not have been the perfect place for a family moment such as that one, but I did watch as they both dropped the animosity between them enough to give their love another chance.

Bartell was still waiting for me out in the corridor, and he held his hand out the second I walked out to him.

"I don't know where you managed to pull that from, Carter, but geez man, what a surprise."

"Neither do I," I said as we shook, and while I wanted to tell him the truth, I figured it best he just assumed I was a genius. What's a career without a little bit of healthy banter and competition?

Linda joined Grace and me shortly after Bartell continued on his merry way, and the three of us stood around waiting until Kat eventually walked out of the courtroom. Nobody was surprised to see her holding the hand of her mother, the two of them finally looking like family again. Kat walked close to me and leaned in a bit.

"If it's OK with you, my mom wants to drive me home. She offered me my old room back."

"Hey, that's fantastic," I said. "Maybe you and your mom would like to come down to Placido's Restaurant later to celebrate. Say around six?"

"Yes, we would love to," Lois said with a smile on her face, and while I didn't say anything, I did want to tell her how much better she looked with one.

It was no surprise to find a waiting media pack outside the courthouse, and I spent quite some time answering as many questions as possible. Now that I had effectively won the case and given Kat back her freedom, who wouldn't want to front such a pack of inquisitive people? That was where lawyers basked in their glory, sharing the news with the world and later watching themselves on television. I gladly stood there answering questions while Kat and her mother snuck off to their waiting ride.

Once I finished with the media pack, I did honestly consider my professional day done, but of course, there was one more small detail to contend with. It turned out that Linda had been busy once again while I was inside finishing up the case and then caught up answering questions for the media. She'd made a call herself and shared the news with someone who also needed to know the result.

Riccardo Costa wasn't the kind of man to miss an opportunity to put on a show, and boy, he didn't let anybody down. Ten minutes after receiving Linda's phone call, he drove down to the courthouse to congratulate me personally. He even rolled up in a huge stretch limo, ensuring that some of the television cameras would catch his arrival.

He passed by a couple of reporters and ignored their questions completely as he held a hand out to me. We shook, the crime boss animatedly pumping my hand up and down while smiling for the cameras. His teeth appeared almost painted, the brilliant white comically bright.

"This has to be the smartest son of a bitch working the courts, doesn't he?" He laughed, gave my hand another shake, and then let go as he waved the reporters away. "I was beginning to lose faith in you," he whispered once we were alone again, Grace and Linda standing a few feet behind me. "I truly didn't want to hurt the girl, but then again, if she was found guilty..."

That was when two things happened almost at once. First, several cops ran up to our group with their guns drawn and aimed at the crime boss, and second, Riccardo Costa's grin vanished in an instant.

You know that revelation Linda told me about that I promised to share with you at the right time? Well, hang on to your pants because it's coming at you now. It turned out that my investigator had pulled a fast one and didn't bother to let me in on it. I guess it was a good thing because it paid off...this time. That moment when we were sitting in Franco Costa's living room and Linda walked over to admire that Babe Ruth card? I had never known Linda to care about any sort of collectible, but I forgot to ask her about it afterward.

It turns out that while I was sitting on the couch, she placed a tiny video recording device between a couple of the other collectibles and managed to capture Riccardo Costa murdering his brother in a full 4K video from a front-on angle just a couple of hours later. The woman even managed to link the device to the resident's own Wi-Fi in the seconds while we were waiting for him to answer the door, so it streamed directly to her cell phone. When she handed the footage over to her contact at the police station, they used it to acquire an arrest warrant and, well, you know how that part of the story ended.

The awakening that appeared the second the handcuffs slapped around his wrists is something that I'll never forget. It wasn't anger, as such, more like surprised frustration. One of the cops revealed the charges and then read Costa his rights. He listened to them quietly while his bodyguard slowly slithered away until he jumped into the back of the limo and disappeared.

Given the amount of money Costa had, I knew he'd manage to hire himself the best team of lawyers available, but even still, it felt good to see him finally in cuffs. Unfortunately, his mouth was the only thing not under control, and he had no intention of giving that power up.

"What is this? You think you've got something on me?" He looked from the cops to me. "I knew you had balls, Counselor, but this is stupid, even for you."

"Explain it to a judge," I said. "No accident you ending up here like this. Your brother didn't deserve to go out like that."

"Accident?" The grin returned. "You want to talk about accidents, Ben Carter?" He tried to walk a couple of steps closer to me, but the cop held him back. "You know something, it's rare to lose a loved one through an accident. You lost someone like that, didn't you?" He shot me a wink as the cop led him away, and something inside me shifted. I watched until he was put into the back of the police cruiser before turning my attention back to Grace, who was still standing next to Linda.

"Let's get the hell out of here," I said, finally glad to have the case officially end.

After I insisted on catching my own Uber back home, Grace and Linda finally headed to their respective cars, and I gave each of them a final wave when they drove past while waiting for my ride. It didn't take me long to get home. Even with the afternoon traffic not playing fair, my driver managed to take a couple of shortcuts down some side streets and still managed to pull up out the front of my building some thirty-five minutes later.

The shower I had shortly after walking into my apartment must have been one of the best I'd had in a long time. It felt like an actual cleansing, the dirty residue of an active murder investigation finally washing away once and for all. I stood in silence for a long time while thinking about the final hour of the case and the confession that had revealed the truth behind the lie.

I also thought about Riccardo and his arrest. Linda had handed me a copy of the video she'd managed to capture with her cleverly hidden camera. While I couldn't help but smile while thinking about how she went about catching the crime boss, it quickly faded away again when I considered the way things could have ended. If we had failed…if Linda didn't set that camera up and we failed to convince Cafaro that we knew whom he'd paid, what would the outcome have been?

There was no denying that Riccardo Costa would have ended Kat's life, and I don't think she would have lasted the night if a guilty verdict had been read out. The prison had been his plan all along, and now that he was trapped inside it himself, I wondered how he would handle such an unforeseen ending.

"Oh, he's not finished," Linda whispered to me later that evening after we had taken our seats at the restaurant. "You can bet your bottom dollar he would have prepared for such an outcome. He's probably planned for it his whole life, given the things he's involved in." Grace leaned in from the other side of Linda.

"Think he'd escape?"

"I wouldn't put it past him, although given how high profile he is, I doubt it," Linda said. "He'd have to skip the country entirely, and given how much he enjoys the attention?"

"He's not escaping," I whispered as I spotted Kat and her mother climbing out of a taxi. "He won't need to."

We each got up to give Kat a hug and her mother a handshake before we all sat down again. It wasn't long before the drinks were flowing for those who indulged and sodas for everyone else. The food? Wow...Italian with a Southern twist. I think they called it Tuscan Fusion on the menu. I ate well beyond my fill and afterward felt like I needed a wheelchair to get to my ride. I even managed to squeeze in a piece of rhubarb pie before admitting defeat and tapping out with half a piece left on my plate.

It wasn't until later, while we were celebrating Kat's release with a final glass of champagne, that Grace turned to me and asked something I'd been thinking about since hearing it. I don't know why I hadn't considered the statement more other than to say it frightened me.

"What do you think Riccardo meant with that whole losing a loved one through an accident?" she asked as I took a sip from my glass of champagne.

"I have no idea," I said as that familiar uneasiness fell onto me. "But I know I'm going to find out."

Don't miss THE HITMAN'S LAWYER. The riveting sequel in the Ben Carter Legal Thriller series.

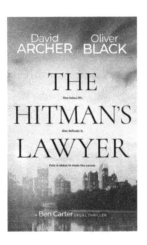

ONE TAKES LIFE. ONE DEFENDS IT. FATE IS ABOUT TO MAKE THE SWITCH.

When a middle-aged businessman enters the office of Ben Carter and hires him for a murder case, nothing could have prepared the lawyer for the cat-and-mouse game that follows. Tasked with defending a woman accused of killing local businessman Dale Rich, Carter soon finds himself asking more questions about the man who hired him than the woman he's been sent to defend.

Corinne Lucas appears as nothing more than a victim trapped in a nightmare, caught up in a frenzied murder that screams wrong place-wrong time. When the evidence begins to pile up and appears to implicate the woman in multiple ways, it's up to her lawyer to separate truth from fiction. Carter quickly uncovers a possible motive for the killing and when it turns the entire investigation on its head, how can he protect himself when all the evidence points to the unlikeliest of suspects?

Purchase at: www.righthouse.com/the-hitmans-lawyer
(Or scan the QR code below.)

NOTE: flip to the very end to read an exclusive sneak peek...

DON'T MISS ANYTHING!

If you want to stay up to date on all new releases in this series, with these authors, or with any of our new deals, you can do so by joining our newsletters below.

In addition, you will immediately gain access to our entire *Right House VIP Library*, which currently includes six original novels!

righthouse.com/email

(Easy to unsubscribe. No spam. Ever.)

ALSO BY DAVID ARCHER

Up to date books can be found at:
www.righthouse.com/david-archer

ROGUE THRILLERS
Gates of Hell (Book 1)
Hell's Fury (Book 2)
Ice Burn (Book 3)

BEN CARTER LEGAL THRILLERS
Dead Man's Jury (Book 1)
Trial by Murder (Book 2)
The Hitman's Lawyer (Book 3)

JACOB HUNTER THRILLERS
The Kyiv File (Book 1)
The Bogota File (Book 2)
The Havana File (Book 3)

PETER BLACK THRILLERS
Burden of the Assassin (Book 1)
The Man Without A Face (Book 2)
Unpunished Deeds (Book 3)
Hunter Killer (Book 4)
Silent Shadows (Book 5)
The Last Run (Book 6)
Dark Corners (Book 7)

Ghost Operative (Book 8)

A Fire Burning (Book 9)

Dawnlight (Book 10)

ALEX MASON THRILLERS

Odin (Book 1)

Ice Cold Spy (Book 2)

Mason's Law (Book 3)

Assets and Liabilities (Book 4)

Russian Roulette (Book 5)

Executive Order (Book 6)

Dead Man Talking (Book 7)

All The King's Men (Book 8)

Flashpoint (Book 9)

Brotherhood of the Goat (Book 10)

Dead Hot (Book 11)

Blood on Megiddo (Book 12)

Son of Hell (Book 13)

Merchant of Death (Book 14)

NOAH WOLF THRILLERS

Code Name Camelot (Book 1)

Lone Wolf (Book 2)

In Sheep's Clothing (Book 3)

Hit for Hire (Book 4)

The Wolf's Bite (Book 5)

Black Sheep (Book 6)

Balance of Power (Book 7)

Time to Hunt (Book 8)

Red Square (Book 9)

SAM PRICHARD MYSTERIES

ABOUT US

Right House is an independent publisher created by authors for readers. We specialize in Action, Thriller, Mystery, and Crime novels.

If you enjoyed this novel, then there is a good chance you will like what else we have to offer! Please stay up to date by using any of the links below.

Join our mailing lists to stay up to date -->
righthouse.com/email
Visit our website --> righthouse.com
Contact us --> contact@righthouse.com

facebook.com/righthousebooks
x.com/righthousebooks
instagram.com/righthousebooks

EXCLUSIVE SNEAK PEEK OF...

THE HITMAN'S LAWYER

CHAPTER ONE

HAVE YOU EVER MET SOMEONE WHO IMMEDIATELY MADE YOU feel like you've known them your entire life? You might use the word charming to describe them, but that doesn't quite fit the immediate connection you feel to them. There seems to be something inside them that goes beyond any sort of verbal descriptions you could use to explain the interaction.

That's how I found Walter Morris the first time I met him. The warmth in his smile, that particular glint in his eyes. Even the handshake had just enough squeeze to imply somewhat of a familiarity without going over the top. The expression on his face when he first introduced himself reminded me of someone conveying, *Hey, pal, how's life been treating you since the last time I saw you?* It felt almost as if he already knew each and every day of my existence, and asking the question was just a formality.

When the man walked into my office behind my

assistant, Grace introduced him as Mr. Morris. To me, I could tell the man had class, and his suit alone perhaps cost more than some people's monthly mortgage. When I threw in the manicured nails and the neatly trimmed beard, I could tell that he was a man who took care of himself. He wasn't exactly ripped, but for a man in his early 50s, he certainly did look to be in great shape, someone who obviously worked out regularly and avoided the desert bar as best he could.

"Please, call me Walter," the man said with that same smile, and when I asked him to sit after thanking Grace, he first set his briefcase down beside the chair.

"Can I offer you a coffee or some water?" I asked before retaking my own seat, and when he waved a hand to decline the offer, I dropped down to my previous position.

"I'm sorry for dropping in unannounced like this, Mr. Carter, but the matter I need your help with is somewhat time-sensitive."

"Call me Ben, please, and why don't you tell me how I can help you?"

I don't know whether it was confidence, perhaps arrogance, or maybe even a mixture of both, but the way the man held his emotions in perfect balance was how I believed he projected a kind of calmness about him. At the time, I wouldn't have been surprised to learn that he had a good number of grandchildren with whom he enjoyed quality time most weekends. Hell, he probably would have made for the perfect Santa Claus, given his demeanor.

"Have you heard of a man named Dale Rich, by any

chance?" Morris asked, and the name immediately raised a recent memory without bringing forth a face.

"The name sounds familiar, yes," I said.

"But you're not quite sure why?" He smiled, adding a slight nod. "Understandable. From what I understand, Mr. Rich wasn't the kind of man who enjoyed the spotlight too much. He was an antiques dealer, for the most part, trading in exotic pieces which he peddled to collectors across the country."

"Was?"

"Yes, unfortunately, Dale Rich was murdered two nights ago out behind the Kimpton Hotel Monaco."

That was when the penny dropped, my brain finally catching up and reminding me of the newspaper headline I'd seen two days earlier.

"From what I read in the paper, he was also quite connected within City Hall, if I'm not mistaken."

"I believe he went to school with the mayor's wife, yes," Morris said.

"OK, but I'm not understanding my purpose, though, unless you're under suspicion for the murder?" Morris chuckled somewhat.

"The police arrested a woman named Corinne Lucas last night and are currently holding her down at Zone 1. I believe that it is the connection Dale had with Corinne within the antiques business that is the reason she's been arrested. I'd like to hire you to defend Ms. Lucas, if I may. I will be paying all necessary costs, as well as expenses incurred, for you to clear her name. If need be, I could deposit an upfront fee into a trust fund for you to draw upon as needed."

"Who is she to you?"

I don't think he expected the question. For the briefest of moments, I could see his focus break just enough for his eyes to narrow as he considered me. The moment, however, didn't last long.

"A friend, you might say. Someone who I consider dear to me."

"A murder defense can be expensive," I said. "We're not talking small change here. Weeks, perhaps even months of ongoing work, a trial, a full-time investigator."

"Like I said, I'll cover all necessary expenses," Morris said as he doubled down on his request.

While I normally would have jumped at the chance of such an offer, something held me back, stopping me from jumping in head first. It wasn't that I didn't find the man's offer appealing. On the contrary, in fact, it sounded like one of the best offers I'd received in a very long time. I imagined Dwight pushing me aside to shake the man's hand, ensuring a significant case with the potential to keep the lights on in the building for close to a year. And yet, something held me back, something that didn't go unnoticed by my prospective client.

"I sense your hesitation," Morris said. "Not entirely surprising, given the case."

"It's just that your proposal sounds a little too good to be true," I said and immediately heard the lie from my own lips. That wasn't the reason at all.

What I found hard to believe wasn't the proposal at all; it was the man himself. He just came across as a little *too* perfect, a little *too* sincere. I couldn't work out whether that was just how he was or if this was some kind of elaborate ruse to...to what? That was the thing I couldn't figure out. If he *was* being disingenuous, for what purpose?

"How do you know Ms. Lucas?" I asked, posing the same question with a different approach.

"We were neighbors for a long time. Her ex-husband ran off with my ex-wife, and you might say that I feel a certain sense of responsibility for their betrayal."

"So you are kind of like her protector, figuratively speaking."

"Yes, I guess that's one way of putting it. Corinne is a good woman. She didn't deserve what happened to her, and she certainly doesn't deserve this."

"So you don't think she did it? The murder, I mean?"

"Most definitely not," Morris said. "Not only do I know her to be one very courageous woman, but she wouldn't have it in her. She's a very gentle woman, if you know what I mean."

I'm not sure at what point I finally managed to push aside my apprehension, but before I knew it, I half stood out of my chair and reached out a hand toward my new client.

"All right, Mr. Morris...Walter...you have yourself a defense attorney. I'll get my assistant to put together the necessary paperwork and have it emailed through to you this afternoon."

"One other thing," Morris said when he reached the door and turned back around to face me.

"Yes?"

"I know this might sound a little left field, but I'm wondering if you might keep our agreement between us?"

"You mean from the press?"

"I mean from your defendant," Morris said, surprising me yet again.

"You want me to keep you hiring me away from Ms. Lucas? Why on Earth would I need to do that?"

"Corinne isn't the kind of woman to accept help. Or should I say *my* help?"

That's when a vision came into my head, the one which painted Morris as the kind of man who couldn't take no for an answer. Either through guilt or obsession, I imagined him to be the kind of person who needed more than a simple no to quit. Maybe that was the moment when I should have changed my mind and recanted my acceptance of the job. Looking back now, it was probably at that very moment when I could have still backed out of the entire case and let it continue without me, having never gotten involved. Instead, I went against every instinct telling me not to continue.

"I'll make sure it remains between us" was what I said, and after giving me a final nod of approval, Walter Morris left my office.

What followed was perhaps the longest fifteen minutes of my life as I stood at my window, staring out across the parking lot long after my new client's Maserati had pulled out onto the road and disappeared into the day. It was his ghost that I couldn't take my eyes off, the last place where he stood before climbing into his car and vanishing from my view. It was his words rolling around my head, the ones about not letting the defendant know of his involvement, the woman who was "just a neighbor" but whose suffering he took responsibility for.

"Grace, would you please start collecting everything you can find on the Dale Rich murder?" I asked my assistant once I managed to get back to my desk.

While there were an extensive number of articles on the Internet I found for myself, they didn't delve anywhere deep enough to the level I needed them to. Information was key in any murder investigation, and details mattered almost as much as time itself. When I read through one of the first news articles I came across, what I found was a story I'd heard many times before.

The details mirrored too many others in our state, perhaps throughout the country. A lonely businessman cutting through an alleyway to get to an appointment was attacked and left for dead. His wallet, cell phone, and watch were found to be missing by authorities, the only suspect being the one person nearby that security footage picked up as having entered said alley minutes before and left moments after the crime. Nearby witnesses reported hearing screams and, when they investigated, discovered a fifty-two-year-old man lying in a pool of his own blood. Despite frantic efforts by said witnesses to stem the bleeding, the victim died from his injuries before paramedics arrived at the scene.

It took law enforcement officers less than twenty-four hours to locate and arrest their prime suspect, a woman witnesses described as being highly agitated in the moments before the killing. She'd been talking on a cell phone at the time and appeared to be engaged in an aggressive conversation when seen entering the same alleyway. Witnesses didn't recall seeing her leave.

The one thing I knew for sure was that the investigation would need the best person on the case. Thankfully, I already had that person on my payroll, and I sent Linda a text after reading that first article a couple of times, asking if she had time to drop into the office later that afternoon. There was something I needed to do first.

Be there with bells on was her reply just a few seconds later, and I smiled at the image in my head. My investigator certainly had a way with words, and I responded with a simple thumbs-up emoji. With Linda coming to see me later in the day and Grace out at her desk accumulating what I needed to get a better understanding of the case, there was just one more thing to do to get myself into a prime position for taking on a new case.

Before getting up, I first leaned back in my chair and gazed up at the ceiling, closed my eyes, and tried to envision the scene for myself to get myself into the moment, if you will. A woman arguing on a cell phone entering an alleyway, a man following her but maybe a minute or two behind, perhaps taking a shortcut to whatever destination he was headed. She attacks him, robs him of his belongings and then simply vanishes.

I opened my eyes again when the scene just didn't play out the way the news reports described it. It just didn't flow right. Usually, mainly when the accused is eventually found guilty, each moment seems to slip effortlessly into the next, the minutes passing as if floating along a river. Not so with the one I was trying to envision, and that was why I pushed myself out of the chair, grabbed my briefcase, and headed for the door. It was time to go ask the kinds of questions that built a defense.

CHAPTER TWO

THE MIDDAY SUN FELT ALMOST UNBEARABLE DURING THE BRIEF walk from the building to my car, and once I slipped behind the wheel of my Mustang, I didn't hesitate to fire up the engine so I could max out the A/C. I'd only had the car a little over a month after that whole debacle with the SUV. Oh, that's right. I haven't brought you up to date on that part.

After losing my previous ride to a failed bombing attempt the previous year, I somehow talked myself into getting an SUV instead of another Mustang. It was the comments from some of my colleagues, most of whom drove the usual range of expensive and classy German-made automobiles. Several preferred the prestige of riding higher than the average vehicle, giving them a somewhat superior position in traffic. Personally, I didn't think I cared either way, but after a couple of test drives, I opted for this BMW that set me back a pretty penny. Fast forward six months, and I absolutely hated it.

It certainly felt like being force-fed a giant piece of humble pie when I eventually walked into the Ford dealership, but the feeling of betrayal quickly fell away when I saw my new ride for the first time. I didn't even need to wait; the floor model suited me perfectly. And when the salesman threw in a few optional extras plus a couple of the services for free, I knew I couldn't say no.

There's just something comforting about returning to an old favorite for me. I just couldn't get used to driving above the majority of traffic, the sensation feeling almost snobbish, in a way. I'm not someone to look down on people, either proverbially or physically, and appearance isn't something I've ever taken seriously. Yes, I know that lawyers like to drive all manner of fancy cars to convey success, but to me, it's just another form of deception. A person's character isn't determined by how flashy their vehicle is or what label their clothing is. Give me a good soul any day.

It took just a minute or two for the temperature to drop to a more comfortable level, and once on the road, I turned the car into traffic on my way across town. I settled in behind a cab that, surprisingly, nearly followed my exact same route. It ended up leading me almost all the way to my destination, only turning off a street before the police station. I found a spot to the right-hand side, and either through fate or just perfect timing, someone pulled out of one of the few spots shaded by trees.

"Thank you very much," I muttered under my breath when shooting the departing vehicle a wave and quickly slipped into the space.

When I climbed out, the heat immediately slapped me in

the face, and the difference in temperature felt like a wall. I recalled the weatherman forecasting a high of ninety-three during the news broadcast the previous evening, but I swear it easily felt above a hundred. Given the speed with which the sweat on my brow began to build, I made getting inside the building a priority.

Thankfully, the A/C in the station was doing its job with some efficiency, the transition from the outside temperature to the inside one again feeling like slipping between two different planes of existence. The sweat immediately reversed course, and by the time I reached the counter and asked to meet with my new client, all hint of the uncomfortable stickiness had vanished.

"One moment," the woman manning the reception area said once she confirmed my client's location and asked me to take a seat.

I didn't bother with sitting, per se, and just kind of hovered near the back of the waiting area with the rest of those in limbo. For the next ten minutes or so, the number of people waiting see-sawed up and down. Every now and then, someone new would be called up while someone else walked in to join the rest of us. I ended up being one of the longest-waiting people, not being called up until all of the original people in waiting had gone.

"Mr. Carter, come on through," the same woman called out to me and led me through to the back of the station, where a couple of interview rooms were located. She pointed me into one, and I took a seat while my escort disappeared again.

This time, I didn't have to wait nearly as long, footsteps

almost immediately clapping down the hall before slowing right outside my door. A cop walked in first, rounding the corner ahead of a woman whom I immediately recognized from the only photo I'd seen of her on the website I'd used.

From first impressions, I had to agree with the man who had hired me for the job. Corinne Lucas didn't look like the kind of woman capable of murder. She didn't even look like the kind of person able to raise her voice enough to offend anybody, let alone hurt someone. She was tiny, barely five feet tall, with arms the size of twigs. Aged in her late thirties, she hadn't yet given in to the course of time that wears us all down, still hanging on to her youthful looks in every way possible. She'd tied her long dark hair back into a ponytail that exposed her face in all its beauty. Even without makeup, I saw barely a hint of wrinkles or any blemishes; her skin was almost perfect.

If someone had asked me if I thought the woman was attractive, I would have agreed wholeheartedly. Even under pressure and with the weight of the world on her shoulders, it was impossible to deny her beauty. It wasn't until she looked over at me with her dazzling blue eyes that her real beauty hit me.

The cops left the handcuffs on her, but unlike some of the more dangerous criminals I'd spoken with, they didn't tie them to the bench. I waited until the escort had left the room and locked the door before greeting my new client.

"I'm Ben Carter," I began. "How have they been treating you?"

"All right, I suppose," she said, her voice low and lacking confidence. "Why are you here? I can't afford a lawyer."

"My firm tends to keep an eye on the forums, and every now and then, my boss gives the go-ahead for one of us to offer free representation."

It wasn't *exactly* a lie, aside from a couple of subtle facts, but I didn't think they would matter in the long run.

"I need to get out of here," she said, not entirely unexpectedly.

"That's what I hope to make happen, but first, I'm going to need information from you."

"I don't know what I can tell you. I didn't kill Dale Rich."

I could sense her close to tears and understood the trauma she must have been going through. Facing a murder charge is no easy thing, the prospect of life behind bars one of the scariest prospects a person can deal with.

"Did you know him at all?"

"Not in the sense that these people seem to think. I met him once during a fundraising ball, but that conversation lasted all of about a minute."

"Any reason why?"

"He hit on me, and the wedding band on his finger was enough to convince me not to take things any further."

"How do you think you both ended up in the same place at nearly the same time? The police seem to think it might have been planned."

"I had a dinner reservation with a friend at Wang's. The place has a back door that's open to anybody. I was on the phone with my ex at the time and wasn't exactly in a great mood. I didn't want to make a scene out on the street, so I took the conversation down the alley."

"You didn't hear the scream from Rich when he was attacked?"

"No, I'd left by then. My friend Donna texted me at some point during the phone call I was having, saying she couldn't make it, and I didn't even bother taking a seat. Wasn't about to sit there alone."

Her story made sense, and if I could prove all the minor details, then I figured I could use them in such a way as to strengthen our case. I still wasn't sure about the police evidence—hadn't had enough time to access it—but I didn't think it would have been anything physical. If all the evidence the authorities had on my client was circumstantial, then my bid for winning her parole should have been a slam dunk.

"I need to ask. Have you ever been in trouble with the police before?"

She shook her head without hesitation. "Got a speeding ticket once, but that's about it."

"What about anybody you associate with? Boyfriends, colleagues, exes?"

"No, not that I know of. My latest ex is a Marine and about as clean as you can get. I doubt he'd let a shoelace hang too long, if you know what I mean."

"How long were you together for?"

"Four months. Not exactly award-winning, but it was good while it lasted."

"Corinne, I need to warn you. This isn't going to be an easy case to win, not by a longshot. If there is anything, and I mean *anything*, in your life the prosecutor can use, believe me, they will. Now is the time to tell me."

For a minute, she just stared back at me with those frightened eyes of hers, the iridescent blue almost intensified by the stress. It also highlighted the distinctive black ring running around the edge of her iris, only adding to the beauty of them. In another time and place, I might have considered them hypnotic and found myself caught in their power.

"I'm not one to have secrets, Mr. Carter. I lead a very simple life. I work, I pay a mortgage, I have a dog. This kind of thing doesn't happen to people like me."

"Actually, you'd be surprised by how many times this happens to people like yourself. More than you could imagine."

"And are they guilty?"

"Sometimes."

We spoke for a few more minutes before the detectives investigating the case joined us, and not long after, Corinne Lucas was formally charged with first-degree murder. The process didn't take long but did offer me a chance to request access to the evidence they had against my client. Once we had gone through all of the formalities, I spent around another ten minutes or so with Corinne alone, but that was just to take her through a few things planned for the immediate future.

When the time came for me to finally leave my client again, I did note a slight change in her demeanor. She no longer looked quite as vulnerable and confused as she had when I first saw her. I think with a bit more understanding of the process and perhaps sensing some hope that she might actually have a chance at freedom again, Corinne walked out of the room with her head held up a lot higher. She walked with a sense of purpose, and that gave me hope that she might actually have the strength to spend time in lock-up.

Once back in my car, I first took care of the A/C so as to bring the car's interior back to habitable levels before pulling out my cell phone and calling Grace. Now that we had somewhat of a direction to go in, it was time for us to take the necessary steps to get the wheels rolling. Organizing and sorting through the brief of evidence and arranging a bail hearing was at the top of the list, and Grace was the perfect person to take charge of both.

www.righthouse.com/the-hitmans-lawer